Praise for Kimberly Belle and *The Last Breath*

"Painstakingly emotional…will surprise readers to the very end…
it's so worth it!"

—*RT Book Reviews*

"Belle's engaging debut brings the reader into [an] emotionally tangled
world."

—*Booklist*

"Belle's a smooth writer whose characters are vibrant and truly reflect the
area where the novel is set."

—*Kirkus Reviews*

"*The Last Breath* will leave you breathless. This edgy and emotional
thriller will keep you guessing until the very end."
—*New York Times* bestselling author Heather Gudenkauf

"Powerful and complex with an intensity drawn out through each page,
The Last Breath is a story of forgiveness and betrayal and one I couldn't put
down!"

—*New York Times* bestselling author Steena Holmes

Also by Kimberly Belle

The Last Breath

MIRA

Recycling programs
for this product may
not exist in your area.

ISBN-13: 978-0-7783-1786-9

The Ones We Trust

Copyright © 2015 by Kimberle Swaak-Maleski

For questions and comments about the quality of this book, please contact us at
CustomerService@Harlequin.com.

www.MIRABooks.com

Printed in U.S.A.

First printing: August 2015
10 9 8 7 6 5 4 3 2 1

THE

ONES

WE

TRUST

KIMBERLY BELLE

To the women and men who risk their lives every day for our country, and for the people who love them.

THE

ONES

WE

TRUST

Part One:
Murky Truths

1

There's a thin, fragile line that separates us all from misfortune. A place where life teeters on a razor's edge, and everything boils down to one single, solitary second. Where either you will whiz past the Mack truck blissfully unaware, or you will slam into it head on. Where there's a before, and then, without warning or apology, there's an after.

For the past three years, I've rewound to those last *before* moments, moments I was still blissfully unaware I was about to be blindsided. I've tried to pinpoint the very spot when tragedy struck. It wasn't when Chelsea took her last breath, though that was certainly a tragedy. No, the tipping point was somewhere in the days leading up to her death, when her story was barreling like a deadly virus across the internet, snowballing and mutating and infecting everyone it touched. Infecting *her* with words I wrote and sent out into the world. I guess you could say I poisoned her with them.

To the rest of the world, Chelsea Vogel looked like any other white, American, middle-class mother in her early thirties.

On the dowdy side of forgettable, one of those women you acknowledge with a bland smile as she pushes her cart by yours in the grocery store, or idles patiently in her car while you hang up the gas pump and climb back behind the wheel of yours. You see her but, for the life of you, couldn't pick her out of a lineup five minutes later.

But underneath all that dull suburban facade burned a big, bright secret.

I had no idea of any of this, of course, that rainy Tuesday afternoon I walked into her slightly shabby offices south of Baltimore to interview her for iWoman.com, the online news magazine I was reporting for at the time. I only knew that as the founder and CEO of American Society for Truth, Chelsea was an outspoken opponent of gay rights, one who preached about God-ordained sexuality and the natural family to anyone who would listen. And people seemed to be listening, especially once she became a regular contributor on conservative news senders.

"I'm Abigail Wolff," I told the receptionist, a slight woman by the name of Maria Duncan. "I have an interview with Mrs. Vogel."

Maria offered me coffee and showed me to the conference room. I noticed her because she was pretty—short pixie hair, a fresh face, clothes that were fashionable but not flashy. But I remember her because two weeks later, she slid me the story that ended my career.

"Here," she said to me that day, shoving a file across the table before I'd settled into the seat across from her. "This is for you."

I'd known when she asked me to meet her at a Cracker Barrel in Linthicum Heights just south of Baltimore, it wasn't to become friends over sweet teas and biscuits. But never in a million years would I have guessed what greeted me when

I opened that file. Dozens and dozens of photographs, each one dated and timed, of a naked Maria and Chelsea. In bed, on the backseat of a minivan, atop both of their desks.

"Who took these?" I said, flipping through them. Judging by the low resolution and awkward angles, I was placing my money on a hidden camera, and an inexpensive one.

Maria shook her head. "Doesn't matter. They're real. There's a DVD in there, too, with about twenty different videos."

I pushed everything back into the file and closed the cover. Maria was well above legal age, probably somewhere in her mid to late twenties. That didn't mean, however, that Chelsea Vogel wasn't a predator, or that the affair wouldn't be one hell of a story...and a byline.

But still. If this story hit, Maria needed to know what she was in for.

"What do you think your family will say when they open up their morning newspaper and see these?"

Her chin went up. "There's no one to see it. The only family I had left died last year."

"Your friends, then. Do any of them know you're sleeping with your female boss?"

"I don't..." She glanced down at the table, then lifted her gaze to mine, clinging to it like maple syrup, thick and sticky. "I just moved here from Detroit. The people here aren't exactly friendly."

I took this to mean she hadn't made very many friends yet.

I gestured to the envelope between us. "So, what's this about, then? Is it to get attention? To prove to people that you're loved? Because I can guarantee you people are going to think a lot of things when they see these pictures, but not much of it's going to be nice."

"I don't give a shit what people think. This isn't about getting noticed. This is about Chelsea Vogel taking advantage of me. She was my *boss*, and she used her position of authority to make me think she loved me."

"So this story is about revenge."

"No." Maria's answer was immediate and emphatic. "This story is about justice. What she did to me may not be a crime, officially, but it was still wrong. She should still be punished."

"Take it to the HR department. They'll make sure Chelsea Vogel is fired, and they'll be inclined to keep things quiet."

"Chelsea *is* the HR department, don't you get it? American Society for Truth is *her* project. And I don't want to be quiet. I'm done being quiet. I'm the victim here, and I want Chelsea to pay."

I told myself it was the righteousness in her tone, the resolve creasing her brow and fisting her hands that convinced me, and not the idea of my name attached to a story that I knew, I *knew* would go viral.

"I'll do what I can to protect your identity, but you need to be aware that there's a very real probability it'll get out, and when it does, every single second of your life will be altered. Not just now, but tomorrow and the next day and the next. This scandal—and make no mistake about it, this is a scandal for *you* just as much as it is for *her*—will follow you for the rest of your life. You'll never be anonymous ever again."

She swallowed, thought for a long moment. "I think I still want you to write the story."

"You think? Or you know?" I leaned forward and watched her closely. Not just her answer but also her body language would determine my course of action.

"I know." She straightened her back, squared her shoulders and looked me straight in the eye. "I want you to write the story."

So that's what I did. I wrote the story.

I did everything right, too. I checked facts and questioned

witnesses, volunteers and employees at neighboring businesses and the building janitor. I made sure the evidence had not been digitally altered, compared the dates and times on the photographs to both women's work and home schedules. I held back Maria's name, blurred out faces, released only the least damning of the pictures, the ones where there was no way, no possible way Maria would be recognized. I did every goddamn thing right, but within twenty-four hours of my story breaking, Maria's identity, along with every single one of the photographs and videos in clear, full-color focus, exploded across the internet anyway. Just as, if I'm being completely honest with myself, I knew they would.

Two weeks later, on a beautiful January morning, Chelsea Vogel hung herself in the shower. I wasn't there when it happened, of course, but that doesn't mean I wasn't responsible for her death. After all, those were *my* words that made her drive those five miles in her minivan to the Home Depot for a length of braided rope, then haul it home and knot it around her neck. I knew when I put them out there that *both* women's lives would be changed. I just never dreamed one of them would also end.

Secrets are a sneaky little seed. You can hide them, you can bury them, you can disguise them and cover them up. But then, just when you think your secret has rotted away and decayed into nothing, it stirs back to life. It sprouts roots and stems, crawls its way through the mud and muck, growing and climbing and bursting through the surface, blooming for everyone to see. That's the lesson here. The truth always comes out eventually.

But I can no longer be the one to write about it.

2

It's the strangest thing, running into someone famous.

First, you get that initial rush of recognition, a fast flare of adrenaline that quickens your pulse and prickles your skin with awareness. *Oh, my God. Is that…? Holy shit, it is him.* Your body gears up for a greeting—a friendly smile, a slightly giddy wave, a high-pitched and breathy hello—when you suddenly realize that though this person may be one of the most recognizable faces in greater DC and the nation, to him you are an unfamiliar face, a stranger. You are just any other woman pushing her cart through the aisles of Handyman Market.

And then you notice the red apron, the name tag that proclaims him Handyman, the light coating of sawdust on his jeans, and realize that to Gabe Armstrong, you're not just any other woman.

You're any other *customer.*

"Need some help finding anything?" he asks.

I am not a person easily flustered by fame. I've interviewed heads of state and royalty, movie stars and music moguls, crime bosses and terrorists. Only one time—*one time*—in all those years did I lose my shit, and that was when I interviewed Gabe's older brother Zach. *People*'s Sexiest Man Alive, the Hollywood golden boy who chucked his big-screen career to die in a war that, on the day he enlisted, fifty-seven percent of Americans considered a mistake. But when Zach aimed his famous smile on me that afternoon, a mere eleven days before he shipped off to basic training, I forgot every single one of the questions I thought I had memorized, and I had to fire up my laptop on the hood of my car to retrieve them.

But not so with Gabe here, who is not so much famous as infamous. There's not an American alive who doesn't remember his drunken performance at his brother's funeral, when he slurred his way through a nationally televised speech, then saluted the Honor Guards with a bottle of Jack Daniel's clutched in a fist as furious as his expression.

And his image has only gone downhill since. *Cantankerous*, *obstinate* and *hostile* are some of the more colorful words the media uses to describe him in print, and their adjectives lean toward the obscene when they're off the record. Part of their censure has to do with Gabe's role as family gatekeeper, with his thus-far successful moves to thwart their attempts at an interview with his mother or brother Nick, crouched a few feet away when three bullets tore through Zach's skull.

But the other part, and a not-so-small part, is that he answers their every single question, even "How are you today?" with a "No fucking comment."

I clear my throat, consult my list. "Where do you keep your tile cutters?"

Gabe doesn't miss a beat. "Snap and score or angle grinders?"

"Wet saw, actually. I hear they're the best for minimizing dust."

"True, as long as you don't mind the hike in price." When I shake my head, he continues. "How big's your tile?"

"Twelve by twelve," I say as if I'm reciting my social security number.

And that's when the absurdity hits me. I'm discussing tile saws with Zach Armstrong's younger brother. One who so closely resembles his big-screen brother that it's almost eerie. If I didn't know for a fact that Zach died on an Afghani battlefield last year, I might think I'd stumbled onto a movie set… one for *The Twilight Zone*.

Gabe motions for me to follow him. "I've got a table model with a diamond blade that's good for both stone and ceramic. It's sturdy, its cuts are clean and precise, and it's fairly affordable. What are you tiling?"

"A bathroom."

He stops walking and asks to see my list, and I know what he's doing. He's checking it. Inspecting for mistakes. Looking for holes. If he had a red pen, he'd mark it up and tell me to revise and resubmit.

Gabe glances up through a lifted brow. "What's the sledgehammer for?"

"To take out the built-in closet. It'll give me another three feet of vanity space."

My answer earns me an impressed nod. "Are you planning on moving any fixtures?"

They could almost be twins, really. Same towering height and swimmer's build, same dark features and angular bone structure, same neat sideburns that trail down his cheeks like perfectly clipped tassels. I take all of it in and try not to let on that I know exactly who he is.

"Nope. Same floor plan, just a thorough update of pretty much every inch. I'm fairly certain I can do everything but the plumbing and electricity myself."

"I can get you a few referrals, if you'd like." He looks up for my nod, then returns to the list. I give him all the time he needs, leaning with my forearms onto the cart handle and waiting for his assessment.

Gabe may be Harvard educated, but I happen to know I've made no mistakes on that list. I approached this project as I do every other these days: by scouring the internet for relevant articles, handpicking the most important facts and condensing them into one organized document. My bathroom has been content curated to within an inch of its life, and that list is perfect down to the very last nut and bolt.

He passes me back the paper with an impressed grin. "You've really done your homework."

"I'm excellent at research."

"Almost excellent." He taps the list with a long finger. "You forgot the silicone caulk."

I straighten, shaking my head. "No, I didn't. I already have three tubes at home from when you guys had your buy two, get two free special."

"What happened to the fourth?"

"I used it last week to re-caulk the kitchen sink."

Amusement half cocks his grin. He nudges me aside to take charge of my cart. "Come on. We'll start on aisle twelve and work our way forward."

And that's just what we do. Gabe loops us through the aisles, loading up my cart as well as another he fetches from the front as we check off every item on my list, even the items Gabe assures me there's no way, no possible way I will ever need. I tell him if it's on the list, to throw it in anyway. The entire expedition takes us the better part of an hour, and by the time we make it to the register, both carts are bulging.

He waits patiently while I fork over half a month's salary

to the gray-haired cashier, then helps me cram all my goods into the back of my Prius.

"Are you sure you don't need anything else?" He has to lean three times on the hatchback door to click it closed. "Because I think we might have a couple of rusty screws left in the back somewhere."

"Old overachiever habits are hard to break, I guess." I grin.

He grins back, the skin of his right cheek leaning into the hint of a dimple. "It was a pretty fierce list. Very thorough. One might even say overly so."

"I told you I was—"

"Excellent at research," he interrupts, still grinning. "I remember. But preparation is only half the battle."

His tone and expression are teasing, and I imitate both. "Are you doubting my competence?"

"Hell, no. Anyone who can make a list like yours is fully capable of looking up instructions on the internet. All I'm saying is, if you happen to run into any problems with the execution and need an experienced handyman…" He cocks a brow and gestures with a thumb to his apron, *Handyman* embroidered in big white letters across the front.

I laugh. "I'll remember that."

This is when he smiles again, big and wide, and it completely transforms his face. It's a smile that's just as fierce, just as sexy and magnetic as his look-alike brother's, yet somehow, Gabe makes it his own. Maybe it's the way his left cheek takes a second or two longer to catch up with his right, or the way his eyeteeth are swiveled just a tad inward. Maybe it's the way his eyes crinkle into slits, and that dimple grows into a deep split. Whatever it is, Gabe's smile is extraordinary in that it's so *ordinary*, lopsided and uneven and unpracticed for red carpets and film cameras, and in that moment, I forget all about his famous brother. In that moment, I see only Gabe.

But now we've milked the moment for all it's worth, and it's time to go.

"Thanks for everything," I say, reaching for my door. "Really. You've been a huge help."

Gabe waves off my thanks, but he doesn't turn to go. He stands there while I get settled, watching as I start the engine and fiddle with the gearshift, and then he stops me with a knuckle to the glass.

I hit the button for the window. "Don't tell me I forgot something."

"Yes," he says, that extraordinarily ordinary smile nudging at the edges of his expression. "You forgot to tell me your name."

"Abigail." I extend my hand through the window, and his face blooms into a smile I can't help but return. "Abigail Wolff."

"Nice to meet you, Abigail Wolff. Gabe Armstrong."

He shakes my hand, and a surge of solidarity for this stranger-who's-not-quite-a-stranger spreads over my skin. I want to tell him I get it. I understand how one person's death can tilt your entire world into a tailspin, how it can make you reevaluate your life and send you scurrying for a dead-end job in a dusty hardware store, how that one choice, that one event, that one split second can change everything.

Instead, I tell him goodbye, shove the gear stick into Reverse and point my car toward home.

3

The good thing about renovating a master bathroom yourself is that it takes loads of time. Six to eight weeks, including demolition and drying, so says the internet, and if there's one thing I've had since Maria, it's oceans and oceans of time.

It's not that I'm overqualified for my current position as content curator for the nation's leading health care website, though I most definitely am. My job is a forty-hour-per-week slog that, on my worst weeks, I can wrap up in less than half that time. Yes, I'm capable of so much more, but I can't seem to muster up the energy to care. Content curation pays the bills and, as far as I know, has never killed a single soul.

It's funny. Back when I was working—*really* working—as a journalist, there was no such thing as free time. When I wasn't writing or researching or following leads, I was thinking about my next story. In the shower, on the water, during one of my mad sprints through the grocery store. Even my vacations, by definition a break from the daily grind, were not idle, and they were never long. Stolen snippets here and there, half days and federally mandated holidays, spent rowing or climbing or hiking through some forest somewhere, my mind tripping over ideas for my next piece. The harder I pushed myself, the faster my creative juices flowed. I didn't have time to stop moving. Time is money. Time waits for no one. There's never enough time in the day.

Now, though, I have more than enough to cart in all the bathroom supplies from Handyman, organize them by the order in which the internet tells me I will need them, line everything along the wall of the upstairs hallway and still be a good fifteen minutes early for my mid-afternoon skim latte date in Georgetown—even though I know it's just not in Mandy's DNA to arrive anywhere when she says she will. She pulls up at thirteen minutes past three, just as I'm settling onto a sidewalk terrace chair with two fresh drinks, my second and her first.

"Sorry I'm late," she calls from across the street. "Client meeting ran way over, but the good news is, I knocked their sixty-dollar argyle socks off."

"Come on. Socks don't cost sixty dollars."

"Not exactly the point here. The point here is—" an SUV whizzes by, stirring up the early-September air with the first of the fallen leaves, and Mandy disappears behind it, reappearing a second or two later with a wide grin "—they loved me. They gave me the job."

She steps off the curb without checking traffic, without making sure the drivers have slammed their brakes and their tires have screeched to a complete halt. Which they do, of course. Mandy is the human version of Jessica Rabbit, a rowdy redhead with Bambi eyes and bee-stung lips who favors skin-tight jeans, high heels and flowy, flowery blouses. Stopping traffic is her superpower. There's not a man on the planet who gets annoyed at the sight of her jaywalking across four lanes of city traffic as she's doing now.

"She's happily married," I say loudly enough so that the one closest to me, a Paul Bunyan type in a minivan, hears me through his open window. He responds by leaning into the dash to get a better look at her ass.

She collapses onto the seat next to me, snatches up her cup from the table. "Did you hear me? Honeymoon Channel wants me to redesign their app. It's a big deal, Abby. You should be thrilled."

"I *am* thrilled for you."

"Be thrilled for *us*." She lifts her drink in a toast, then pauses for a long pull. "I sold your services, too."

"I already have a job, remember?"

If she rolls her eyes, she's considerate enough to do it behind her mirrored sunglasses. After Chelsea died, Mandy made no secret of her disgust with my decision to shove my press pass to the back of a drawer, and she's spent the past three years encouraging me, rather loudly and relentlessly, to get back in there. To write something good, something meaningful, do something more exciting than my current drudgery.

But what Mandy can't seem to understand is, there's no shelf life on guilt. Someone died because of me, because of words I wrote. Just because I wasn't the one to pull the proverbial trigger doesn't mean I wasn't to blame. Words, even when they're carefully crafted, can be just as deadly as a bullet.

"Come on, Abigail." Mandy shoves her glasses to the top of her head and leans into the table. "I've seen your day planner. You row until mid-morning, you take weekly martini lunches—"

"I take them with you."

She waves off my rebuttal with a manicured hand. "Not the point. My point is, you can do your job in your sleep. In fact,

I'm pretty sure you've done your job in your sleep, and more than once. You have plenty of time for the one I'm offering."

I shake my head, confused. Mandy is a technological genius who peppers her sentences with terms like *HTML* and *search engine optimization* and *JavaScript*. Half the time, I have no idea what she's talking about. Why would she hire me for anything?

"I know nothing about apps," I tell her, "except how to order pizza off them."

"No, but you know about writing." When I don't respond, she cranks up her pitch a notch or two. "Have I mentioned it's for the Honeymoon Channel? We're talking beaches and cruises and European getaways. How is that going to harm anyone, except maybe with jet lag or a sunburn?"

"That's not the point, and you know it."

She sighs. "I know, I know. Your muse has vanished, your well's run dry. But surely you have enough talent still lurking in there somewhere to spit up a few thousand words of catchy advertising copy."

I turn and stare down the street, not eager to rehash this stale argument—yet again—with my well-meaning best friend. No matter how many times I've told her, she refuses to believe my not writing is so much more than just me missing my muse. It's that I *can't*. What happened with Chelsea didn't just mess me up mentally but also physically. I know this because for the past three years, every time I sit down at a blank computer screen or pick up a pen and paper, my fingers freeze up. My brain shorts out. The words are piled up somewhere deep inside of me, but they refuse to come out to play.

If anything, I'd always thought it would have been Maria. After all those pictures hit the internet, I'd obsessed about her welfare. Did she find another job? Had she made friends, come out of the closet, settled into a normal life? Was she living on the streets? But Maria had gone dark. Her phone was disconnected, her apartment empty, her email address unrecognized.

And then Chelsea surprised everyone by tying a noose around her neck and dangling herself from the showerhead—not an easy task, considering she had to rig the rope just right to support her weight and keep her knees bent as the oxygen stopped flowing to her brain. But she succeeded, and while the rest of the world shook their heads in compassion or tsked their tongues in holier-than-thou judgment, a chain of two words repeated in an endless loop through my brain. *My fault—my fault—my fault.*

And because Mandy knows me better than just about anyone, she heard them, too.

"Abigail, repeat after me," Mandy said when I called to tell her the news, now coming up on three years ago. "I am not responsible for Chelsea Vogel's death."

"My phone and email are blowing up with people, my freaking *colleagues*, asking me how her death makes me feel."

"Tell them it makes you feel unbelievably sad. For Chelsea, for her family, for everyone who ever knew her. Tell them her death is a tragedy, but do not, do *not* accept responsibility for that woman's suicide."

My fault—my fault—my fault.

A loud, exasperated sigh came down the line. "How many times have I listened to you preach about public enlightenment, how it is the foundation of democracy? That, as a journalist, it is not only your job but your *duty* to seek truth and report it to the world?"

"Yes, but I was also supposed to be sensitive and cautious and judicious in order to minimize harm, which clearly I didn't, because I'm pretty sure suicide is the mack-fucking-daddy of harm."

"If Chelsea Vogel didn't want her dirty laundry aired, then

she shouldn't have had any in the first place. You reported the facts, Abby. Fairly and honestly and comprehensively. Just like you were trained to do."

"Yes, but—"

And just then, a terrible, awful, horrible thought entered my mind unbidden. It was like an invasive weed that couldn't be killed, climbing and coiling through my consciousness like kudzu, suffocating every other thought in its path.

And the thought was this: yes, I had been sensitive and cautious and judicious with Maria, perhaps even overly so, but I could have done better by Chelsea. I could have shown more compassion for how she was about to be involuntarily outed not just as a predator but as a lesbian. I could have thought a little longer about her husband's and son's response to the news, what would happen when they opened up their morning paper or switched on their morning talk shows. I could have been more sensitive to her right to respond to the allegations, could have been more diligent in seeking her out. I *should* have done all those things, but I didn't.

"Yes, but what?" Mandy said.

"I have to go."

"Not until you answer me, Abigail. Yes, but what?"

I hung up on her then, and she never badgered me about it again—a decided lack of interest that's very un-Mandy-like. I suspect she heard those words, too. The loud and insistent ones I didn't know how to smother, the ones telling me that while I might have done everything right with Maria, with Chelsea I did everything wrong.

"Earth to Abby," she says now, waving a hand in front of my face.

I shake off the memory with a full-body shudder. "Sorry. What?"

"I said just think about it, okay? This job's a great way to ease back into writing, and I really could use the help. The last copywriter I hired was a total dud. He missed every single deadline."

"Great. So now I'm your last resort?"

She gives me a teasing half smile over her Starbucks cup. "You know what I mean."

I nod because I do know what she means, even though my answer is still no. "No offense, but if I ever write again, it will not be for an app. It will be because I can't keep the words inside. Because the story demands to be told. As awesome as tropical beaches are, I don't think they qualify."

But instead of being disappointed as I figured she'd be, she looks as if she wants to stand up and applaud. "Look at you, having a breakthrough."

I snort. "Hardly. I didn't say I was going to write. Only that I'm self-aware enough to know it has to be for the right topic. And honestly? I can't imagine what that topic would be."

"Maybe BenBird21225 can help you."

For a moment, I'm confused. How does Mandy know about BenBird21225, the faceless handle who's been badgering me by email and text for weeks now, his messages increasing in frequency and urgency. I have no idea who he is, why he's contacting me, how he got my phone number, because the only thing he ever actually says in any of them is that he wants to talk to me.

She points to my phone. "He's texted you ten times in as many minutes. Who is he?"

I pick up my phone and scroll through at least a dozen shouty texts. Ben wants a MEETING. He has something VERY IMPORTANT to say that must be said IN PERSON. Once upon a time, I would have followed this lead. I would have written back to Ben—asking for more details, setting up a time to talk, feeling him out as a potential source—instead of writing him off as I do now.

I delete them all, every single one, and toss my phone back onto the table.

"He's nobody."

4

When the doorbell rings in the middle of the day, nine times out of ten it heralds the arrival of the UPS man or a band of Jehovah's Witnesses on a mission to save my soul. Today, like pretty much any other day, I ignore it. I'm not exactly in a position to go to the door anyway, my body wedged uncomfortably under the bathroom sink, both hands prying loose a particularly stubborn drain nut. This happens to be a crucial moment, one the internet tells me is best handled equipped with a bucket, a mop and an endless supply of rags.

But when the doorbell rings again, and then again and again and again, I retighten the nut, wriggle myself out, dust myself off and head down the stairs.

The person on the other side of the door is a kid, twelve or thirteen maybe, with long shaggy hair that falls in a honey-colored veil over eyes I can't quite see. He's prepubescent skinny, his beanpole limbs sticking out of baggy shorts and a faded Angry Birds T-shirt, his bony ankles tapering off into orange Nike sneakers. White earbuds dangle from his shoulders, the long cord trailing down his torso and disappearing into his pants pocket. He shifts from foot to foot in what I read as either a bout of sudden impatience or the sullen annoyance typical of kids his age, almost-teens with a laundry list of things to prove to the world.

"Can I help you?" I say, glancing beyond him to the street for an idling car. No bike or skateboard, either, and I wonder if he's one of the neighborhood kids. Once they hit middle school, they shoot up so quickly I stop recognizing them.

"I'm Ben," he says, and when my brow doesn't clear in recognition, he adds, "The dude who sent all those emails?"

"Ben. As in BenBird21225?"

"Yeah. How come you never emailed me back?"

There are a million reasons I haven't emailed him back, none of which I'm willing to go into with a twelve-year-old kid. I settle on the one I think would be easiest for him to comprehend. "Because I didn't feel like it."

He makes a face as if I just offered him raw broccoli. "I thought you were a journalist. Aren't you supposed to, like, follow every lead or something?"

"I'm not a journalist. I'm a content curator."

"Huh?"

"I mine the internet for content relevant for today's active seniors." It's my elevator pitch, and I typically pull it out only when I want the person across from me to stop talking. It almost always works or, at the very least, results in slack jaws and glazed eyes and a very swift change of subject.

But Ben here doesn't take the bait. "Like, Viagra and adult diapers?"

"No," I say a bit defensively, even though Ben's right. Viagra and adult diapers are relevant to pretty much every senior, even if it's only just to brag about how their still youthful, virile body doesn't yet need them. "Do you need a ride? Or for me to call your mom to come get you?"

"I'd love for you to be able to do that, but my mom is dead." He runs his fingers through his messy bangs, pulling them off his face, and recognition surges. I know those gray-blue eyes. I've seen them before. I know the gist of his next words before they come out of his mouth. "She hung herself in the shower."

From the start, I knew this day would come, though I always thought it would be Chelsea's husband or one of her three sisters who showed up on my front porch, not her son. After all, journalists are threatened all the time by the people they expose. I've been bullied, intimidated and terrorized. I've gotten death threats on my car and answering machine, found knives stuck in my tires or front door, and once, a decapitated rat in my mailbox.

I get it, too. I understand why. It's not a pleasant thing to have your dirty laundry aired for all to see. Chelsea never asked for that crew camped out on her front lawn, for the camera-wielding reporters that followed her around like a pack of hyenas, for the humiliation and discomfort that came with having her transgression plastered across every American newspaper, television and computer screen—and neither did her family.

And once your secret is out there, there's no taking it back, ever. It's so much easier to blame the reporter who broke the story than it is to admit your wife or mother or sister molested one of her employees.

But Ben here doesn't look the least bit vengeful. He slips his hands in his pockets and waits, watching me from under his bangs with an intent expression.

"Look," I say, my voice coming across surprisingly strong

and even, "I don't know why you're here or what you want from me—"

"Because you haven't read any of my emails," he interrupts. "If you had, you'd know that Maria Duncan is driving around Baltimore in a brand-new BMW convertible. She lives in a condo in some downtown high-rise, the kind with a doorman and a pool on the roof, and she carries a different designer handbag every day of the week. She also has the biggest boobs I've ever seen. They're fucking ginormous."

"You shouldn't say the F-word."

The kid rolls his eyes, and honestly, who can blame him? His mother preached loudly and to anyone who would listen about God's message of one man and one woman, and then she molested her female secretary. What's a little curse word compared to his mother's front-page hypocrisy?

"That's it?" he says. "That's your answer, is don't say 'fuck'?"

I shrug. "Maybe Maria has a rich girlfriend."

"She has *boy*friends. *Boys*. A billion of them. And none of them last for longer than a couple of pictures on Facebook and Instagram."

"So she went through a phase with your mother. So she experimented for a bit. Lots of girls do."

"You don't think it's weird that she's suddenly so rich?"

"Maybe. But there are plenty of ways to get rich quick. Just because she's found one doesn't mean the money is connected in any way to what happened between her and your mom."

"Okay, then." He slips the iPhone from his pocket, fiddles with the screen for a few seconds, then flips it around so I can see. "How do you explain this?"

It takes a beat or two for the film to load, and then it's Maria, all right. I recognize her sharp cheekbones and delicate ears, her ruffled pixie cut, her thin, suntanned frame in a skimpy red bra and nothing else. And Ben was right about the boobs. They are inflated to ridiculous, porn-freak proportions, swaying up and down, up and down to the rhythm of the man riding her from behind.

"Should you be watching this?" I say. Even with the blurring and voice distortion, this video is pornographic, and far too hard-core for a twelve-year-old.

My question earns me another mouth twist. "Please. Nothing can shock me these days."

I return my attention to the film, and I think how much Maria has learned since her last go-round with Chelsea. The lighting is softer, the images are clearer, the angles less awkward. It almost looks professionally shot, as if all the clip needs is some cheesy background music and a willing pizza delivery man to make it a halfway decent, if not predictable, porn flick.

And then I see the man's hand, and what looks like an expensive watch winking on his wrist above a wedding band. He says something I can't quite make out in a voice that's distorted to be less dark bedroom and more Darth Vader. This isn't a porn flick. This film is exactly the same as that decapitated rat some asshole once left in my mailbox: a threat.

Because it's not a very far stretch to assume that whoever this man is, he would prefer his heaving, sweating, married face not be revealed on the internet, and his manicure and jewelry tells me he likely has the money to pay to make sure it doesn't. Which means that the person who uploaded this film—and after what Ben just told me, my money is on Maria—did so with an intent to harm.

"You should take this to the police. Blackmail is a crime, and it's punishable by law."

Ben shakes his head so hard, his hair slaps him on the cheeks. "No way. That dude's married. What if he has kids? What do you think will happen to them if his identity gets out? I'll tell you what will happen. They'll be fucking traumatized."

This time, I let the "fuck" slide. Ben is right. They *will* be fucking traumatized, and so will his wife, his friends, his family, his colleagues, everyone he ever knew. The scandal will likely die down quickly, but by then it will be too late. The married man will have lost his family, his job and most likely a good deal of his savings.

Still, though. It's really not any of my business.

"What do you want from me, Ben? I don't write those types of articles anymore. I can't..." I lift my shoulders and search for the words, settling finally on a definitive, "I can't."

"I don't want an article. I only want to know that my mom was not the bad guy here. That she didn't go after her secretary but the other way around. I want you to tell me that."

I think about what he's asking, for me to take another, closer look at Maria, to search for clues that she might have been a not-so-innocent victim of the affair with Ben's mom, her boss. I think about what it cost him to come here, to the front door of the journalist who outed his mother and ruined his life, requesting not a retraction or even an article refuting my original claims against his mother, but an answer. All he wants is an answer.

But I meant what I told him before. Maybe she's having an affair with a wealthy married man. Maybe she's an amateur porn star on the verge of her big break. Maybe the money and film are not connected at all. I don't know. My point is, there are unlimited possibilities, and the answer isn't necessarily the one Ben is hoping for.

"What if I can't tell you that? What if I do a little digging and find my original claims still stand?"

Ben thinks about it for a moment, lifts his bony shoulders. "Then at least I'll know for sure. I'll have closure."

"I don't know..."

I *do* know. The thought of reopening that old wound sends

an army of fire ants skittering over my skin, biting me not with old guilt, but with new terror. After Maria's pornographic performance, I'm terrified of what I'll find. What if Ben's right? What if Maria really isn't as innocent as she made me think?

"You owe me." Ben jerks his head sharply to one side, whipping his bangs off his eyes long enough to bore his gaze into mine. "You owe me everything."

Those last few words come with a whiptail lash, and I stand there for a moment, waiting for my skin to stop stinging, for the spots to stop dancing in my vision, for the rope to stop squeezing my heart and lungs. But his words don't settle. The knot around my middle doesn't loosen.

Because, hell's bells, Ben is right. I owe him everything.

I sigh, but it comes out more like a groan. "I'll call you as soon as I know something."

5

As soon as Ben leaves, I sit down at my desk and pull up Maria's video, trying to ignore the shoveled-out feeling in my gut as the images light up my screen, trying to quiet the million questions that pull and tug at me, reeling me toward them with the appeal of an impending train wreck. I don't want to see this clip. I don't want to see it, and yet I have to look. Ben was right; if nothing else, at the very least I owe him an answer.

I prop both feet on my chair, wrap my arms around my legs and watch from the space between my knees. Now that I'm looking at the video on a bigger screen, I see I was wrong before. The angle is a little strange, as if the camera is wedged only a few feet or so away from Maria's face and trained up. It gives me a fish-eye view of the left side of her face, her swinging breasts in all their porn-star glory, the man's heaving chest and his hand as it slaps, over and over and over, a red splotch onto Maria's ass. I don't blink, I barely breathe, and I study every pixel for clues.

About halfway through, I drop my feet to the floor, hit Pause and zoom in on the frame. The man is middle-aged, somewhere in his mid-to-late fifties. Flabby skin over muscles fighting gravity, a few stray gray hairs on his chest. I lean in and zoom some more, see his wedding ring is a plain gold band, the watch a classic gold model, unadorned and without flash. He could be one of a million men in this town.

I push Play and watch the rest. There's a lot of grunting and slapping, mixed in with some dirty talk—him—and exaggerated moans—her—and then, at the very tail end of the video, when the activity crescendos into a loud and rather explosive grand finale all over Maria's back, I see it. What I missed the first time on Ben's tiny iPhone screen. What plunges my stomach into the crawl space under my office floor.

Maria looks straight at the camera...and smiles.

The empty hole in my gut fills in an instant, swelling with a churning mush. I push back from the desk with a hard shove. "Fucking hell."

Could Maria really be that brazen and greedy to have sex with someone, record it, then use it to squeeze some cash out of him? Could she really be so evil and coldhearted, especially after what happened with Chelsea? My nausea rises up, crawling through my stomach and strangling the calm, reasonable voice telling me surely, *surely* Maria couldn't be that evil.

I rewind the last ten seconds and watch them again, stopping on the exact moment when her pretty lips twist in so much more than a smile.

They twist in a deliberate taunt.

With her face still filling up my screen, I reach for my phone and scroll until I find the number I'm looking for, the one I haven't dialed in almost three years.

Floyd picks up on the second ring. At first all I hear is background noise—a shouted command, an explosion, the staccato stream of gunshots. I'd be alarmed, except I happen to know the battleground sounds come from a video game.

"Well, well, well, if it isn't Abigail Wolff. I thought you'd gone off and died on me," he says in the rapid-fire Baltimorese I'd forgotten he spoke.

I force myself to slow down long enough for small talk, then summon a tone friendly enough to smother my rolling stomach and hammering heart. "Hey, Floyd. How are you?"

"Not bad, not bad. I played fifteen rounds of Spartan Ops last night and ranked up from twenty-six to thirty-three."

"I have no idea what any of that means."

"Halo 4, hon. It's the bomb."

Though Floyd and I have never actually met, I've always pictured him as the type of guy who lives in his parents' basement—hair a little too unwashed, social skills a little too awkward, middle a little too mushy from a constant diet of pizza and Cheetos. But if anyone knows how to flush out Maria's shenanigans, it'll be him. Floyd is a computer whiz who specializes in financial investigations, and one thing I know for sure is that money almost always leaves a paper trail.

"My bad," I concede, then steer us on to the reason I called. "As much as I'd love to hear all about your mad PlayStation—"

"Xbox."

"—your mad Xbox skills, I need you to check on some-one's finances for me."

"An assignment, huh? I thought you quit."

"I did." I search for an explanation, then decide on the truth. "This one's personal."

It's all I needed to say. The background noise plummets into a muted silence, and Floyd's tone makes a drastic U-turn, from fun and Xbox games to all business. "Give it to me."

I relate a quick lowdown on Maria, being careful not to re-veal any more detail than absolutely necessary. Her name, her moving-on-up lifestyle and very little more. I don't mention a word about her five minutes of internet fame. If that's connected to her bank account in any way, I want Floyd to ferret it out by himself.

"You got it," he says, and I already hear his fingers flying across a keyboard. "I'm kinda slammed, so it might take me a week or two to get to you. I'll call you as soon as I know anything."

"Thanks, Floyd."

"Oh, and, Abigail?" He pauses, and I can hear his smile. "Welcome back, hon."

After I hang up with Floyd, I wander through my house, looking for something to take my mind off Maria. I could unload the dishwasher and mop the kitchen floor. I could finish removing the drain in the bathroom and take out the shower pan. I could sort through the million emails in my inbox. Nothing sounds even remotely appealing. Maria's images replay on a constant loop through my mind, shooting ice water through my veins, knocking me sideways with that smile, because my gut...my goddamn gut is telling me—three years too late—that I missed something the first time around.

I change into shorts and a T-shirt, shove my feet into my sneakers and bang out the front door to burn off my frustration in a long run through the district, but my feet get tangled up in something unexpected on my welcome mat. A large brown envelope. No address, no postage, no writing or stamps on it anywhere at all. I cut a quick glance up and down my quiet street, which is, of course, ridiculous. Whoever leaves an unmarked, unstamped envelope for a person on their front doorstep doesn't wait around for that person to find it.

And while we're at it, why me? This is the kind of thing

someone leaves for a journalist, not a washed-up ex-journalist turned health care content curator.

I look up as a car slides by. A neighbor from up the street waves from behind the wheel, and I'm too frozen to wave back. I check up and down the street again, even though I know the effort is futile. Whoever left the envelope is long gone.

I carry the package into the house, hook a finger under the seal and rip it open.

At first, what I find inside doesn't make any sense. It's about twenty pages of sworn statements, a written transcript of someone's testimony. Someone by the name of Corporal Daniel Kochtizky, a surname so uncommon that I recognize it from this past year's news coverage.

Corporal Kochtizky was the medic for Zach Armstrong's platoon.

I return to the papers, skimming the testimony. The first few pages contain a lot of back and forth on details like name, rank, title, then moving on to dates, locations, logistics of the battle. Pretty standard fare, and nothing I haven't read before and in a million places.

I skim the testimony, refresh my mind of the details of the army's most famous soldier, whose death became its worst nightmare.

Zach's death was like one of those perfect-storm cases, where one little thing sets off a chain of seemingly innocent events that end in disaster. In his case, it all started with a broken-down valve on an armored vehicle that brought the entire platoon—thirty-five soldiers spread out over eleven vehicles—to a screeching halt. A spare part was summoned, the platoon was split, a battle ensued. Zach Armstrong took three bullets to the head. His brother Nick, crouched a few feet away, was the one to recover his body.

But what nobody seems to be willing to talk about, what the US Army has refused to even discuss, is who shot him. Even more suspicious, the army spent the first few months after Zach's death touting him all over town as a hero. They awarded him medals and posthumous promotions in elaborate, nationally televised ceremonies. They built memorials and slapped his name on bridges and highways. They created scholarships and grants in his name. Meanwhile, nobody else was reported killed or wounded in that battle, not even the enemy.

Jean Armstrong called foul, and she demanded answers in the form of a congressional investigation into not just who pulled the trigger of the weapon that killed her son, but also the army's subsequent handling of his death. General Rathburn—we're not technically related, but he is my godfather—is one of the three-star generals being investigated. The other is General Tom Wolff. My father.

I've just flipped to the fifth or sixth page when it occurs to me.

This document has not been censored. There are no dark stripes of marker, no blacked-out names or classified details. Every single letter is there on the page, lit up like strobe lights.

I rush through the living room to my office and my computer. After a bit of poking around on the internet, I find the censored version of the same document on the Department of Defense's website and hit Print.

As it's rolling out of my machine, I nab a pink highlighter from the drawer and lay the pages side by side, highlighting the blacked-out words on the DOD's version in pink on my gifted copy. The name of the investigating officer. Others in the chain of command. Comments that could be construed as opinion, the medic's version of what happened, hearsay and accusations. And then, on page seven, I highlight a name I've never seen before.

Ricky Hernandez.

According to the medic, Ricky was present on the scene when Zach was killed, and he was one of the thirty-six eye-witnesses briefed back at the base. *Thirty-six.* My pulse explodes like a bottle rocket.

So why does every single transcript the army ever released, every news magazine article ever printed and every evening news report ever broadcast maintain there were thirty-*five* soldiers on the field the day Zach was killed? And now there are thirty-six?

Thirty-six.

The word travels through me like electricity, rushing through my veins at the speed of light. I stare at the pink-striped papers fanned across the surface of my desk, feeling my scalp grow hot, then cold, then hot again with the realization that I'm looking at classified information. Whoever sent it to me is someone with inside knowledge of the operation—a soldier? an army investigator?—and wants me to know the truth. They want me to know about Ricky.

I turn back to my computer, fingers flying across the keyboard. A few hours later I've compiled a mountain of papers to sort through. Every document the army and DOD have ever released around Zach Armstrong's death. Every hit on Ricky and all four Armstrongs—soldiers Zach and Nick, mother Jean, brother Gabe—that my content curation software spits out. Thousands and thousands of pages.

A slow sizzle begins somewhere deep in my gut, heating me from the inside out. What if Ricky Hernandez watched three bullets tear through Zach's skull on the battlefield that day? What if he saw whoever pulled the trigger? What if he pulled that trigger himself? At first, the warmth feels like a phantom limb, vaguely familiar and not entirely real, and then I remember.

This is what a story feels like.

I toe off my sneakers, lean back in my chair and get comfortable. I'm going to be here awhile.

6

Early Saturday evening, I'm studying my menu in Bar Dupont's sleek lounge when a rhythmic *thump-click, thump-click* pierces the chatter around me like the steady beat of a drum. I twist on my bar stool, as do half the people in the place, and find my former boss, Victoria Santillano, coming at me on crutches. She's wearing an oversize black boot on her right foot and a dragged-down expression, heavy with equal parts crankiness and effort. All long lines and sharp edges, Victoria has always had the hardscrabble air of someone who's forgotten to exhale, only now she looks pissed about it.

"What the hell happened to you?"

She juts her chin at the dirty martini that, just two seconds before, the bartender slid in front of me. "If that's vodka, extra cold and extra dirty, I need it far more than you do."

I signal to the bartender for another and push my still full glass in front of the empty seat next to me. Victoria hobbles up to the stool, flings her crutches against the bar and drinks half the glass in one giant gulp.

"Jesus, that's good," she says, smacking her lips.

"Please, tell me that boot isn't just a scheme to get free cocktails."

She snorts. "Now that you mention it, it is one of the better perks. But, alas, no. Damn ankle broke in three spots, can you believe it?"

I can't, actually. Victoria is one of the most indestructible women I've ever met. She's trekked through deserts and jungles, crawled through caves and fields of land mines, chased down thieves and dictators and drug lords, and lived to talk about all of them in front-page, top-billed feature articles. The woman survives on adrenaline and vodka and caffeine, and the only thing I've ever known her to break is a nail.

"Were you rappelling off an Afghani cliff? Skydiving into a war zone? Scaling the Kremlin with fish wire and Scotch tape?"

"I fell down the stairs." Her long, unmanicured finger comes within millimeters of my nose. "And if you tell anyone that's how I broke my ankle, I'll have you murdered in your sleep." She plucks an olive from her glass with two hooked fingers. "So what's new and exciting in content management these days?"

"Not one goddamn thing."

"Excellent," she says, nodding sagely. "Business services, was it?"

"Health care. Health&Wealth.com is the leading health care web magazine for today's active seniors."

"Mmm-hmm. Sounds fascinating."

Victoria buries her nose in her glass, and I do the same with the fresh one the bartender hands me, neither of us quite willing to rehash old arguments. She was there when I broke the Chelsea Vogel scandal three years ago, and she was there two weeks later, after Chelsea was found hanging in her Herndon shower, when I shoved my press pass to the very back of my kitchen junk drawer and handed in my resignation letter. She never questioned my decision to quit. She never, not once, tried to talk me out of it. She just told me to call her when I found my balls.

For the next six months, I sent her every type of ball I could come up with. Soccer balls, baseballs, tennis balls and footballs. A ten-pound bag of meatballs and a monogrammed bowling ball. A framed vintage poster of Lucille Ball. A custom Magic 8 Ball where every side of the triangle popped up as "Hell, yes!" Finally, when I paid a delivery service to dump a box containing a thousand ping-pong balls onto her office floor, she sent me a one-word email. "Uncle," it said in the subject line, and nothing more. After that, we picked up where we'd left off, with regular email check-ins and cocktails every time she swings through town, which is often.

But we never broach the one subject that hangs between us in gleaming, glittering strobe lights—that by walking away from the Chelsea Vogel aftermath all those years ago, I walked away from my duty as a journalist to seek the truth and report it to the public.

Only now I've spent the past thirty-six hours researching an article I'm not writing, looking into a story I'm not covering, and though I'm not certain I've found my balls, I have, without a sliver of a shadow of a doubt, found a thirty-sixth soldier. One who was in Zach Armstrong's convoy of vehicles rumbling down an Afghani street when small-arms fire rained down from the upper level of an abandoned building. One who fought alongside both Armstrong brothers and was returning fire when Zach took three bullets to the head. One whose interview was cataloged and then buried, whose name disappeared from every army account except one—the uncensored transcript I'm not supposed to have.

"What?" Victoria says, studying me with squinty eyes.

"What do you mean, what?"

"I mean, what's going on here? You have that look about you, like maybe I should check between your teeth for canary feathers."

My skin prickles, and my scalp buzzes with the thrill of new knowledge I can't hold in another second. "Okay, so I'm not saying I'm writing anything, but say I know something that no one else knows about the Zach Armstrong story. Something new. Something earth-shattering and groundbreaking."

"How earth-shattering and groundbreaking?"

"Enough that the DOD buried it."

Victoria takes in my words like a seasoned journalist who's seen and heard it all, with a pursed-lipped nod. She reaches for her martini. "I see. And what exactly did they bury?"

"A name."

She looks up from her glass with an arched brow, the same arched brow I've seen her use on rapists and swindlers and serial killers, when she asked them if perhaps they shouldn't have wiped down the door handle after leaving their prints all over it. "A soldier's name?"

I confirm it with my own pursed-lipped nod, but I don't reveal anything more. The thing is, as much as I like Victoria, she is completely ruthless when she smells a story. Even back when I worked for her, when she served as both my boss and my mentor, I was always careful to never reveal too much until I sent her the final copy. I didn't trust her, not completely, to not run off with my story.

But since Ricky's name has been wiped from every report the DOD or army has published, I'm fairly certain that no matter how hard Victoria looks, she'll never find him.

"Where's my Magic 8 Ball when I need it?" Victoria pounds

a fist on the polished maple bar, and her next words pierce the music and bar chatter like a bomb siren. "Hell, yes! I *knew* it!"

Packed with corporate executives and political insiders, the Bar Dupont crowd is a seen-it-all-heard-it-all kind of crowd, but still. More than a few heads swing our way at Victoria's outburst.

I try to ignore their curious looks. "Knew what?"

"That you'd be back eventually. Send me what you've got whenever it's ready. If I don't have a spot for it, I'll make one. How many words, do you think? Three thousand? Four?"

"Hold up. I never said I was writing anything."

"Please." She waves a palm through the air, takes a long pull from her glass.

"Please what?"

She rolls her unmascaraed eyes and thunks her glass onto the bar hard enough to send liquid sloshing over the sides. "Please, stop fooling yourself, because you're not fooling me. The very fact that we are sitting here, talking about Zach Armstrong, is proof you're already writing the piece in your head. You didn't tell me about the additional soldier because you were filling me in on what's been going on in your life. You were looking for validation, and you knew I'd give it to you."

Well, hell. Does Victoria have a point? Did I come here looking for her to tell me to write the Armstrong story? It's a theory I hadn't thought of yet, though I certainly am now, and the answer is maybe.

The truth is, discovering Ricky's name has cracked something open inside of me, something that feels as if it's been hibernating for a really long, really harsh winter and now might be ready to step into the early-spring sunshine. And while I'm certainly not already writing the piece in my head, why not hand him over to Victoria instead?

Because he's my *lead.*

At the unwelcome thought, a familiar and greedy rush, as uncomfortable as an old, itchy sweater, warms my blood and coats my skin like a rash.

Victoria must read the indecision on my face, because she drains her glass, signals for another round, then twists on the bar stool to face me.

"I'll tell you what the wisest journalist I know once said, and that is this. *Our profession holds the power to be a force for good, and in the end, credit will go to the ones of us in the ring, the ones covered in sweat and blood and tears, and not the ones watching from the safety of the sidelines. Get out there, and be fully informed, fully aware and fully engaged. Be part of a force for good.*"

"*You* said that, last year in a graduation speech at Princeton."

"Harvard, but that's neither here nor there. What matters is the message. Are you or are you not going to be part of the force for good?"

"I *was* part of the force for good, remember? Until I became the cause of something bad."

"How many times do I have to say it?" Victoria leans into me, her tone fierce and forceful. "Chelsea Vogel's death was a tragedy, but you did exactly what you were supposed to do, and that was report the facts. The decisions and actions were all Chelsea's. She slept with her female assistant, she took her own life. As much as you seem to enjoy playing the part of martyr, you are not responsible for her death."

"I'm not sure I agree." I tell her about Ben Vogel's surprise appearance at my front door, and my taking another, closer look at Maria in light of her nouveau-riche lifestyle and pornographic internet performance. "Only, if what I now suspect is true and Maria is not as innocent as she led everyone to believe, then I'm even more responsible than I thought."

"Not necessarily. Maybe Maria didn't realize her sexual prowess until she gained some with Chelsea. Maybe it took seeing how those videos went viral the first time around for her to come up with a plan to do it again, this time for a wad of cash. My point is, Chelsea's story is not finished. There's more to tell, and there's no one on the planet more qualified—or more justified—to tell it than you. Expose Maria as a conniving slut who ruins lives and sleeps with anything with money or power if that's what she is. Set the record straight."

"Maybe she's not a conniving slut at all. Maybe she won the lottery or...I don't know, found a pot of gold."

"Only one way to find out."

Victoria doesn't say the rest. She doesn't have to. She's telling me to dig deeper into Maria's story, to do the research, to search out the facts. But she doesn't have to tell me to do that, either. I've already got Floyd on the case. No matter what I end up doing with the answer—handing it over to Ben or stuffing it in a box and pushing it to the very back corner of my mind—I already plan to find out.

But still.

"What if I write something, and it happens all over again? What if somebody gets hurt?"

"Somebody always gets hurt, Abigail." Victoria lifts her shoulders high enough to brush the ends of her fringy bob, then turns back to her drink. "But if you do your job right, nine times out of ten it's the bad guy."

7

The next time I walk through its double glass doors, Handyman Market looks more like a haunted house than a hardware store. Orange lights and black streamers and miles of fake cobwebs are slung from every display and shelf unit, hanging above tombstones, cauldrons, smoke machines and every other front yard decoration imaginable. I walk down the middle aisle, past the ghouls and ghosts and glow-in-the-dark skeletons, sidestepping a grinning witch straddling a broom, in search of Gabe. I find him atop a ladder in the electrical department, loading boxes onto a top shelf.

Recognition flashes across his face in the form of that extraordinarily ordinary grin.

"Abigail Wolff is back, and less than a week later, which we all know can mean only one thing." He swings himself down off the ladder, the metal rungs squeaking under his weight. "You flooded your house, didn't you?"

I pretend to be insulted. "Do you really have that little faith in my abilities?"

THE ONES WE TRUST   53

He leans in, and his grin widens. "That bad, huh? Come on. I'll show you where the shop vac and drying fans are."

"Ha-ha. My bathroom is demolished, and look—" I hold up both hands, wiggle my fingers in the air "—still have all ten. No water damage, either."

Well, *almost* none. There was a little excitement when a pipe snapped clean in two as I was unscrewing the showerhead, drenching me and the bathroom floor in the process, but I had the rags and the mop, and the water turned off in thirty seconds flat. The only real damage done was to my blowout and a wall I was already planning to paint over anyway.

He holds out his hand, palm to the sky. "Let's see it, then."

For a moment, I'm confused. "See what?"

"Your list." He steps closer, and I can smell the detergent on his clothes, the sawdust coating his apron, his shaving cream spicy and complex. "Does it have *Find Handyman ASAP* written anywhere on it, because I'll bet it does."

His sarcasm, his teasing tone, his half-cocked grin. So far I like everything about him, and it's distracting me. His closeness is distracting me. His thick shock of hair is distracting me. His looks as if it hasn't been combed in days, but instead of making him look ungroomed, it makes him look really good in a way that makes me uneasy. Especially in light of what I came here to tell him.

A bitter taste pools on my tongue, as if I'm sucking on old pennies. This is going to be so much harder than I thought.

Because if I've learned anything from Chelsea's death, it's that I have a lot to make up to the universe for my hand in it. When I set in motion events that ended in her lifeless body hanging in the shower, I upset the universal balance just as surely as pitching the planet a few degrees would transform the earth's climate. In order to tip the karma scale back to good,

I have to *do* good. I have to do what's *right*, which means I have to tell someone about Ricky.

And it has to be one of the good guys.

Just say it, I think, glancing around, my gaze skimming over the lone customer all the way down at the end of the aisle, an elderly man sorting through a markdown bin. He doesn't seem to be paying us much attention, and he probably can't hear us from here, but I lean in and lower my voice anyway.

"I need to talk to you about your family's case."

Gabe freezes in momentary confusion, but it doesn't take long for him to catch on, and his expression to catch up. The muscles tighten in his jaw, his mouth, the skin around his eyes, and three vertical trenches slash up the center of his forehead.

"My family's case?"

I nod.

"My family's *case*."

"Yes."

Gabe takes two small but significant steps backward. "Are you a journalist?"

"I'm a *former* journalist, and I've found something that—"

"Jesus!" he says, and fiercely enough that the man at the end of the aisle looks up in alarm, dumps his items back in the bin and scurries around the corner. "I can't believe I actually bought your ridiculous bullshit story about renovating a bathroom. Unbelievable! Is your name really Abigail Wolff, or was that a load of crap, too?"

"Okay, so admittedly, my skills at approaching sources are a little rusty, but, yes." I take a step in his direction, but he holds me off with two palms in the air. "My name is Abigail Wolff, I *used* to be a journalist, I have the credit card bill to prove I'm renovating my bathroom, and I came here with information that could make your family's case take a hard left turn."

"I'll make this very simple for you, then. My family is in

the middle of a federal investigation. None of us are allowed to talk about the case. If you had done any background research at all, you would know that."

A fleeting frustration zings up my spine, but I swat it away. I remind myself that Gabe sees me as the enemy, as a member of the same media who has painted him and his mother as ferocious and unreasonable. And with valid enough reason. He doesn't know me, doesn't know anything about me. No wonder he sees my coming here as an ambush.

The realization pushes a friendly smile up my face, softens my tone to placating. "I don't want *you* to talk, I want you to listen to what I have to *tell* you. Did I mention this information could change the course of your case?"

"You mentioned it, and now it's my turn to talk. No fucking comment."

And there it is, I think. The infamous *no fucking comment*.

Gabe doesn't wait for me to argue it, just does an abrupt about-face, cursing under his breath and crossing the entire length of the aisle, past the extension cords and rolls of electrical wire and every kind of lightbulb imaginable, in three angry strides. At the end, he hangs a sharp left and ducks around the corner. I hustle to where he disappeared from sight and lean my head around the corner.

"I found a thirty-sixth soldier."

My revelation stops him as I knew it would, as instantly and absolutely as it stopped me when I discovered it. His back goes ramrod straight, and he turns, that famous Armstrong jaw clenched and tight, those legendary eyes raking me up and down. I can tell he's trying to decide whether or not to believe me, so I decide to help him out. I step into the aisle with square shoulders and a high chin, looking him straight in the eye.

"I've studied every single document that's been released,"

he says, stalking back up the aisle, his boots thumping out ominous notes on the hard floor until he pulls up right in front of me. "Read every single interview and report and transcript there is. There's no thirty-sixth soldier."

"That's because you've only seen the censored versions."

"And you haven't." His jaw is set on neutral, but there's the slightest crease between his brows, as if maybe he doesn't believe my claims, but he doesn't quite dismiss them, either.

"I have every single unmarked letter, period and comma of the medic's transcript, which include the name of a thirty-sixth soldier that was censored from the version the DOD released." I reach into my bag, pull out a business card and pass it to him.

He glares at it for a second or two, then looks back up. "What does Health&Wealth.com have to do with my brother's case?"

"Nothing, that's what I've been trying to tell you. Send me some times that work for you and your mother, and we'll set something up."

"My mother. Of course. There's no thirty-sixth soldier, is there? This is all just another bullshit ruse to get an interview with *her*."

I can't hold back the exasperated sigh that pushes up from my lungs. "Of course there's a thirty-sixth soldier. Why would I make something like that up?"

Gabe looks at me as if I might be coated in anthrax, his eyes narrowed into tiny slits. "I don't know. That's what I'm trying to figure out. Why don't you just give the copy to *me*?"

I don't tell Gabe that I seriously considered doing exactly that, passing him Ricky's name and washing my hands of the entire episode. But the more I thought about it, the more I contemplated my reasons for wanting to give the Armstrongs Ricky, the more I realized giving Gabe his name would be like confessing my sins to the priest's secretary. I need to go straight to the top, which means I need to hand Ricky to his mother.

"Look, Gabe. I realize you're suspicious of my intentions, and honestly, I can't say I blame you. Journalists are pretty ruthless when they smell a story, and they've crucified you and your mother for daring to take on the US Army, but again, and I'm just being completely honest here, it's exactly because of the behavior you've shown me in the past five minutes."

He hauls a breath to respond, but I don't give him the chance.

"You don't have to explain. I get it. You lost a brother, you're allowed to be angry. But your mother lost a son, and in my book that means she needs to be in the room when I hand over the name. Believe me or don't. Call me or don't. I've never met your mother, but I think I know enough about her to know that if she were standing here right now, she wouldn't let that soldier just walk away."

And then that's just what I do. I turn and walk away.

Because even though my skills at approaching sources may be a little rusty, I can still read one like a book, and I know one thing for sure. Gabe might not want to, but he believes me, and he'll call.

Twenty minutes later, I'm walking through my front door when the text pings my phone.

Wednesday, 3 pm. 4538 Davidson Street. Gabe

8

Jean Armstrong lives in a traditional brick colonial on a quiet, tree-lined street just outside the western beltway. I ease to a stop at the curb, gazing out my car window at the lace-hung windows, the perfectly clipped boxwood hedges that lead to the front door. So this is the house where the Armstrong boys grew up. Where they took first steps and left for first dates, where they swung from a tire on the hundred-year-old magnolia and roughhoused on the wide, grassy lawn, where only ten months ago, a solemn-faced chaplain and uniformed CNO trudged up to the sunny yellow door, carrying a task heavier than holding the front line.

I reach for my bag and climb out of the car, smoothing my skirt as I make my way to the door. For some reason I didn't give too much thought to at the time, I dressed to impress. Makeup, hair, heels, the works. Part of my effort is that the more that I read up on Jean, the more I really like her. The few quotes she's given the media have been so smart and thoughtful, and I've always been drawn to smart, thoughtful people. And besides, it's hard not to feel affection for a grieving mother.

But there's more to it than just wanting Jean to like me. As much as I hate to admit it, I can't deny my glossy hair and five-inch stilettos are also a teeny tiny bit for Gabe. To remind him of the first time we met, before my accidental discovery torpedoed our connection, when he seemed to like me enough to ask my name. I don't know what that says about me that I want him to like me again, but there it is. I do.

I climb the few steps to the door and aim my finger at the bell, but before I can make contact, the door opens and Gabe steps out, swinging the door shut with a soft click. He's in those same faded and worn jeans, but he's traded his apron for a T-shirt and nice wool sweater, and accessorized them both with what I'm beginning to recognize as his trademark scowl.

"Here's how it's going to go down," he says without so much as a hello. "We go inside, you give Mom the papers and answer our questions, and then you leave. You don't get to ask us anything, and you sure as hell can't use anything we do or say in your article. All of it, every single second, is off the record. Do you understand?"

"I've already told you—" *and at least a dozen times* "—I'm not writing an article."

He gives me a get-real look. "Right."

I'm getting awfully tired of his assumptions and accusations, but in light of what happened with his brother, I'm also giving him a long, long rope. I let it go.

"Did you bring the transcript?"

I pat my bag and summon up a smile. "Got it right here. Along with my notepad, digital camera and voice recorder."

"Jesus, seriously?"

"Of course not. Journalists don't use paper these days, not since Evernote." I give him a toothy smile to let him know

I'm kidding, but when his scowl still doesn't relent, my eyes go wide. "Come on, Gabe, it was a joke. I'm not… You know what? Never mind. Let's just get this over with, shall we?"

"Gladly." He flings open the front door and takes off in long strides down the hall.

I breathe deeply and step inside, taking in what I can of Jean Armstrong's home as I follow in Gabe's fumes toward the back of the house. Light, rambling rooms filled with flowers and painted in warm, sunny colors. Thick carpets and overstuffed couches begging to be sunk into. Smiling family photographs everywhere, decorating the walls and covering corner tables. It's a home filled with laughter and love, much like the one I grew up in, though you'd never know it from the man marching in front of me.

We emerge in an enormous kitchen on the back of the house, where it smells like flowers and vanilla and something else, something warm and delicious. Jean Armstrong hovers over a whistling teapot at the stove, lost in thought.

"Mom," Gabe says, his tone warm and obliging, much like the first day we met. It's such a drastic transformation from the one he used with me just a few seconds ago that I feel almost disoriented, at the same time as this new animosity between us wrings my insides in a way I don't want to consider too closely. "Abigail is here."

Mrs. Armstrong switches off the gas. She's much prettier in person than on screen and in print, her auburn hair richer, her eyes brighter, her skin more glowing. She's smaller than I expected, too. Her sons must have inherited their height from their father, who died when Zach was still in grade school.

I cross the room and wrap both palms around her tiny, birdlike hand. "I know these are not the happiest of circumstances, Mrs. Armstrong, but I hope you don't mind me saying, it's an honor to meet you in person."

She pats her free hand over mine. "Now, why would I mind you saying something so lovely? I was just making some tea. Would you like a cup?" At my nod, she reaches for her son's arm. "Gabe, be a dear and get the mugs, would you?" She turns back to me, points me to a washed pine table by a wall of windows. "Have a seat, Abigail. We'll be right there."

I head over and drop my bag on the table, looking out at a garden worthy of a Martha Stewart magazine cover. Even now, when most plants should have wilted and shriveled in the last of the Indian summer's heat, Jean's garden is still full and lush and filled with color. It's the kind of garden that can belong only to a master gardener, one who spends the bulk of every dry-sky day coaxing plants out of the ground.

While Gabe pours the tea, I sink onto a padded chair across from Jean. "I assume Gabe's told you why I'm here."

Jean and Gabe share a look, then Jean says, "He told me you have information you'd like to share about Zach's murder."

Though it's not the first time I've heard Zach's death referred to as "murder" from one of the Armstrongs, it startles me all the same. I take it in with a nod and move on.

"As I told Gabe earlier this week, I've found evidence of a thirty-sixth soldier in Zach's unit." I slide the transcript from my bag and across the table. "His name is Ricky Hernandez."

Gabe flips the papers around, and he and his mother bend over them. I give them all the time they need, sipping at my tea and taking another good look out the window. Jean's garden really is beautiful, meticulously maintained and wild at the same time. As picturesque as, well, a picture.

Gabe is the first to speak, and the hard edge is back in his voice. "Where did you get this?"

"Someone left it on my doorstep."

"Who?"

I give him one of his own get-real looks, a pretty decent

imitation judging by the way the creases in his scowl fold in on themselves even further. "He didn't exactly stick around to introduce himself."

"Then how do you know it's real?"

"Because, first of all, why would anyone go to the trouble to doctor up a fake version for me? Especially since I'm not a journalist. And second—" I slide another packet of papers across the table, the censored version from the DOD's website "—it matches up exactly to this one. Word for word, letter for letter. Except for the blacked-out ones, of course."

There's a long, stunned silence. Finally, Gabe swipes a palm up the back of his head. "Those motherfuckers."

Mrs. Armstrong backhands him with a light slap on the chest. "Language."

I bite the inside of my lip, a smile tickling under my cheekbones. The gesture makes me like Jean even more, and not only because it makes Gabe look so properly chastised. There's just something sweet about a mother still disciplining her thirty-three-year-old son.

"Okay," Jean says, returning her attention to the transcripts, "so who's Ricky?"

"I don't know."

"Well, was he interviewed?"

"If he was, they didn't release his transcripts."

"Was he in the first convoy or second? Where was he positioned when Zach was killed? Did he see it happen, did he see who pulled the trigger, was it him?"

I lift both palms from the table. "I don't know. I'm sorry. I even put him through my content curation software. There were seven and a half million hits for Ricky Hernandez, most of them Facebook and Twitter profiles. A couple athletes, an author, a youth minister, a sound designer, but unfortunately, no soldier. There were a few possibilities in the military databases but none of them our Ricky, which means I've kind of hit a wall."

Gabe snorts. "I thought you were excellent at research."

I stifle a sigh and smother my rising exasperation with her son in a sugary smile I aim at Jean. "No matter how many times I try to convince your son otherwise, Gabe insists on thinking I'm here because I'm writing an article. But let me assure you, unless he's somehow relevant to health care for active seniors, my boss at Health&Wealth.com couldn't care less about Ricky Hernandez."

Jean's brow crumples, but I can't detect even an ounce of the suspicion that darkened her son's brow when I told him much the same thing. To me, Jean only looks confused. "Then why are you here?"

Because you're one of the good guys. And despite your son's volatile temper, I think he is, too.

"Because I don't know why the DOD buried his name and testimony, but I do know I can't just sit on him. Maybe he's nothing, but maybe he's the person who blows this investigation wide-open. Either way, I believe you have the right to know he exists, and that he was there, fighting in the battle that killed your son."

"But why?" I must look as if I still don't understand, because she adds, "Everybody wants something, Abigail. What is it that you want?"

I blow out a long breath, thinking through how to give a simple response to such a complicated question. Where to begin? With Chelsea's suicide and how I feel responsible? With my karmic imbalance, and my hope that by doing right by the Armstrongs, I can atone for what I did wrong by Chelsea? Those answers are all too complex, and far too lengthy, to condense into a few short sentences.

But my coming here is more than just for atonement.

It's also because of a sense of righteousness.

Jean Armstrong lost a son, and under what she has always insisted were suspicious circumstances. Now that I know Ricky exists, I'm beginning to think she may have a point.

So even though my father is one of the generals on the other end of her pointer finger, even though by coming here I might be handing her something that could look bad for his defense, I needed to come here anyway. I felt morally obligated to do something that could be construed as immoral…or at the very least, disloyal to both my father and the organization he spent his entire adult life serving.

"I come from a military family," I tell them both, but mostly Jean. "My father was in the army, as was his father and the one before him. I'm not a soldier, but that doesn't mean my father didn't teach me to live by the seven army values. They were hammered into me from the day I was born, and they're what brought me here today. So, to answer your question, I want a healthy conscience."

Gabe pushes away from the table so fast, he almost topples backward on his chair. "Un-fucking-believable."

His mother flaps a palm in his direction, but she never takes her eyes off me.

"You're General Wolff's daughter."

It's not Gabe's words that skitter up my body like a battalion of scorpions, stinging my skin and straightening my spine, but his mean and spiteful tone. I feel my face flush and my body heat, but somehow I manage to sit still. I will not apologize for being a Wolff, even though I feel as if I'm being x-rayed, as if my skin is being stripped off to reveal something he clearly finds repulsive.

"Yes." I lift my chin and superglue my glare to his. "I'm his daughter. General Rathbun is my godfather."

Gabe stands, his entire body shaking with barely contained fury. "Get out."

The words fall into the air between us with finality, like Donald Trump saying *you're fired*, or a spouse saying *I want a divorce*. There's no going back from a statement that absolute.

I reach for my bag, push to a stand.

"Gabe…" Jean says, his name a one-word warning for him to calm down, sit down, pipe down.

"No, Mom. If I had known she was General Wolff's army brat—" the way he says it—*Wolff's army brat*—as if he's talking about a child molester or a serial killer, crawls across my skin like a bad rash "—I would've never let her in the door. She lied to me in order to gain entry into your *home*, and I want her gone. Now."

And this is when I've had enough, when that little fire that's been sending up smoke signals from the pit of my belly roars to life, licking at my organs, sizzling through my veins, growing and pulsing with heat. Gabe Armstrong doesn't know me or my father. He doesn't know anything about us.

"When would have been the appropriate time to fill you in on my lineage, Gabe? When we were discussing the different types of shower drains? I never lied to you about my name, and I certainly never made a secret about my motivations for coming here."

Gabe's gaze slides to me, and it burns me clear to the bone. "No fucking comment."

"For the last time. I came to give you that transcript, the operative word here being *give*. And though I don't need your gratitude, I certainly don't need all your suspicion and hostility, either." I give his mother a tight-lipped smile. "Thank you for the tea. Your home, especially your garden, is lovely. I wish you all the best."

She blinks at me in surprise, and that's the last thing I notice before I march out of her kitchen, down the hallway and out her sunny yellow door.

9

I'm halfway onto the driver's seat, residual heat from Gabe's enmity still pulsing my insides like a back draft, when I hear Jean's voice, calling to me across her front lawn. "Abigail, wait."

For a good second or two, I seriously consider ignoring her. Just leaping into my car, ducking my head and gunning it for home.

But now it's too late. Jean is already halfway down the stone walkway, one hand waving in the air for me to stop, and she's gaining. I don't bother disguising my exasperation as I step out of the car and swing around to face her.

"I wanted to apologize for my son's temper." She steps off the curb and rounds the back of my car to where I'm standing on the street, keys clutched in a fist. "I really have taught him better. I promise." Her expression, clear and pleasant, friendly even, sucks some of the steam from my anger.

"Sorry, but shouldn't he be apologizing for himself?"

"Of course, dear, and he will eventually. It's just that this rage he carries from his brother's death…he lets it eat him up from inside. I know that's not an excuse, but I hope you can at least understand what's driving his grief. It's one thing to lose the brother you idolize, another thing entirely when the country he died for isn't honest about the circumstances surrounding his death."

I'm kind of taken aback by her matter-of-fact tone, as if she's talking about a new car purchase or the vacation she just booked to Florida rather than discussing one son's grief at another's death. From the start, Jean Armstrong has made no secret of her disgust at the way the army has been neither transparent nor honest about what happened to Zach, but I can't sense an ounce of her anger now, only concern for Gabe.

Still. I can't help but point out, "You seem to be managing very well."

"Yes, well…" She smiles, and I catch a whiff of Gabe in it, the way one cheek is a little slower to rise, how the other folds into a dimple. "All these wrinkles don't come for free, you see. I'm wiser, but that's only because I'm ancient."

Jean Armstrong is older and wiser, definitely, but she's also got a force about her I can't quite pin down. The media calls her fierce, and she certainly is when it comes to defending her sons, but it's more than that. Much more. It's a force that makes her seem stronger than she should be in her situation, sharper and more intense, as big and tall as any one of her boys. It's a force that draws me into her field as surely as it must stave plenty of other people off.

"Take a walk with me, dear, would you?" She crooks an elbow in invitation, which is as endearing as it is ridiculous. In my heels, I have a good half foot and twenty pounds on her, and if anyone should be crooking an elbow here, it's me. But because she's Jean, because so far I haven't discovered a single thing I don't like about her, I toss my bag onto the seat, lock my car and loop my arm through hers.

She leads me around the side of her house, down a lavender-scented path and through a simple wooden gate, into her back-yard. If I thought it was impressive before, from the few glimpses I got from her kitchen window, it's a billion times better up close. Raised beds of blooms nestled between clumps of bushes and swaying grasses. Secret pathways leading to hidden clear-ings, and trellises dripping in vines. Benches and chairs every-where, secluded under arbors or tucked behind fragrant plants, providing front-row seats for stargazing or butterfly watching.

"Beautiful," I say, and the word seems absurdly lacking. "Did you do all this yourself?"

She laughs. "I would say it's cheaper than therapy, but it would be a lie. That patch of tiger lilies alone could have fed all three of my boys for a month." I follow her outstretched arm to a tall clump of yellow flowers, their trumpetlike blooms swinging in the breeze under the limbs of a massive oak. "Nick broke his arm in two places on that spot when he was eight. I swear, that boy would've lived up in that tree if he could have. I'd come outside and he'd be all the way at the top, waving down at me from the highest branch. It was only a matter of time before he fell out and broke something. I guess I should be thankful it wasn't his neck."

Now that I'm out of the spotlight of Gabe's hateful glare, the knots in my shoulders unwind, and I find myself return-ing her smile. "He sounds like a handful."

"He was nothing compared to those brothers of his. Gabe and Zach were the real troublemakers..." She shakes her head, but the gesture is more wistful than sad. "Do you know those two once removed every single item from their chemistry classroom and re-created the lab smack in the middle of the gym floor? I'm talking desks and microscopes and pencils and lab coats, all the way down to the very last petri dish. Don't ask me how they got into the school on a weekend, because I never knew, and I still don't want to. I'm pretty sure I wouldn't like the answer."

I laugh. "I bet their old teachers are still talking about that one."

"Those two were two peas in a pod. I always said God meant for them to be twins."

I think about the sudden and overwhelming sense of déjà vu I got when I saw Gabe coming at me at Handyman Market, how for the second time in my life, I found myself getting flustered by those famous Armstrong genes. "They certainly do look the part."

"That they do." We round the corner, and Jean gestures to two chairs burrowed in a patch of wispy ferns. "Let's sit, shall we?"

We settle in, and the early-October sun makes kaleidoscope patterns on my bare shins through the trees. I lean back onto the chair's warm wood and think for possibly the hundredth time how much I like this woman sitting beside me. That if things had been different, if we'd met under different circumstances, through mutual friends at a party or volunteering for some local nonprofit, Jean and I might have been friends.

"I met him once," I find myself saying. "Your son Zach, I mean. I interviewed him right before he left for basic training."

"I know, dear." I must look shocked, because she laughs at my expression. "I don't just let anyone in my home. Unlike Gabe, I did my homework before you came over. Don't take it personally, but I need to know who's walking through my door these days."

I think back to her questioning my motivations for coming, how she didn't look the least bit surprised when I admitted my connections to the army. But if she already knew, then why not just call me out on it? Why not confront me? It occurs to me then that maybe it was something else entirely. Maybe her questions were a test.

"In your article," she says, "you accused Zach of enlisting as a publicity stunt."

Yes, I think. Definitely *a test*.

I twist on my chair and give her my answer. "I didn't accuse him. I questioned his motivations. Zach enlisted the same year President Obama began pulling out of Iraq, and to fight in a war that a solid majority of Americans didn't want us fighting. I was only trying to figure out why then, why, if his motivations to serve were as pure as he claimed they were, it took him so long to enlist."

"You compared him to a Kardashian."

"True, but then I concluded that his motivations were completely unselfish, and that everything about him was very un-Kardashian-like. I believe I called him *the real deal*, but only because my editor restricted my use of the word *heroic* to three."

"I'm not criticizing you, dear, I'm complimenting you. As the daughter of a three-star general, it would have been far easier for you to praise the pants off my son, but you didn't let him off that easy. Yourself, either. I imagine your connections with the army made it difficult for you to come here today, no?"

A flutter of guilt where my father is concerned worms its way under my skin. Handing the Armstrongs proof about Ricky might have been the right thing to do, but my father will certainly not see it that way. His loyalty is to his country and the army first, and I'm pretty certain he will see my coming here, to the home of the family who has accused him, loudly and publicly, of misconduct, as a betrayal.

But as for me, my biggest loyalty is to my conscience. My

conscience compelled me here. Objectively I know I should be loyal to my father, and that he will never understand, but the conscience isn't objective. I had to come. I had to do the right thing. Zach Armstrong gave up everything for his country, including his life. I had to tell his surviving family what I found.

"I see," she says, taking in my expression. "I'm sure once Gabe calms down, he'll see what this visit is costing you, too."

I look beyond her and across the yard, over swaying leaves and bobbing blooms, back up toward the house. Under the ruffled kitchen valance, Gabe is posed like a statue—legs wide, arms folded across his chest, big form taking up a good part of the window. I can't make out his expression from this far, but I'd bet my every last penny it's not pleasant.

"Anger can be like a buoy," Jean says, following my gaze. "Sometimes it feels like the only thing holding your head above water, but you have to let go of it at some point. Otherwise, you'll never make it back to shore." She turns back to me, smiles. "He'll get there."

I don't answer, mostly because I'm not entirely sure I agree. After what I've seen of Gabe thus far—his stubborn suspicion, his firecracker temper—I think he might not let go of that life vest anytime soon. But instead of saying any of this, I pose the question that's been piling up on my tongue for the past twenty minutes. "Why did you bring me here? Why didn't you just let me get in my car and leave?"

"We've not had the best experience with the media, as I'm sure you know, and the journalists we've interfaced with have been far too overzealous to be pleasant. No offense."

Why do I feel as if she's on a fishing expedition? As if I'm trying to dodge a hook I can't quite see?

"No offense taken," I say. "Journalists can be pretty hardcore."

"But not you."

"I already told you. I'm not a journalist."

"But you were. And to use your own term on you, you were *the real deal*." She cocks her head and studies me in a way that makes the breath freeze in my throat, my muscles tense for the head-on collision I can't see but can sense coming. "That Chelsea woman really did a number on you, didn't she?"

My breath leaves me in a loud whoosh, and I blink away a sudden burning in the corners of my eyes. I wish I'd grabbed my sunglasses from the center console of my car to hide behind, to protect me from Jean's superhuman scrutiny. It's an uncomfortable thing, being seen so clearly by a virtual stranger, one who seems to know the skeleton I've tucked away in the back of my closet, knows that much like her son, I cling to my guilt like a life buoy, too. Beating myself up for what happened feels so much easier than actually forgiving myself, or asking for others' forgiveness.

"Yes," I say, looking away. "She did."

"I want to tell the world about Zach. I want to tell his story. And I want you to help me."

And there it is, I think, the hook. Jean got me so distracted, so flustered and discombobulated with her Chelsea questions that I didn't even feel it slide into my side. Or maybe it's more than that. Maybe after stumbling on Ricky, my curiosity has come alive. Maybe Jean's hook simply doesn't hurt as much as I thought it would.

"Why me?"

Jean smiles, not unkindly. "Because of all the things we've already talked about. Your connections with the army. Your experience with Chelsea. Both those things will make you very careful with your words, with how you choose to frame Zach's story."

"I haven't agreed to frame *any* story."

"What if I told you I plan to find Ricky?"

"I would say I have absolutely no doubt you will. But that doesn't change my answer."

"Actually, dear, you haven't *told* me your answer."

I open my mouth to say no. Helping Jean write Zach's story isn't just sticking a toe into the early-spring sunshine. It's stepping into the sun at high noon, without clothes or blankets to keep me warm, without SPF or shades to protect myself from the sun's harsh glare.

And yet I find myself considering the possibilities.

Because all those things that made me want to become a journalist are still there, have *always* been there, lurking just under the surface. Discipline and determination and temerity and a curiosity that, as evidenced by the very fact that I'm still sitting here, on a chair in Jean's sunny backyard, just won't stop.

But do I have the courage to try again, to trust myself not to make the same mistake I made with Chelsea all over again this time around, with Jean? That my words will not do someone harm?

Then again, they wouldn't be my words, would they? They'd be Jean's.

So how could any words poison her or her family, when essentially what she's asking is for me to help her write *hers*? How would helping Jean be any different from what I'm doing now, with health care? The content would be all hers. I would just be curating it.

Jean reaches across the ferns, wraps her bony fingers around mine. "At least tell me you'll think about it, will you?"

Before I can stop myself, before I know that I even intended to speak, I find myself saying to Jean, "I will."

Part Two:
Wicked Lies

10

On Saturday, I steer my car across the border into Maryland, and the tax brackets rise like floodwaters all around me. The houses grow progressively bigger, their lots stretch wider and deeper, their lawns become greener and lusher. Minivans and hatchbacks give way to eight-cylinder SUVs and expensive German sports cars. They weave in and out of afternoon traffic on their way to the gym or the driving range or the mall, zipping around runners and pedestrians with diamond rings the size of marbles.

It's here, at the tail end of a quiet residential street in Bethesda, that I find my brother Mike's ten-thousand-square-foot monstrosity of stone and shingles. I ease to a stop behind my sister-in-law's navy Range Rover, pluck the gift from the passenger's seat and head up the herringbone walkway to the bleached oak double doors.

I punch the bell, and from somewhere inside a dog barks, a baby screams and my brother yells at both of them to quiet down. And then a door opens to reveal my niece, Rose, wearing a bright pink princess dress covered in what I sincerely hope is tomato sauce.

"Abbyyyyyyy! You came!" She pounces on me, wrapping herself around my right thigh like a monkey. Their dog, Ginger, comes sliding around the corner, and I brace for her attack to my other leg.

"Of course I came, goofball. I wouldn't miss your third birthday party for the world."

She looks up with wide and impossibly green eyes. "No, I'm four!"

"Silly me. I guess that's why I got you a present, isn't it?"

"But you already got me a present."

Admittedly, I might have gone a little overboard with the giant pink-and-purple castle playhouse I paid the toy store to install in her backyard this past week, but I adore this child, would throw myself in front of a bus for her, hope if I ever have a daughter of my own she will be exactly like my adorable niece.

I hold out the bag. "I got you another one."

Rose hops off my leg. A determined Ginger takes her place, licking frantically at the sauce on my jeans while Rose rips the package open in record time. "It's a *teapot*!" she squeals as if she's sixteen, and I've just given her the keys to a cherry-red convertible Mercedes. "And *cups* with *saucers*!"

"You and me, girlfriend, tea party in the castle. Just let me say hi to everyone first, okay?"

Rose gathers up her gift, hangs the bag from a handlebar on her tricycle, then peddles off down the hall.

My brother and his wife, Betsy, have a gorgeous home, rambling and gleaming with polished marble and dark hardwoods. Its rooms would be magazine worthy, were it not for the two toddlers who live here. Sippy cups and empty food wrappers and a trail of toys leading from room to room, like a messy Hansel and Gretel chain of clues. It's as if Mike and Betsy, who before they had kids would roll their eyes with disdain at their less tidy friends, have given up trying to maintain any semblance of order. I don't know what their descent into disarray means for me, the least organized person of the family, should I ever have kids, but it can't be good.

I head through their chef's kitchen, pausing to admire Rose's cake, a sugary concoction shaped like stacked gift boxes smothered in buttercream bows and flowers, then follow the sound of voices and laughter toward the backyard.

I'm halfway down the back hallway when I hear my father's voice in the den, fueled by authority and something much angrier, something that sticks my soles to the antique Aubusson runner. "If you have a point you'd like to make, I suggest you do it right here, right now, to my face. We've been friends for too long for stunts like the one you just pulled."

My godfather's familiar chuckle answers, but something about it pinches my insides like a swarm of mosquitoes eating me from the inside out. Especially when he follows it up with a rather testy, "I don't like your tone, or what you're accusing me of. And if you wanted to keep handing down orders, then perhaps you shouldn't have retired."

General Chris Rathburn is not technically my uncle, but I've known him all my life and I love him like one. He and Dad met in basic training, and they climbed the army ranks as friends and equals, landing with three stars apiece and matching general's salaries up until my father retired last year. So why does Uncle Chris sound so condescending now?

"Fine. I'm asking you, then, as my longtime friend, as my brother in arms, to not take this any further. I'm asking you to do the right thing." Dad's tone is grave and humble and… unfamiliar. Tom Wolff is a man used to giving orders, not asking favors.

Uncle Chris doesn't seem inclined to bow, either. "The right thing, according to whom? Besides, you and I both know it's out of my hands now. Regardless of what you think of me and my involvement in this matter, I'm not the one fueling this investigation. Jean Armstrong is."

Her name whips a lightning bolt up my spine, sticks the breath in my lungs. I know I shouldn't be listening, but I can't seem to move. I lean my upper body closer to the doorway, tilt my head so I can better hear.

"I'm not talking about the investigation, and you know it."

"Look, Tom. You and I want the same thing here, and that's for that family to back down. Where we disagree is how to go about getting there. But you're no longer in charge here." There's a long, long pause, then Chris's voice, darker now. "I am."

The silence that spins out lasts forever. It's the kind of silence that wraps around you like a shroud, the kind that turns the air thick and solid, the kind that makes you want to hear the answer as much as you dread it. I hold my breath and lean in, straining to hear what comes next.

Finally, it comes in the form of Rose's high-pitched squeal from right behind me. "Everybody's *outside*, silly!"

And then, before either my father or Uncle Chris can respond or come storming around the corner, I latch on to Rose's hand and drag her out the door.

Rose and I emerge onto a stone terrace that could be on the cover of a Frontgate brochure. Designer wicker couches, teak dining tables, cushioned chaise longues in front of a rolling lawn as perfectly manicured as any golf course. Pretty, but with not even the slightest nod to the family who lives here.

Mom greets me as if she hasn't seen me in months, as if I didn't just meet her for coffee this past Thursday morning.

"Abigail!" she says, pushing a kiss on my cheek and strangling me in a hug. "How *are* you, dear?"

Margaret Wolff is the storybook version of a mother. The kind of mom who alphabetizes recipe cards and embroiders Christmas stockings and can whip up hot, hearty meals on a moment's notice. While my father climbed the army's ranks, collecting pins and adding stars to his sleeves, she stayed at home with me and Mike, packing our lunches and drilling us for spelling bees. Whenever I picture her, she always looks as she does now, in simple makeup, sensible shoes and a cheerful, frilly apron.

She releases me, and I dole out hugs to the rest of the family. My brother, Mike, hovering at the edge of the terrace with a Heineken and his orthodontist's smile, toothy and white. His wife, Betsy, stretched out in an Adirondack chair nearby. Their son, Tommie, dressed in a diaper and onesie and waving an empty bubble container in a fist. Chris's wife, Susan, my godmother, who gives Mom a run for her money when it comes to enthusiastic hellos.

By the time I've made my rounds, Dad and Uncle Chris are coming out the terrace door, and neither of them look particularly happy. Their knowing gazes land on me, lighting me up inside like a bonfire...or maybe that's my own guilt at getting caught red-handed, eavesdropping on their conversation.

Uncle Chris breaks away from my father and comes across the terrace with a wide grin. "How's my girl?" He tucks me under an arm and drops a kiss on my temple. "Isn't it time for another one of our monthly lunches?"

"Way past. But you canceled the last two times."

"Sorry, sugar. But things have been a little hectic, as I'm sure you know, with the Armstrong case."

All around us, everyone has gone back to their conversations. Mom and Aunt Susan are exchanging recipes, Mike and Betsy are bickering about whose turn it is to change the baby's diaper, Rose is sweet-talking Tommie into a bite of his cookie. Only my father is silent. His gaze is pinned to mine as if I might be concealing an IED. It's more than just anger at the eavesdropping. It's as if he's searching for something in my answer.

I keep it as innocuous as possible. "I'll bet," I say, returning my gaze to Uncle Chris, and that's that.

The party progresses the way most four-year-olds' birthday parties do, with half-eaten hamburgers and puddles of spilled milk and more cake than any person should ever eat in one sitting. Dad barely says a word. Even worse, he spends most of every minute pumping a muscle in his jaw and glaring across the table at the man he always claimed was the brother he never had. Yet I can't find even an ounce of affection between them now, only animosity. Whatever I walked into in that hallway is much bigger than the few sentences I overheard. There's an electricity that crackles the air between them, and it soldiers every hair on my arms to attention.

Finally, when Tommie's sugar high crashes into a sticky, sweaty meltdown, Mom takes him inside for a nap, and Rose and I escape with her tea set and a pitcher of lemonade to the castle playhouse at the back of the yard, nestled at the base of a big oak tree.

"I have a secret," Rose tells me in an ironic twist. Another secret, this time from the four-year-old. Apparently, folks in this family learn early. "I'm asking Santa for a dog."

Rose and I are seated cross-legged on the grass, the tea set spread out between us. Outside the plastic castle, the early-October sun is still beating down, but thanks to the playhouse's position in the shade and a cross breeze blowing through the half-shuttered windows, inside the air holds the cool nip of fall.

I laugh and hand her a miniature teacup, delicately balanced on a miniature saucer. "You already have a dog."

"I want a littler one." Rose chugs her lemonade, then holds out her cup for a refill. "Jenny Kilkelly has one that'll fit in a shoe. That's the kind I want."

For the next few minutes, Rose fills me in on every kid in her pre-K class, as well as a few of what I suspect are imaginary friends. Olivia threw up on Sam's brand-new sneakers in the car-pool lane. Noah wants to be a girl for Halloween. Bridget and Bella, who are apparently identical twins, wear matching bows in their hair every day. Joseph has learned how to fly.

"Fly?" I say. "As in, flapping his wings like a bird?"

She gives me a don't-be-dumb look. "No, silly. In an airplane. His dad taught him how."

"Oh." Schooled by a prekindergartener.

But Rose has already moved on, and to a girl by the name of Annie, who is going to live with her mother and brand-new father in Omaha, when my father's voice booms from outside the castle roof. "Knock, knock."

Rose springs to a stand and throws open the plastic shutters. "Grandpa! Want to come inside for some tea?" She leans her head out and lowers her voice to a shout-whisper. "It's not really tea. It's lemonade."

"Thank you, sugar, but I wanted to talk to Abigail for a minute. How 'bout you run up to the house and see what Nana's up to?"

She shrugs as if she couldn't care either way, then takes off for the house, announcing loud enough for all of Bethesda to hear, "Nana, I gotta *pee*!"

As soon as she's gone, I crawl across the grass and wedge my adult-sized body out the kid-sized door. "Is this about what happened in the hallway? Because I didn't mean to overhear. I was walking out and—"

"Not exactly," he says, cutting me off with a palm in the air. The sun hangs high in the sky above his head, backlighting him like an apparition, making him look even more stony-faced than I see he still is. "What I need to know is why you're calling meetings with the Armstrongs."

At first I think I must have heard him wrong. After all, it's not as if I've told anyone other than Mandy and Victoria that I've had contact with either of the Armstrongs, and neither of them would pass the information on to my father.

I unfold myself, brushing the grass off my jeans. "Are you spying on me?"

"Answer the question, Abigail. Are you or are you not writing about the Armstrong case?"

By glossing over my question, my father has unwittingly also answered it. He's been spying, all right, though I'm not sure if it's on me or the Armstrongs. Dad may have retired four months into the investigation, but that doesn't mean he's not still involved—though, involved enough to spy on his own daughter? The idea seems as impossible to me as unicorns or counting to infinity or eating only one french fry.

"Whatever my conversations have been with the Armstrongs, they have nothing to do with you."

"Of course they have to do with me. My department is under investigation because of Jean Armstrong. Where's your loyalty?"

His condescending tone lights a fire under my temper. "Funny you should mention that word, because loyalty is *exactly* why I'm talking to the Armstrongs. One of the seven reasons why, actually, and I'm sure you can guess the other six."

A muscle ticks in the general's jaw. Dad knows I'm referring to the seven army values, the same ones he drilled into me from the moment I could talk, and he doesn't like that I'm throwing them back in his face now. "Stop playing around here, darlin', and tell me about your conversation with the Armstrongs. Because I can only assume you didn't get together to talk about nutritional supplements for seniors or swap health care reform stories."

Dad's sarcasm doesn't mitigate his message. He sees my contact with any of the Armstrongs as a personal betrayal, just as I suspected he would. Sure, I felt a tiny ping of guilt when I passed Ricky's name on to the Armstrongs, but it was nothing compared to the one I would have felt if I'd sat on that transcript.

But still. Ricky Hernandez is sort of a gray area. I decide to gloss over him for now and give my father a very brief summary of the conversation's conclusion instead. "Jean asked me to help her write Zach's story."

Dad makes a face as if he just bit down on a sour apple. "And? What'd you tell her?"

"I take it you've met her."

He nods, one sharp dip of his chin.

"Then you know what a mighty woman she is."

He dunks his chin again.

"Did you know she's set up a foundation in Zach's name, and that she's raised and donated over a million dollars to other military families in the past year alone?"

I read all sorts of things in his hesitation but mostly impatience. "I know more than I care to know about Jean Armstrong. Spit it out, darlin'. What are you trying to say?"

"I'm trying to explain to you why I told her I'd think about it."

"Because she's philanthropic?"

"No. Because she's *likable*. I *like* her. Jean Armstrong knew who I was before I walked through her door. She knew you were my father, she knew my writing, and she still picked me.

How awesome is that? She wants me to help her write what I'd imagine is the single most momentous project of her life. Beyond the fact I was supremely flattered, she sparked something inside me. Something that makes me think I might want to write again, Dad. Something positive and good and important."

"Maybe or for sure?"

"I haven't decided yet."

My father clamps down on his lips, watching me for a long, drawn-out moment. In the military, walking away from duty for any reason is a serious offense, and though he's never said as much out loud in the years since Chelsea, I know he never agreed with my decision to walk away from mine. So on the one hand, while he might be thrilled *in theory* at my step back into the sunshine, that doesn't mean he's not going to try to talk me into another subject matter.

"Believe me when I say you do not want to get mixed up in this matter. And that's not the general talking, that's your father. Stay away from the Armstrongs. You do not want to open that Pandora's box."

"Why not?"

He shakes his head. "I can't tell you that."

"Is it because the Armstrongs' allegations are true? Have they hit a nerve?"

"You know I can't tell you that, either."

"Okay, then. What *can* you tell me?"

"I can tell you that as of today, there are 6,717 other American mothers who've lost a son or daughter in the war on terror. Other mothers who've been torn apart by grief and have somehow figured out how to put themselves back together without starting a federal investigation. Write about one of them."

"That's basically telling me nothing."

"Then how about this—the Armstrongs are off-limits, Abigail. You are not to talk to them, you are not to visit them at their house or place of business, and you are most certainly not to write about them. Not one word. And that's an order."

His tone is forceful, unrelenting, and his words ambush me. I hold his glare and my breath, trying to rein in my temper. Last time I checked, I was not one of his subordinates, but his thirty-two-year-old daughter. I pay my own way, I make my own decisions, and I don't take orders from anyone but my boss. Especially ones as questionable as the one my father just gave me.

Because, in ordering me to stay away from the Armstrongs, he's also telling me there's more to their story. More he knows, more they don't, and more he doesn't want anyone, including me, to find out. Much more.

Ricky Hernandez rips through my mind, and not for the first time I wonder who he is, where he is, what he saw. Because if anything, this conversation with my father has convinced me that Ricky is as big a lead as I thought he was. Instead of talking me out of Zach's story, my father seems to be doing exactly the opposite.

"Sorry, Dad. I'm still thinking about it."

My father fixes me with a stare stony enough to make the thundercloud on his face settle onto my chest, pushing down like an elephant-sized weight. I hold my breath and his gaze until, without another word, he turns and marches off toward the house.

I've been dismissed.

11

Maria's convertible comes roaring out of her condo's garage, and I hit the start button on my Prius.

So far, Ben's intel has been spot-on. Maria has upgraded not only her bustline but her entire life. She's traded in her Honda for a fancy BMW convertible, a sporty hardtop with every option imaginable. She lives in a two-story condo on the twenty-second floor in The Mansion, one of Baltimore's swankiest high-rises on the waterfront in Locust Point. And she drapes her new curves in the latest fashion, designer dresses and red-soled heels and calfskin bags that cost three times more than I make in a month.

She goes by Maria Davidson now, though even with the new name, it wasn't very hard for me to find her. All I needed was her old cell phone number and a fleeting memory of her telling me she moved here from Detroit. Everyone leaves a digital trail. You just have to know where to look.

For days now I've been trailing her as she goes about her business, and it's been every bit as thrilling as it sounds. I've followed her to the grocery store, to the nail salon, to CVS and the mall and Starbucks, everywhere but to an office. *Never* to an office. As far as I can tell, Maria Davidson is not employed...at least not in the conventional definition of the term.

I pull into late-morning traffic and trail a good three or four cars behind Maria's BMW, keeping a careful watch as she zips in and out of lanes. She takes a left up the ramp to 95, then merges onto the beltway heading west. I follow for another half hour, until we've looped all the way around to the northern end and exit in Pikesville. We weave past businesses and restaurants, schools and synagogues. A doctor's appointment? Another shopping spree? I grip the wheel a little more tightly and keep a close eye on her back bumper.

We take a left onto a tree-lined street, and then another into a complex called Sunnybrook Springs. The place screams assisted living, from the clusters of squat buildings to the wide doors and easy-access ramps to the folks milling about the manicured grounds. Maria pulls into a lot on the far side of the grounds, climbs out of her car with a bouquet of flowers and heads across the pavement to a brick building that, anywhere else, would look like a two-story block of apartments. The plaque to the right of the building tells me it's Sunnybrook's Villa, and judging by the measures Maria has to take to make it through the double doors, it's highly secured.

I back my Prius into a spot at the far end of the lot with a clear view of both the door and Maria's dark and silent BMW, and reach for my phone.

Floyd picks up on the third ring and greets me with, "You little minx."

"Excuse me?"

"You could have warned me what I was getting into. Good thing I wasn't in public when I pulled up that clip. Imagine what the lunch crowd at Panera would have thought."

I smile at what I know is a joke. Floyd isn't stupid. He wouldn't work anywhere but at home, on his own highly secured, impenetrably firewalled network. He's thorough, too. I figured it was only a matter of time before he found the clip. "Does this mean her money is connected to the videos?"

"Well, seeing as she hasn't shared a penny of that income with Uncle Sam, I think that's a safe assumption. But again, at this point, it's just an assumption. Oh, and her name's not Duncan. Your girl was born Maria Elizabeth Daniels and hails from Toledo, Ohio."

I frown. "I thought she was from Detroit." In fact, I found at least three different addresses when I went looking for her there, which tells me that if nothing else, she lived there for a while. Toledo's not too far down the road from Detroit, but still. What other lies did she feed me? What else have I missed?

"Anything else?" I say.

"You can't rush genius, hon. I'll call you when I call you."

While Mandy's superpower is stopping traffic, mine is the ability to talk myself through any door. It's a skill I honed in my time as a journalist, this innate ability I have to read a complete stranger, to be so attuned to their sensibilities that I know what to say, how to act, what cards to play to make me seem just the right mix of friendly and sympathetic. Sometimes getting invited inside is as simple as slipping them a crisp bill, but more often than not, it's about gaining their trust, about making whoever's on the other side of that door think you're one of them.

And so, as soon as Maria motors away with a throaty vroom, I'm dusting off my old talents with the sourpuss nurse behind the Villa's double glass doors. Leslie, according to her name tag. She glances up when I come through and holds up a finger, indicating I'm to wait until she's off the phone.

"Exit twenty," she says in a short, I've got better things to-do-here tone, then gives the person on the other end half-assed directions from the beltway. While she's talking, I take a good look around.

The Villa's lobby is light and friendly, the walls smeared a buttercream yellow and hung with the kind of framed pictures you'd expect in an assisted living facility—cheerful flowers and frolicking farm animals set against sunny landscapes. My gaze zooms in on the visitors' log, on handwriting I recognize immediately. The neat block letters that are fat and round, their slight slant to the left. Maria Daniels, here to see Matthew Daniels, room 213.

A relative?

But Maria doesn't have any family. I distinctly remember her telling me the last of them died in the year prior to Chelsea.

Then again, Maria hasn't exactly proven to be the most trustworthy source.

Leslie hangs up, hauls a mammoth sigh. "Can I help you?"

I'm careful not to give her too big of a smile. Overworked and underpaid types like Leslie here want validation, not an ass-kissing.

"Yeah, my boss sent me over here to check out your facility. Apparently, Sunnybrook comes highly recommended for his disabled son, who I didn't even know he had until it was suddenly in my job description to vet out his son's new living arrangements." I plant both forearms onto the counter and lean in conspiratorially. "Next thing you know, he'll be asking me to bring him coffee and pick up his dry cleaning."

She gives me a half-amused snort. "Sounds frighteningly familiar."

"I'll bet. Anyway—" I make a show of looking around "—this place looks nice. Do you maybe have a brochure or something?"

She fishes a packet from a drawer and passes it to me. "What type of disability does your boss's son have?"

I give her a wry smile, wrapping my words in a what-can-you-do tone. "You and I might think sharing his disability would be essential information for vetting out a place, but we'd be wrong. My boss didn't tell me anything other than the address."

"Probably help your employee review, then, if I gave you a tour."

"Omigod, totally. It might even get me my very first *good job*."

Leslie squeezes out a smile, heaves herself out of her swivel chair and buzzes me through.

See? Easy as pie.

I trail her through the building as she gives her sales pitch, making notes on a blank page in the back of the brochure. I pepper her with questions about the resident population and the varying levels of care, on the campus and all its facilities, on the programs that are designed to enrich and empower. I don't have to pretend to be fascinated by her talking points. Whoever Matthew Daniels is, he's somewhere between early twenties and late thirties, moderately to severely mentally challenged and highly supervised.

A cousin? A brother? After everything I've learned from Ben, after everything I've seen here today, I'm starting to wonder if any of what Maria told me three years ago was even close to the truth.

We're making our way through the second floor when a sudden and high-pitched squeal slices through the air and pierces my eardrums. Leslie looks more annoyed than surprised at the interruption. "Sorry," she screams over the noise. "We're going to have to cut this short."

I nod and follow her around the corner toward the stairs,

but we pull up short at the mass of residents clustered at the far end of the hall by the window. Their backs are huddled together, their hands pressed tightly over their ears. Leslie pushes through them like a linebacker, pausing for only a second or two in front of the glass, and then the crowd parts again, and my heart gives a lurch at the sight of Leslie's expression as she reemerges. Without even a glance in my direction, she barrels past me and disappears into the stairwell.

A few moments later, the fire alarm stops its deafening shriek, as abruptly as a needle yanked from a record. The silence that follows is so heavy it's tangible, a whole other noise punctuated with the soft sniffs of someone crying.

"What happened?" I say, pushing up onto my toes, trying to see, but a good dozen shoulders block my view. All I can make out from my spot behind them are treetops and the blue sky beyond.

One of them, a pudgy woman with the round and plump face of a muppet, turns back, her already impossibly large eyes bulging with an uninhibitedness that reveals her condition. "Another fire."

"He set another fire," someone wails between wet sniffs.

"Who did?"

"Matthew," another says, and my ears perk up. Matthew Daniels? "It's 'cause Maisie was just here. He always does bad things when Maisie's been here."

Something about the name teases the edges of my memory. *Maisie.* It flits away before I can grab hold.

"Who's Maisie?" I ask.

"His sister." Muppet Face presses hers into the window. "She's pretty."

Maisie Daniels.

There's something about the name, a gritty taste behind my teeth I can't quite place. I pull out my phone and type the words into the search field. The image that fills my screen hits me like a Fireball shot, lighting me up from inside. The cheesy backdrop, an obviously fake library background. The lopsided pigtails tied with red yarn. The chipped and bucked front teeth pushing through the slight smile. I see it, and my breath dries up.

"Fucking hell," I mutter, and more than one person giggles.

It's Maria's—no, *Maisie's* second-grade picture. The same one that was circulated back in 1996, when she was snatched from her bedroom in the middle of the night. The same one I stared at for the good part of my junior year in college six years later, when I wrote my term paper singing the praises of the media, which I maintained made a greater contribution than the Toledo police force in pulling her filthy, undernourished but still breathing body from that man's basement. By the time the police got their act together and sent out a search party, the media had already plastered her face on every newspaper, milk carton and television screen across the continental United States. All the cops had to do, I argued, was wait for someone to recognize her.

My professor gave me a D-minus, but only because he liked me enough not to flunk me.

What I didn't understand then, what I understand all too well now, is that media attention can be a double-edged sword. In Maria/Maisie's case, the media saved her life, and yet it also exposed a scared, scarred eight-year-old girl to the world. It revealed all the awful things that man did to her, to her no-longer-innocent body. It imprinted her face, her story, every awful, horrific, gruesome detail, on the collective American memory.

You don't survive a trauma like the one Maisie did undamaged. You don't come out the other end unchanged. But damaged and changed enough to let others use her body for money, to put it on the internet for the world to see, even after it drove a former lover to suicide? An icy chill hijacks my spine at the answer: *yes*.

"Lady, are you okay? You don't look too good."

I look up into a pair of sweet, caring eyes. "No," I say, "I don't think I am."

When I return home from Sunnybrook, Mandy is sitting at my desk, flipping through the Zach Armstrong printouts.

"Hi," I say from the doorway, but she doesn't answer. Her brow is furrowed in concentration, and she's twirling a long strand of auburn hair around a finger as she always does when she's thinking really hard. It's not unusual that she's here. Mandy is one of the few people with a key to my house, and she uses it often. I work from home. She works from home. Impromptu work sessions like this one are a regular thing.

Except Mandy's not working. Her laptop lies closed and dark on the bookshelf behind her.

"Hi," I say again, this time with a bit more muscle, and she startles, catching a good few inches of air on the chair.

"Jesus! Give a woman a warning, would you?" She presses a palm to her chest, blows out a long breath.

"I did. Twice now." I cross the room to my desk, pull up my content curation software and begin entering the keywords for searches for Maria, Maisie and her brother, Matthew. It takes only a few seconds, and once I'm done, I swivel in my chair and gesture to my once-neat piles, now scattered across the surface of my desk as if a windstorm picked them up and dumped them there. "What are you doing here? Besides making a mess of my papers, that is."

She spreads her arms wide. "The question is, what are *you* doing? If I didn't know better, I'd say writing an article about Zach Armstrong."

It's no use not telling her. The only person on the planet with a curiosity determined enough to compete with mine is Mandy, and if I don't admit to why I've plowed through a good chunk of the Amazon rainforest for printouts of everything ever written about Zach, she'll hound me until I do. I give her a quick recap of my initial run-in with Gabe at Handyman and how, two days later, an anonymous package arrived on my front doorstep, revealing the name of a thirty-sixth soldier.

Mandy's eyes go wide. "You don't think that's a little co-incidental, meeting Gabe one day and finding this mysterious package on another? I mean, what are the odds?"

"Questionable at best. Which means whoever gave me that transcript wanted me to find Ricky, which as far as I can fig-ure means they wanted me to reveal him to the world."

"Are you going to?"

I shake my head. "Hell, no. I already told you, I'm done with that part of my life. But I had to do something, so I gave a copy of the transcript, unedited version, to the Armstrongs."

"Oh, my God. What did they say? What did your *father* say?"

"Gabe told me to get lost, Dad cornered me in Mike's back-yard, and Jean asked me to help her tell Zach's story."

Mandy sits back in the chair, her eyes going even wider than before. "Like, ghostwrite it?"

I lift a shoulder. "I guess. We didn't really go into the details."

"And what did you say?"

"I told her I'd think about it."

She smacks both palms on the desk. "Are you crazy? Call her up right now and tell her you'll do it. Tell her you'll get started tonight. I'll help."

"What about my father and Chris? What about Gabe?" She dismisses Gabe with a flick of a manicured hand, but I'm not so ready. "He'll accuse me of scheming this outcome all along, of planning the whole thing. He probably thinks I hypnotized his mother or cast some evil spell that bewitched her into asking me. He'll think I went there with the intention of walking out with a book deal."

"Did you?"

"Absolutely not." Regardless of my interest in Ricky—who he is, what he saw—I did not in any way sweet-talk Jean into asking me for help writing Zach's story. Jean's request came out of the blue, and it was all her own. I had nothing to do with it, other than maybe giving her the honest answers she wanted to hear.

"So, what do you care what Gabe thinks?" Mandy says, handing me her cell phone. "Jean's the one you should be trying to impress. Call her. Say yes. You know you want to."

I stare at her, but I don't argue. As my best friend for almost two decades, Mandy knows me better than pretty much anybody on the planet, and she's right. I *do* know. I roll Jean's request around for the hundredth time, and the temptation is hot caramel on my tongue.

"And as for your father and Chris?" She shakes her head. "Whoever gave you that transcript was trying to tell you something, and it doesn't reflect favorably on either of them."

Another good point, and one that's occupied the better part of my mind since tripping over the envelope on my front doorstep. I think about who would have purposefully breached OPSEC to give an unmarked, uncensored copy to me. Someone who has it out for my father or Uncle Chris? Possibly, but then why give it to me? Why not give it to the *Washington Post* instead?

There's something I'm missing here.

Something that's maybe in the transcript.

I dig through the papers on the desk in search of it, but there are over two thousand pages of printouts here, and Mandy has made such a mess of my piles, it will take me forever. "Where did you put the transcript?"

"I didn't." When I look up in surprise, she adds, "I never saw it. When you mentioned it just now, I figured you'd put it somewhere safe." She takes in what feels like a frantic expression on my face, purses her lips. "Please, tell me you put it somewhere safe."

"It was on the top of Zach's pile. You must have seen it. About twenty pages smothered in pink highlighter."

Mandy shakes her head, and the first niggle that something is wrong rises in my chest.

I lick my finger and flip through the top of each stack for a second time, and then a third, my eyes peeled for swipes of hot pink.

But on every page I come to, there's only black and white.

"Okay, so when did you see it last?" she asks.

At the reminder, I pop out of my chair and rush over to the copy machine. The last time I touched the transcript was when I was making a copy for the Armstrongs. But when I lift the cover on the machine, there's nothing there. The glass is empty.

"Those machines usually have a memory function, you know. Let me see."

While Mandy fiddles with the buttons on the screen, I search my desk and the cabinets and bookshelves. I search under the rugs and in the magazines and under the potted peace lily in the hallway. I search in the recycling bin and the pile of mail by the microwave and in the junk drawer and under every piece of furniture in the entire house. I search everywhere I can think of. The only things I find are a few stray socks and more dust bunnies than I'd care to admit.

By the time I return to the office, my hands as empty as when I began, Mandy is pulling a fresh copy off the machine.

But still. A transcript appears A transcript vanishes. Both under suspicious, and suspiciously criminal, circumstances. A jolt of something creepy shoots through me, knotting my shoulders and wringing my stomach like a wet rag.

Mandy looks over, and I can tell her thoughts are colliding with mine. "Maybe you should call the police."

"And tell them what? That someone snuck in and stole a document I wasn't supposed to have in the first place? And anybody who doesn't break a window or bust down a door is not going to leave prints."

"Okay, but what if they come back?"

"Why would they come back, when clearly they already got what they came for?"

She holds the fresh copy in the air, an unspoken reminder that my statement is not quite true. "But who would give it to you in the first place? What do they want?"

"I don't know, but I intend to find out."

"How are you going to do that?" she asks, but she's already smiling, already nodding as if she knows what's coming, and she approves.

"I'm going to find Ricky."

12

After a weekend behind my computer, I've made zero progress. I still haven't found Ricky. I haven't heard a peep from Floyd. I've stared at the transcript until the letters blur and run together. By Monday morning, I'm sick and tired of thinking about all of it, and my veins hum with cooped-up energy.

Outside my windows, the temperature has taken a nose-dive, and the heavens are unloading a steady stream of rain, so I release my frustration the old-fashioned way. Upstairs in my bathroom with hard, physical labor.

I spend the day cutting and spacing the floor tile—a smooth, square porcelain that looks as if it might be stone unless you happen to notice the price per square foot, which was a total steal. I use the spacers Gabe threw into my cart just in case, and I start from the middle of the room as the internet told me to do.

I must admit, something about the work is soothing. Maybe it's the rhythm. The buzz of the saw, the swish of the trowel, the rake of the mastic. Or maybe it's the way it takes all my concentration, giving my mind a much-needed rest. Even though my loudest thoughts are still there, percolating under the surface—Maria's shenanigans, Ricky's whereabouts, my father's objections, Jean's request—the work drowns out their constant loops through my consciousness.

When the last tile is set, I push to a stand, stretch out my creaky bones and head down the hallway for the shower.

The doorbell rings as I'm drying myself off. I run across the hall, throw on some clean clothes—an ancient rowing sweat-shirt and a pair of yoga pants—and hurry down the stairs in bare feet and wet hair.

The face that greets me on the other side of the door is just as wet. Actually, everything about him is soaked—his hair, his shoes, his bomber jacket of brown-and-black leather. Gabe, of course. I'm as surprised as I would be to find Elvis dripping on my front porch floor.

"Sorry to just show up unannounced, but I was out for a walk and…" A frigid gust sends a whirlwind of leaves and rain across the yard, and Gabe and I shiver simultaneously. He looks beyond my shoulder, casting a longing look down my centrally heated, dry hallway. "It's probably really warm in there, isn't it?" His gaze returns to mine, and to my locked-down expression, the way I shift to fill up the opening in the doorway. "Right. Of course not. Never mind."

"What do you want, Gabe?"

I know I'm on the wrong side of rude, but the last two times I saw Gabe, he accused me of lying, called me names and ba-sically threw me out of his mother's house, so I don't exactly feel inclined to let him into mine. He doesn't look angry or combative, but still. Unless he's here to thank me for sliding him Ricky, he can stand outside on my freezing doorstep in his wet clothes all night as far as I'm concerned.

And then he shoves his hands in the front pockets of his jeans and says something even better.

"I wanted to apologize. For losing my temper with you, twice now, and saying some things that were a little out of line." My eyes widen, and he amends. "Okay, okay. *Way* out of line. Especially the part where I called you an army brat and threw you out of my mother's house. And I might have said 'fuck' more times than I care to count, but in my own defense, I cuss a lot, so you probably shouldn't take it personally. Regardless, I'm sorry."

Everything about his change of heart seems sincere—his repentant tone, his remorseful expression, the way his gaze sticks to mine the whole time it took him to say it—but the thunderhead that rolled onto his expression when I told him about Ricky is still imprinted on my brain. I picture his big form silhouetted in his mother's kitchen window, all rage and repulsion that a Wolff army brat would dare darken her door, and a question elbows its way up my throat. "How much of that did your mother make you say?"

One brow slides up his forehead, and he puffs out a laugh. "You don't pull any punches, do you?"

"How much, Gabe?"

Another sharp burst of breath. "Okay, if you really want to know, it was my therapist. He urged me to come here and express my frustration and anger in a 'healthy, productive manner.'" He pulls his hands from his pockets to make quote marks in the air, then gives me a rueful grin. "The apology, as shitty as it was, was all mine."

I find myself softening just a tad at this little glimpse of the first Gabe I met, the one who was witty and friendly and personable, who didn't take himself too seriously as he helped me gather all the items on my list. I liked that Gabe then, and I like him now.

But that doesn't mean I'm ready to let either Gabe in just yet, literally or figuratively. Not until I know we're on the same page. "I assume she told you what we talked about in the garden."

He nods.

"As well as my answer."

Another nod. He looks at me inquisitively, opens his mouth to say something, thinks better of it.

"You walked all the way over here in the freezing rain, Gabe. Why don't you just say what you're thinking?"

"Why does that feel like a trick question?" He follows up his words with a good-natured grin, but when I don't share in his lightheartedness, his expression grows solemn. "Okay, fine. What I don't get is how you can be so adamant you're not a reporter one minute with me, and then one little request from Mom and you're suddenly agreeing to write Zach's story."

"Okay, first of all, I didn't agree to anything other than to think about it. I'm *thinking* about helping your mother write Zach's story because I like her and she asked. And ultimately, I wouldn't be writing anything. They're her words. I would only be helping put them in the right order."

"It would still be one hell of a byline."

"It's not about the byline. It's about the story."

"Which, if you help write it, is also your byline."

"I already told you, I don't give a shit about the byline." I frown, shaking my head in frustration, and start to close the door. "I don't expect you to understand."

Gabe presses a wet palm to the wood, stopping it at halfmast. "It's cold as balls out here, but I'm still here, and I'm listening. Try me."

Gabe slips his hands into his jeans pockets and waits as if he's not freezing his ass off, and I protest with a sigh, short and sharp, even as the words begin to take form in my head.

The thing is, I *want* him to understand. I *want* him to know I didn't walk into his mother's house with the goal of walking out with a book deal. Other than the rhythmic patter of the rain and the occasional swish of tires rolling through puddles, the street is quiet, and Gabe's eyes are wide and questioning.

I decide to give him the answer he came here for.

"Three years ago, my career imploded. I'm not telling you this because I'm looking for sympathy or encouragement or even understanding, because what happened was completely, one hundred percent my fault. My mistakes, I own them, and I deserved every bit of the fallout. But the thing is...all I've ever wanted to do was write, and not blurbs about hip replacements and dementia drugs like I'm doing now, but real stories, about subjects that *I* care about, that are relevant to me."

Gabe clearly wasn't expecting my answer, but he manages to look only slightly puzzled by it. "My brother's story is relevant to you?"

I shake my head, immediately and emphatically. "Ricky Hernandez is relevant to me. Who he is, what he saw, is relevant to me. The *truth* is relevant to me. And whatever it is, if it's as momentous as my gut is telling me it is, I can't just sit on it. I have to send it out into the world. The public has a right to know the truth, even if it's bad. *Especially* if it's bad."

"So if all that's true, what is there to think about? Why didn't you just say yes?"

He doesn't sound accusatory, only genuinely curious, and so the truth simmers up before I've made the conscious decision to share it. "Because words can be just as deadly as warfare."

Gabe doesn't ask anything further, but from the way he watches me, earnestly and with a sudden tenderness I didn't expect, I am pretty certain he knows about Chelsea. Maybe his mother told him, maybe he did his own research. I don't know, and it doesn't matter. What matters is that he seems to understand.

"Well, hell," he says, flashing me a bemused grin worthy of one of his big brother's rom-coms, except not the least bit practiced. "Mom told me I was being an ass-hat, and now, as usual, she was right. I should have used that in my apology, now that I think about it. That even my own mother thinks I'm an ass-hat."

I smile despite myself. "I doubt she used the word *ass-hat*."

"Nah, that one's all mine, too. But that apology from before? Let me just add that I misjudged you. I assumed you were giving us Ricky for all the wrong reasons, that you came over there looking for a story, and I'm sorry. I'm an ass-hat, and I'm sorry." He blows into his hands, shifts his big body back, pointing it away from my door. "So anyway, now that I can no longer feel my extremities, I'm just gonna…"

And that's when we hear it, a tinny *thock thock thock* that echoes up my street. Gabe looks over his shoulder, and the noise moves nearer, growing louder and sharper, crescendoing into an earsplitting roar as hail the size of golf balls kamikaze-dives from the sky, bouncing off the roofs, the pavement, the cars, the grass of my tiny front lawn.

He turns back with a half-cocked grin. "I didn't plan that, I swear."

I laugh, grab him by the sleeve and pull him inside.

In the shelter of my hallway, Gabe dries off as best he can with a towel I fetch him from upstairs, and I hang his coat over a chair in the kitchen to drip on the white tile floor. While I'm in there, I snag a bottle of wine, an opener and two glasses from the stretch of cabinets by the back door, and carry them into the living room.

I hold everything up for Gabe to see. "It's not brandy, but it'll warm your blood."

"Nice, thanks."

Gabe hangs the towel around his neck, and we settle on the couch. While he goes to work on the cork, I search for neutral ground, for something that won't heave our fragile peace accord into a full-on nosedive like the Titanic, right before it snapped in two.

I settle on, "I really like your mother."

He glances up from the bottle, grinning. "She really likes you back, which is kind of a big deal these days. She says no one was more surprised she asked you to help her with Zach's story than she was, but you passed all her tests with flying colors."

"With *her*," I remind him. "I passed the tests with *her*."

The cork pulls free with a light pop, and he pours a generous glass of wine, then another.

"Yeah, well, Mom has always been light-years smarter than I am, not to mention a great deal more levelheaded." He shakes his head, thunks the bottle down on the table. "My therapist tells me I'm a work in progress, but between you and me, I think that's psych-speak for *you're a real asshole*."

I laugh. "At least he's diplomatic."

"It's because I pay him a shit-ton of cash." He picks up the glasses and passes one to me. "So, Abigail Wolff, are we good?"

I think about his question, tip my glass toward his. "We're good."

We sip for a moment in silence, and I watch him over the rim, thinking how he looks so much like Zach but also doesn't. They both share that famous Armstrong bone structure—angular and strong and utterly masculine—but Gabe's angles are not quite as knife-edged, his forehead not quite so wide. Zach was the Hollywood version of Gabe—too shiny, too stiff, too perfect. Gabe's good looks are real and rugged and raw, and now that I've seen both brothers up close, I'd choose Gabe over Zach any day.

"I'm sorry about your brother," I say, and Gabe's face takes on that solemn but standoffish quality I've seen a million times on the news. "I can't imagine how much it sucks to lose a sibling, and then to lose him like that…" I curl my legs under me, turn to face him on the couch. "I'm really sorry. I wish I'd said it earlier, that first day at the market."

"Nah, you were right. I've thought a lot about what you should have done differently, how I would have handled the situation in your shoes, but the thing is, I don't know. There's not really a good answer. We're in uncharted waters all around."

My head bobs in an enthusiastic nod. "You can say that again. How weird is it that I don't know you, yet I know all these things about you?"

"You know things about me?" One brow slides up his forehead, and a grin twists his lips. It's a cocky expression for sure, but it looks awfully damn good on him. "Like what?"

"Well, I know you went to Harvard on a full swimming scholarship, but despite your coach's prodding and whispers of Olympic greatness, you ditched the pool for an MBA. After graduation, Goldman Sachs whisked you away to Wall Street, where you didn't just climb but bounded up their corporate ladder. You were Manhattan's most eligible bachelor for a few years, until you became engaged to some ketchup heiress—"

"Mustard," Gabe interrupts.

"—sorry, to some mustard heiress. But for reasons I can only assume have something to do with your brother's death, you gave all of that up to come home and stock shelves at a local hardware store."

"Not something." He shakes his head. "*Everything*. My reasons had *everything* to do with Zach's death. Who gives a shit about penthouse apartments and fancy parties when we are getting our brains blown out every day? I didn't then, and I don't now."

"What about the mustard heiress?"

"What about her?"

"How'd she take it?"

"Well, she married some French baron last month, so I'd say pretty well."

A giggle pushes up my throat before I can stop it.

Gabe looks confused, as if maybe he can't decide whether to be amused or offended by my laughter. "What?"

"Really?" I say, a little surprised it's never occurred to him. I laugh again, one of those uncontrollable belly laughs that bubbles up because you're trying to swallow it down. "Now she's French mustard."

Gabe laughs now, too, and whatever doubts I had as to the tenacity of our fresh start float like a bad odor out the window. Gabe refills our wineglasses, then settles his big body back into my couch as if he owns it. He swings an arm up and across the back, points a long finger at my face. "All right, then. Fair's fair. You know all these things about me. Now tell me some things about you."

"Okay..." I lean into the couch, feeling the soft leather crinkle and give under me, and think for a moment. "Rowing scholarship to UVA undergrad, followed by a master's in journalism from Georgetown. After that, I slogged through a couple of shitty jobs until I found one I liked, which paid me approximately one-sixteenth of what you earned at Goldman Sachs. And I was never most eligible anything."

"Engaged?"

"Almost. We lived together for a while, and we talked about it for longer than that."

"What happened?"

"Timothy was a reporter, too, and his schedule was even crazier than mine. Most of the time, we were more like ships passing in the night than a real couple. Anyway, he didn't like it much when I turned in my press pass. I think I was home too much for his tastes."

Weird. Usually, talking about Timothy, about all the reasons we crashed and burned, is something I'm hesitant to do. I don't like the way it awakens all those old feelings of hurt, the way his name on my lips tightens a sharp and rusty barbed-wire band around my chest.

But not tonight. Tonight I say the words without pausing to consider the subject, and then I brace for a pain that doesn't come. What does come is a sense of instant and giddy relief at its absence. Huh.

If Gabe senses it, he doesn't let on. He lifts a shoulder, a no-big-loss gesture. "In my experience, people who don't stick around during the hard times weren't worth having around anyway. That's one of the few perks from this shit show, actually, that it sure cleans out your Rolodex."

Even though I can't detect a trace of bitterness in his voice, I read all sorts of things in his response. I read that in losing his brother, he's lost a lot of others, too, either by watching them walk away or by cutting them loose. I read that some partings were met with a good-riddance attitude and some were more painful, and I can't help but wonder which category the French-mustard ex falls into. And I read that, now that his Rolodex is trimmed down to a core group of people he knows and trusts, he's not quick to add any new names into the mix. Will mine make the cut?

A yearning wells up inside me, and I bury my nose in my glass. All those things I thought and felt those first two times at Handyman Market still ring true. The more I learn about

Gabe, the more I like him, and the more I want him to like me back. I don't trust myself to say anything.

Outside my window, the sky has stopped dumping and the wind has settled, and the usual evening traffic has picked back up, people walking their dogs, cars sloshing past on the still drenched streets. But inside, it's warm and dry.

Gabe reaches for the wine. "Can I pour you another?"

"Sure." I hold up my empty glass.

Much later, by the time he finally gets up to leave, we've polished off the whole bottle.

13

The mind has a habit of getting hung up on one way of thinking. It's kind of like that old riddle, the one where you imagine you're on a sinking boat surrounded by hungry sharks. How will you survive? Your brain is so busy mulling over the possibilities—I'll punch them in the nose, I'll swim like the dickens, I'll pray to every god there is for a miracle—that it misses the most obvious answer: stop imagining.

Kind of like how my mind got hung up on where to look for Ricky.

Because up to now, it's been so hung up on searching for Ricky Hernandez on the American military websites, that it hasn't considered other possibilities. What if he's a foreign coalition soldier? What if he's not a soldier at all? He could be a military contractor, or even an embedded journalist. The possibilities roll through my head in the middle of the night like an army on attack, plucking me from my dreams and lurching me upright in my bed.

I throw off my covers and launch myself out, snagging my robe from a chair on the way out of my room.

Downstairs at my computer, it takes me three hours and five cups of coffee to find Ricardo Manuel Hernandez, and when I do, my heart plummets at the address of the site I find him on: americancontractors.org, a website tracking casualty counts for Iraq and Afghanistan.

According to the website, Ricky was killed on January 12, a mere two months after he may or may not have watched Zach die on a nearby battlefield. A link sends me to WAVY, a local NBC affiliate near Virginia Beach, with a lousy four-paragraph report on the basics of his death.

VIRGINIA BEACH, VA—A civilian contractor for Intergon from Virginia Beach was killed in a roadside attack near Kabul, Afghanistan, on Sunday.

Ricardo Manuel Hernandez, 38, died while on duty for the private contractor when the vehicle he was driving was attacked. An explosive hitting the windshield killed Hernandez and another security worker, sources said.

A former mechanic, Hernandez worked for ten years at Portsmouth Auto Repair. His body is expected to arrive in Portsmouth on Thursday or Friday. Funeral plans are pending.

Hernandez leaves behind a sister, Graciela Hernandez, of Portsmouth.

A roadside attack near Kabul. Zach was stationed in Kabul, meaning if Ricky had been there for more than a few months, he and Zach would have been in the same place at the same time.

With unsteady fingers, I type *Intergon* into the search field.

According to their website, Intergon provides shelter, food and comfort to coalition troops across Afghanistan. I skim over their support operations—delivery of food, water and fuel, dining and laundry and housing services, morale and recreation activities—until my gaze glues to four little words at the bottom: *spare parts and maintenance*. I return to the army reports, skipping down to the mechanic sent to fix a valve on the broken-down MRAP.

A mechanic.

I return to the obit and stare, openmouthed and wide-eyed, at my screen. Ricky was a mechanic. *A mechanic.* One who would know, surely, how to fix a broken-down valve on a tank. My heart races and my skin tingles and my blood pressure explodes like a grenade.

I didn't just find Ricky.

I found his connection to Zach.

Only now it's quarter to six, and I'm about to be late for rowing, an offense my teammates do not tolerate. I yank on my clothes and race to my car. By the time I make it to the river, the boat is in the water and the girls are milling around on the dock, casting annoyed glances at their watches.

I spend the next two hours and fifteen minutes beating out my excitement on the waters of the Potomac, mulling over every possible scenario to explain Ricky's presence on the battlefield the day Zach died, and his absence from the official army reports afterward. He fell asleep in one of the vehicles he was working on, only to accidentally awaken in the middle of a battle. He grabbed a gun and started shooting for his life, taking down Zach in the process. He threatened to expose whoever shot Zach, and someone silenced him permanently. The possibilities are endless.

One thing, however, is clear: Ricky Hernandez was there when Zach died.

And my gut is telling me he saw something he shouldn't have.

Handyman Market is packed with last-minute Halloween shoppers, their arms loaded with orange and black decorations, their bodies lined up in long, snaking lines at both registers. I shoot up the middle aisle in my damp rowing clothes, dodging customers and swinging my head left and right, searching for Gabe.

In the flooring section, I run into an apron-clad handyman, a handsome surfer type named Jeff, and ask if he's seen Gabe. "Sure I have," Jeff says, shoving his hands in his apron. "Gabe's in the back." He grins, and his perfect white teeth are as blinding as his blue eyes.

But as lovely as Jeff is to look at, he's not going to be winning *Who Wants to Be a Millionaire* anytime soon.

"Um, could you maybe go get him for me?"

He starts, and his smile drops a half inch. "Oh. Right. Be right back." Jeff lopes off as if he has all the time in the world, disappearing after an eternity through an Employees Only door.

After he's gone, I stand there for a minute or two, alone amid the waxes and cleaners and mops, shifting from one foot to the other in a bout of caffeinated excitement. I check the time on my cell, then peek through the window on the swinging door Jeff disappeared through. Empty.

I turn back as a heavyset man in a stained Members Only jacket comes around the corner. He passes a disinterested gaze over me, then heads to the display of pumpkins at the back end of the store. Distractedly, I watch him rifle through the pile, picking each one up and inspecting it before exchanging it for the next. He takes all the livelong day with each one, checking for perfect shape and size and color, and I'm about to tell him Trader Joe's has pumpkins twice the size for half the price, when Gabe emerges through the door with a box of hammers.

"I found Ricky," I say the instant I see him.

Surprise flashes across his face before he drops the box onto the floor and shoves it under the bottom shelf with the toe of his boot. "Where?"

"You're not going to like it." I pass him the printout and give him a few moments to read, and digest, Ricky's obituary.

He points to the date the article was written. "This was just two months after Zach."

"I know."

Gabe unties his apron, yanks it over his head and wedges it in a messy ball between spray bottles of carpet cleaner on the shelf. "Let's go. I want to hear the whole story."

"Okay, but did you make the connection? Ricky was a—"

Gabe silences me by wrapping a giant palm around my bicep and pulling me up the middle aisle. "Not here."

We hustle through the store and out the double doors. The street is strangely quiet for a Friday morning, no pedestrians rushing up the block with shopping bags, no cars whizzing past. With no one around to hear us, I feed him the most important line from what he just read. "Ricky was a mechanic."

"Which means he knew how to install a truck valve."

"That's an awfully big coincidence, don't you think?"

Gabe plants his boots at the edge of the curb, pausing to check for nonexistent traffic, then ushers us both across the street. "I don't believe in coincidences, not anymore. But it would explain why Nick didn't remember him. If we're thinking this through right, Ricky would have lagged behind my brothers in the second convoy with the busted truck."

My mind sticks on his words, the ones about Nick not remembering Ricky, and I pull Gabe to a stop outside the glass door to Starbucks. "Gabe, wait a minute. Nick doesn't remember Ricky? What if his name on that transcript was a mistake? Maybe that's why we've never heard his name before."

Gabe grimaces, and he leans his head close, even though there's no one around to hear him anyway. "Nick is a little… confused. Not a lot of what he says these days makes any sense."

Poor Nick, though I guess it's understandable. I imagine any man crouched fifteen feet away when three bullets tore through his brother's skull would be not only confused but scarred for life. In Nick's case, it also sent him squirreling underground. No one has seen or heard from him since his honorable discharge back in the spring.

Gabe tugs on the door handle, and the scent of coffee and autumn spice wraps around us like an invisible fog. "Let's sort through all the facts before we jump to any conclusions."

Starbucks is a little busier than outside, but not by much. There's a cluster of mothers in workout gear in the leather chairs by the front window, a long-haired college student with his nose in a calculus book and a handful of folks behind laptops. Gabe and I settle on a table in the front corner, semi-secluded behind a display of travel coffee mugs, and I hold it for us while Gabe gives the barista our orders.

He returns a few minutes later with a plain black coffee for himself, and a large pumpkin spice latte and two blueberry muffins for me.

"I haven't had breakfast, and I just rowed for two hours straight," I say, feeling an overwhelming urge to explain my order, even though Gabe doesn't seem the least bit interested in my questionable diet.

He points to the article, neatly folded on the table between us. "Start at the beginning."

I do, attacking the first muffin and telling him between sugary bites about my midnight epiphany and my subsequent computer search. I've barely begun when he holds up a hand to pause my story.

"Wait a minute. You've been up since two?"

I nod, swallowing. "I've had a lot of coffee. Anyway, I had been so focused on searching through the military databases, I didn't even consider the fact that he may have been a foreigner, much less a civilian."

"You searched every coalition list?"

"Only the European and Latin American countries. I figured those would be the most likely to have a name like Hernandez."

His eyes widen. "What's that, six or seven countries?"

"Eight. The UK was the largest to comb through, and I would have gone back to check the other countries if I hadn't found him on the American contractors website."

Gabe gives me an impressed look. "You really are excellent at research, aren't you?"

I let out a little laugh, then continue my story of this morning's events. Gabe leans forward in his chair, planting both elbows on the table and listening with squinted eyes. When I get to the part about Ricky being a contractor for Intergon, I explain a few of the theories I came up with on the boat, which widen his eyes and straighten his spine like a series of electric jolts.

"And I checked the map," I say. "The explosion that killed Ricky happened about fifteen miles from where Zach was killed, just two months earlier."

We fall silent, and I reach for my latte, take a long pull. Warm liquid lands in my belly, but it does nothing to chase the chill from my bones. It's one thing to suspect the army is hiding something, another thing entirely to have proof.

Gabe is the first to break the silence. "Call the sister. Set up a meeting. And I want to be there, in the room, when you talk to her."

Something I can't quite put my finger on surges at his request—fear? nerves?—and I swallow it down. "No way. You look exactly like your brother, and your face has been all over the news for the past year. If she owns a television set or subscribes to a newspaper, she'll recognize you. Besides, what am I supposed to say? That we suspect her dead brother is tied to Zach's death somehow? She won't let us anywhere near her."

"So feed her a story that he fixed up your car, or you're old friends from school. You'll think of something."

"You're asking me to lie?"

His answer is immediate. "I'm asking you to go undercover."

I lean back in my chair and consider his request, my heart ramming hard enough to crack my ribs. Whether knowingly or unwittingly, Gabe has just pinpointed a heated debate in the news community. On the one hand, he's not wrong. Undercover reporting *is* a common technique, and not just for a few rogue reporters. Big-name journalists have long been rewarded for crafty approaches to getting a scoop, even if that reward is only a byline.

But for every reporter who's ever lied or misrepresented themselves to a source, there are just as many who are dead set against it, who contend that as reporters, our role is to *tell* the truth, not obscure it.

"Come on, Abigail. Journalists do it all the time. As long as the fib is for the greater good, say, to expose corruption in jails or child labor in factories or bullying in high schools

or racism in the Ku Klux Klan, what's the big deal? You're
manipulating your story to extract a bigger truth."

Gabe is right on this point, too. Journalists often look to
the philosophy of utilitarianism when making these kinds of
decisions. If the actions taken are on behalf of the public, if
they are done for the good of the majority, then what's wrong
with a harmless little lie? The boundaries are vague at best.

But still. Something about it kicks the air right out of me.

"I'm not a journalist, remember?" My voice sounds weird.
Hollow and high and...wrong.

"You're seriously going to sit here and tell me you have zero
plans to write about Ricky?"

"You make it sound like you want me to."

"Somebody has to. Why not you? You're the one who
found him."

I give him a halfhearted shrug, but my lungs won't loosen.
My heart won't settle. I rub a knuckle over my breastbone, but
an ache pulses and pounds behind my sternum, blooming into
a spiky knot that's not from worry or resentment or dread.

It's from longing. Longing clings to me like static electricity
I can't bat away.

I want to be the one to write about Ricky. I want that byline. Even after everything that happened with Chelsea, even
after everything I'm learning about Maria, Ricky's story feels
like *mine*, and I don't like the greedy rush that warms my skin
at the realization.

Gabe misreads my silence as doubt, and he reaches across
the table, across cups and wrappers and crumb-laden napkins,
and wraps his big hand around mine. "Please, Abigail. For me.
Please, call Graciela."

I tell myself it's the double please that does it, or the way
his voice lowers to a rough rumble that rocks me down to the
core. I tell myself it's his expression, so vulnerable and open

it makes me feel self-conscious, or the way his touch buzzes through my skin and mainlines into my bloodstream.

It's shocking what the mind can self-rationalize when it really wants something.

I nod. "I didn't have time to search for her number before practice," I say, and he releases my hand. "I was already late as it was."

"We can use one of the computers at the market." Gabe scoops the trash from our table and jerks his head toward the door. "Let's go."

Outside, the wan mid-morning sun has inched the thermometer up a degree or two, but it's still too frigid for a rowing outfit that is basically head-to-toe Lycra. Now that my excitement has died down and the exhaustion from what was essentially a sleepless night is setting in, my fleece body warmer does little to keep me warm.

Gabe opens the door and I rush into the heat, following him to an ancient computer at the back of the store. He pulls up a very slow internet, types Graciela's full name in the search screen, hits Enter, and we wait an eternity for the screen to load. By some sort of miracle, there's only one Graciela Hernandez listed in Portsmouth. Gabe scribbles her contact information on Ricky's obituary and shoves the paper in my direction.

"What's the strategy?" Frankly, I'm too exhausted to come up with it on my own.

"An old friend?"

"What if she asks me for details? I don't know anything about Ricky."

"Okay, what if you tell her you work for Intergon?"

I shake my head, not liking that one, either. Though I did a little reading on their company website, I don't remember enough to spit out much more than an elevator pitch should she ask. I think, until I come up with something that's a little closer to the truth.

"What if I say I was engaged to a soldier he knew from Afghanistan? One who died. Ricky could be one of the last people to have seen him alive. I could tell her I'm trying to get in touch with people who knew him while he was on tour."

"Perfect."

I pull my cell phone out of my pocket and dial Graciela's number. After four rings, an electronic recording greets me down the line. "Voice mail," I whisper to Gabe. I wait for the beep, and then I begin.

"Hello, Graciela, my name is Abigail Wolff. My fiancé, David, was killed about a year ago in Kabul, right around the time your brother was. I've come across an old letter that makes me think the two of them knew each other, and...well, I know you'll understand when I tell you I'm looking for any sort of connection that will help me keep the memory of David alive. I was hoping we could maybe trade stories, and who knows? Maybe we can help each other find some more people who knew David and Ricky from Afghanistan. My number is 202-555-3761. Thanks, and talk soon, I hope. Okay, bye."

I hang up, and Gabe doesn't say anything, just pulls me in for a long, fierce hug. I wasn't ready for it, wasn't expecting it, and the contact is both shocking and welcome at the same time. I wrap my arms around his middle and hug him back, thinking how nice his big frame feels pressed up against mine, hard and soft at the same time, how perfectly my head fits into the crook of his shoulder, how our bodies slip together like matching puzzle pieces.

"Thank you," he whispers into my hair. His breath warms my scalp, and when he unwinds himself from me, he doesn't let me go. He holds my arms and my gaze, and his face explodes into that extraordinarily ordinary smile. His eyes light up like the sun. I'm the one who put that look on his face, and I don't want to let the moment go.

And then a harried woman comes around the corner and does it for us. "Excuse me, where would I find the floor wax?"

"Thank you," he whispers one last time, and the moment is gone.

Gabe calls that night, as I'm upstairs in my room, getting ready for bed. "Any word from Graciela?"

I toss my hairbrush onto the dresser and dig a tank top out of the drawer. "None."

"Maybe we called the wrong number."

"She said her name on the voice mail."

"Maybe it's the wrong Graciela."

"It wasn't." I wedge the phone between my shoulder and ear and wriggle out of my jeans. I can't be one hundred percent certain of this, of course, but it seems like something Gabe needs to hear. "We called the right one."

"Maybe somebo—"

"Gabe." I wait until he falls quiet, and then I say, in my best calm-a-spooked-source voice, "She'll call." I can't be certain of this, either, but that doesn't mean I don't think it's true. Call it an ex-reporter's hunch. I step out of my pants and kick them toward the laundry pile, a mini-mountain of discarded clothes in the corner. "And the very second I hang up with her, I will call you. I promise."

He's silent for a long beat. "I'm overreacting again, aren't I?"

I sink onto the bed. "Maybe just a little."

"Sorry. I didn't used to be so clueless, just so you know. I used to be pretty decisive." He's taking care to keep his tone flippant, but I can hear something darker pushing up from under the words, something much more honest and true, as if maybe he's testing the waters, checking how I will respond.

"You lost a brother. I think you get a pass."

He makes a sound that's half scoff, half sigh. "Do you know what my specialty was at Goldman Sachs? Fucking crisis management. I was that guy who could manage any meltdown, find order in any chaos. I was the fearless one, the one everybody looked to when the world was tipping."

"And then your own world tipped."

He lets out a sharp puff of air, like a wry laugh. "That's one way to put it."

"You can't beat yourself up about it, Gabe. It will take you some time to get used to your new reality."

"It's more than just a new reality. Losing Zach made me question everything I ever knew. It altered the most fundamental part of me, like…I don't know, it added an extra kink in my DNA or something. There's me before, and there's me after. I'm not the same person I used to be."

I could tell him I understand more than he knows. I get the thin, fragile line that separates the before from the after all too well, but I don't want to make this conversation about me. Gabe sounds as if he needs comfort and reassurance, so that's what I try to give him.

"I didn't know you before, but if it makes you feel any better, I like the person you are now."

"You like ass-hats?"

I laugh. "I like works in progress. I'm kind of one myself."

Gabe laughs, too, and we fall into a comfortable silence. By now it's late. Outside my window the city is dark and quiet, my neighbors all at home in their beds. I scoot up mine and crawl under the covers, my phone still pressed to my ear, and try to picture Gabe. Where is he right now? Reclined on his couch? Leaning against his kitchen counter? Stretched out on his bed? The last image is the one that sticks—one arm cocked behind his head, the other holding his phone, big body sprawled atop the mattress.

"Abigail?" he says, his voice low, almost a whisper.

"Yes."

"Talk to you tomorrow," he says, as if it's the most normal thing in the world. As if I should have known to expect another call.

I smile. "Talk to you then."

14

Washingtonian Magazine recently gave the Oval Room four stars, which means reservations are harder to come by than a sit-down with the president in the Oval Office, only a block or so down the road. Unless you're a three-star general, that is, and unless you want a prominent table in a restaurant like this one—one that, were it not for the overwhelming aroma of roasted meats and buttery sauces and truffle oils, would smell distinctly like power.

The hostess leads me into the dining room, ushering me to the table with a Vanna White move.

Mike and Betsy are seated side by side on the burgundy velvet banquette, and the first to see me approach. Betsy greets me with a happy wave, but my brother acknowledges my arrival with a quick flick of his chin, never missing a word of his monologue.

"…even though Langley Park is not technically that far from our offices in Chevy Chase, we've found our clients aren't willing to travel more than five miles or so. This expands our reach all the way into College Park."

"Hi, Mom." I lean down between my parents' shoulders to kiss her cheek, and then the general's. Circling around his back, I push aside a red silk pillow and take a seat on the banquette next to Mike.

Mike continues as if he hasn't just been interrupted. "Eventually we'll keep going southward, to maybe Brentwood or Fairmount Heights, but we need to absorb the costs of this expansion first."

A waiter appears at Dad's right shoulder with a bottle of red wine, and I can't help but notice the general looks almost grateful for the interruption. That Mike is successful in his career, well on his way to building a mini orthodontia empire to the north of the District, pleases our father to no end, I am certain.

But that my brother equates his success with the number of patients in his multiple offices and the amount of zeros at the end of his tax return, rather than the number of stars on his sleeve, is something I'm not certain my father will ever fully appreciate.

The waiter pours the wine and tells us about the specials, then turns to a neighboring table. Mom picks up the conversation at the other end of ours, something about one of her friends from bridge club who's just had her spleen removed, while I spread my napkin across my lap, straighten my silverware on either side of my plate and pretend to study my menu. Anything but acknowledge my father's gaze, bearing down on me like a nuclear weapon.

"Abigail," he says, clearly fed up with my avoidance tactics.

I try not to wince. Ever since Rose's birthday party, when I overheard his argument with Chris, when my father ordered me to cease and desist any contact with the Armstrongs as if

I were a fresh recruit, we haven't spoken. Dodging his calls seemed easier than dodging the truth, and that is that I'm still thinking about Jean's offer...though I can't deny that finding Ricky has pushed me to the far end of the thinking-about-it phase, the side that juts up against a "hell, yes."

I look up and meet his gaze for the first time tonight. "Yes?"

"Your mother was asking you about your work."

"Oh?" One glance at Mom confirms it. She smiles widely, bobs her head enthusiastically. I wonder if she has any idea what the tension down at this end of the table is about, or if she's even noticed. "What about it?"

"Tell us how your work's going, dear. Any new projects you're working on?"

I pluck a roll, soft and light as a cloud, from the silver bowl in the middle of the table, smear it with butter the waiter advertised as organic and locally sourced, and haul a bolstering breath. But at the very last second, I chicken out. "Medicare is about to start covering lung cancer screening. Have you heard?"

Dad nods at me over the top of his menu, but his forehead doesn't clear. His eyes don't unsquint. The general is a man who misses nothing, including, according to his scowl, the reason behind my non-reply.

So when Mike turns the conversation back to himself, starting in on a long-winded story about some senator whose daughter's double cross bite is going to single-handedly finance the brand-new Porsche Cayenne he just ordered for Betsy, for once I don't mind. I sip my wine and try to look as if I care.

Even though the expression my father is wearing tells me he cares a great deal.

Only something about the way he is watching me makes me suspect it is not Mike's work but mine he is thinking of.

★ ★ ★

Between courses, I slip away to the restroom. I take my time in the plush lounge, washing my hands with scented soap and freshening my lip gloss, inspecting my reflection for far too long. A string of what-ifs whisper through my mind, kicking up dust and picking up speed and swirling into a sandstorm of unease and insecurity. What if Graciela never calls me back? What if it really was the wrong Graciela? What if I can never prove the connection between her brother and Zach? What will I tell Gabe?

That last thought rises up and bites me. *What will I tell Gabe?* I tell myself pleasing Gabe is not the point of this exercise, though I can't deny that the thought of his expression, when I tell him Graciela called with news, makes my heart beat double time.

"Not the point," I tell my reflection, but she doesn't look as if she believes me, either. Rolling my eyes, I pluck my purse from the counter and step into the hallway.

Where I walk right into the general.

I'm too surprised to ask him what he is doing here, and he doesn't offer an explanation. He just wraps a big palm around my bicep and domineers me farther into the hallway, all the way down to where it dead ends into a wall. I know his next question before he even poses it.

"Why are you still talking to the Armstrongs?" he says in his three-star-general voice.

"How do you know I'm still talking to the Armstrongs?"

It's a technique I learned from him, this answering a question with a question, and by the looks of his expression, the way his lips curl and his brows crunch into a crease, he doesn't like it one bit.

But my question is also a provocation, because he and I both know there's only one way he can know I'm still working on the Armstrong story, and that's by spying on either me or the Armstrongs.

His tone softens but just a smidge. "I know lots of things, darlin'. Now I need you to answer my question. The Armstrongs."

I give him an I'm-thirty-two-so-don't-even-go-there look. "Because I'm not one of your subordinates, and I'm not going to stop just because you tell me to. Jean Armstrong asked me to help her write Zach's story, and I'm still thinking about it."

"That doesn't explain why you've been in contact with Gabe."

"What… When… How do you know about Gabe?" I shake my head in disbelief and maybe a little disgust. "Are you tailing me? No, you're tailing *him*, aren't you? *Jesus*."

"Listen to me, Abigail. There are things going on here you don't understand."

"Things like what?"

His expression is like a sluice, locked down tighter than the White House during a terrorist threat. "Things you don't *want* to understand."

"See, Dad, that's where you're wrong. I *do* want to understand what's going on here, and so do the Armstrongs. They lost a son and a brother, and it's not right for you or Uncle Chris or anybody else to keep the truth from them. They deserve to know what happened to Zach."

"He took three bullets to the head. That's what happened to him."

"Yes, but from whose gun? And why was his brother there, on the same battlefield? Aren't there rules for that? The Armstrongs have a right to know those answers, too."

"Just because something's the truth doesn't always make it right."

I shake my head, and rather vehemently. "The truth is *always* right."

I believe this with every ounce of me, from my skin and bones all the way down to a cellular level. I believe that this is where I went wrong with Chelsea Vogel, when I missed the truth about Maria's past and her scheming, and I believe this is where the army messed up with the Armstrongs, by refusing to admit to any wrongdoing or even contemplate the possibilities of who shot Zach. The truth is always right. *Always.* And the public deserves to know.

"I'm gonna need you to trust me on this one," my father says. "I can't explain. I can't tell you anything other than that you do *not* want to get involved in this matter. There is nothing here you need to know."

And this is where my father and I will never see eye to eye. His life, his entire career, has been built on a need-to-know basis, on clandestine operations and restriction of data and security clearance levels. In his mind, the answer is simple. I do not need to know.

My life, on the other hand, is crafted around my inherent belief that *everyone* needs to know. The public, the Armstrongs, myself. *I* need to know.

But this is an argument neither of us will win. Along with my father's hazel eyes and wonky second toes, I also inherited his dogged determination and fierce competitiveness, and pitting us against each other is like throwing two raging lions into a ring—a roaring, snarling fight to the death.

I steer our talk back onto the road, and I throw out my ace of spades. "Okay, then. What about Ricky?"

"What about him?" Dad says, and without missing a beat.

A chill skitters across my shoulder blades. My question was a test, and my father just failed it spectacularly. By tossing out Ricky's name, I was digging into his complicity. In knowing Ricky existed, in burying his testimony, maybe even in breaking into my house and swiping my copy of the transcript. But

Dad didn't even blink, which means that he not only knows about Ricky, he already knew I did, as well.

But he can't know about the copy Mandy pried from my machine's memory, nor the one she transferred to the memory stick on the key chain tucked away in my purse. Nobody knows about those but me and Mandy.

"Why was Ricky's name buried? What did he see? What did he know?"

My father is shaking his head before my first question is finished. "Listen to me, Abigail. Ricardo Hernandez is a dead end, both literally and figuratively. Even if he could talk, he'd have nothing to say about Zach Armstrong's death. He wasn't there. He saw nothing. He was not part of the battle that killed Zach Armstrong. Do you understand what I'm telling you?"

Oh, I understand, all right. I understand perfectly. Dad wants me to believe that Ricky's inclusion on the rogue transcript was a mistake, an oversight, a blunder. He wants me to believe Ricky was nowhere near Zach Armstrong when he was killed. But if that's true, why would someone go to all the trouble to get me an uncensored copy of the transcript? It doesn't make any sense.

Which means I also understand something else. I also understand my father is lying to me. Ricky Hernandez knew something, and it's important enough to the Armstrong case that the army would scramble to bury it. Which means that whatever it is, it doesn't look good for the army.

Dad leans in, and everything about him softens. His posture, his expression, his ten-hut tone.

"I'm asking you, darlin', as the man who brought you into this world, to back off. To drop your search for Mr. Hernandez and let this partnership with the Armstrongs die. Now, I know you want to know all the reasons why, and if I could tell them to you, I certainly would, but I can't. All I can tell you

is, let it go. For the Armstrongs, for yourself, for me. Just…
let it go. Can you do that for me?"

For my father, there's only one acceptable answer, and that
is "yes, sir." I hold his gaze and my breath, not moving, not
speaking, not capable of lying. Not about this. Not without
him seeing right through me.

"Is it a matter of national security?" I say. "Is Ricky a spy
or a terrorist or…I don't know, a being from another planet?
At least give me something to go on here."

"How about this? I am your father, and I'm asking you to
trust me."

I blink into my father's eyes a long moment, realizing that
by turning this argument personal, I've been outplayed. Do
I trust that my father loves me, that he has my best interests
at heart? Absolutely. Without a shadow of a sliver of a doubt.

But for my father, the army has always come first. Duty,
honor, country. Everything else is corollary, including the
people he loves most in the world. After all, none of us would
be here if not for the long, gray line.

He reaches for my hand, tucks it into the crook of his arm,
holds it there with a palm. The gesture is both intimate and
intimidating. "Do you?"

"Do I what?"

"Trust me."

His general mask is gone now, morphed into the man who
not all that long ago tickled my knees, the man who taught me
to drive a stick shift, the man who looked as if he might cry
when at eighteen I told him I was too old to call him daddy.
I look into my father's eyes and nod, but it's sluggish. I know
he expects me to, even as I silently admit to myself that by
doing so, I'm not being entirely honest.

I *do* trust him, just not about this.

"Good." He pats my hand and smiles. As far as Dad is

concerned, the subject is now closed. "Now, let's get back to the table before your mother reports us missing."

Without another word, he leads me there, sinks into his red leather chair and says to no one in particular, "That ricotta cheesecake looks good. Don't you think?"

I respond in an equally passive-aggressive manner. By leaving my third message for Graciela from the car on the way home.

15

Ben suggests we meet in the food court at Arundel Mills, a cavernous mall south of Baltimore. At just before four on a school day, the place is a madhouse, packed with after-school shoppers, harried moms and their screaming kids, and a slew of somewhat sketchier types thanks to the casino next door. By some miracle, I find us a table at the edge of the dining area, sit down and wait.

He shows up ten minutes later, and other than a fresh T-shirt, he hasn't changed much since the last time I saw him. His hair still hangs dirty and long over his eyes, his clothes still dwarf his childlike limbs, his face is still arranged in that carefully disinterested expression. But his eyes find mine from beneath the chunks of his bangs, and I catch their light. He's eager to hear what I have to say.

He slides his backpack off his shoulder, drops it on the floor and sinks onto the chair across from me, pulling the buds from his ears. "Hey."

"Hi, Ben. I didn't know what you wanted," I say, gesturing

to the mini-mountain of Chick-fil-A bags and cups on the table between us, "so I just got one of everything."

His gaze dips to the mounds of food, then back to me. "The cows will be thrilled."

Okay, so maybe I went a bit overboard, as I tend to do, but this offering is fueled by more than just guilt. It's also fueled by worry for the skin-and-bones kid who showed up at my doorstep all those weeks ago, and the fact that he travels all over Baltimore and the District unsupervised. Where is his father? I rip open a bag of sandwiches and hand one to Ben.

"Maria Duncan's real name is Maria Elizabeth Daniels. She wasn't from Detroit, but from Toledo, sixty miles south. She never went to college, never got a degree in business accounting, never worked for any one of those places on her résumé."

Ben drops his sandwich back onto the table uneaten. "So, she lied?"

His prepubescent voice cracks on the last word, and I wonder if it's hormones or emotion that send it into a tailspin. Either way, I soften everything about mine when I answer.

"She lied."

"About everything?"

I nod. "Pretty much."

"But that's...that's insane. The press dug up everything on my mom. *Everything.* Even shit that shouldn't have mattered, like bounced checks and speeding tickets. How could they have missed such humongous things about Maria?"

"Same way I did. Because we were so focused on exposing your mother that we didn't take a closer look at the victim."

"But if Maria's a liar, then she's also not the victim. My mom was."

By making that connection, Ben is grasping a little at straws, and understandably so. No one wants to believe their mother is capable of cheating on their father, of the dishonesty and pretense and hypocrisy of publicly condemning the very thing she is trying to suppress in herself. But Maria's lies don't erase Chelsea's guilt, and Maria was a victim long before Chelsea came along, just not in the way Ben thinks.

"When Maria was eight, she was abducted from her bedroom in the middle of the night. Her captor broke a window, plucked her out of her bed and stole her from her own house. Her parents were fairly prominent, and they were in the middle of a very loud, very public divorce. But because one of Maria's first-grade teachers had reported bruises on Maria's skin a few years prior, the police went after her parents. Her father, specifically. They questioned him for days, while meanwhile across town, a janitor from her school had Maria locked in his basement. Think about the worst thing he could have wanted her for, and that was his reason."

Across from me, Ben swallows, but he doesn't speak.

"The police found her three days later, naked and filthy and abused in every possible way, thanks to a tip from a neighbor. He saw her through a basement window. This was 1996, the year Amber Hagerman's murder prompted the Amber Alert system, but too late to help Maria. But that neighbor recognized Maria that day because of the media, and the way they plastered her face on every newspaper and television set across America."

Ben is silent for a long moment, and then he looks away. I give him plenty of time, watching his gaze roll over an elderly couple in matching green tracksuits sharing a plate of fries, three toddlers wrestling in the aisle, the throngs of people and shopping bags and messy tables piled with fast-food wrappers. He takes several deep breaths, as if collecting himself or his thoughts, deciding what to say, and with each one, his expression smooths out to carefully blank. It's a practiced move, and I'm starting to think the kid's way tougher than I've given him credit for.

Finally, his gaze hitches back to mine. "So, okay...if her parents were prominent, they must have had some money."

"They went bankrupt around the time of the divorce. There were whispers that maybe it was the reason for the divorce. Either way, Maria needs the money. As far as I can tell, she's not working, and she's got a handicapped brother to support." He shrugs, the gesture a silent *so what*, and I plant both palms on the table and lean in. "Look, I'm not in any way excusing her behavior. I'm only trying to explain why I think there's more to her story than we originally thought."

Ben falls silent. Still. I don't want him to get his hopes up for news I can't give him. This time around, I'm not making any assumptions, not until I know all—and by all, I mean every single goddamn one—of the facts.

"Look, Ben. I have someone looking into Maria's finances, but I just want you to be prepared for the possibility I might find nothing."

"You won't."

"I might. If Maria's smart, which she clearly is, she's got the money well hidden and will keep it black, which means we won't be able to trace it."

"Do you think my mom was paying her, too?"

I start to remind him his mother was far from wealthy, but his voice sounds so hopeful, so desperate to believe Maria took his mother for a ride, that I quickly stem my answer.

"Maybe..." I lift both palms from the table and point them to the sky. Even if I do find evidence of blackmail, it won't release his mother from wrongdoing. Chelsea was still a hypocrite and an adulterer, just perhaps a deceived one. "Like I said, I've got somebody looking into it."

"So, basically, you brought me all the way down here to tell me you're still working on it."

"No, I brought you all the way down here to tell you I'm not making the same mistake this time. Maria Duncan-slash-Daniels will not get past me again. I don't have all the facts on her yet, but I will."

"And when you do?"

This time I can give him the answer I know he wants to hear. "You'll be the first to know."

Gabe calls at exactly ten-thirty, as he's been doing for the past four nights, only this time, he doesn't start the conversation by asking about Graciela.

"Hey," he says, then nothing more.

Weird how you can cram so much into one syllable, how you can fill up three little consonants and vowels until they're boiling over in emotion. In that one tiny word, I hear despair and frustration and misery and desperation and loneliness and sorrow. Above all, I hear sorrow.

"What's wrong?"

"Nothing. Everything." He sounds tired, and his words are slow and slushy around the edges, as if maybe he's been drinking. He sucks in a long breath that catches on the end. "It's Zach's birthday."

I freeze in the middle of my living room, my heart pinching in sympathy. "Oh, Gabe…"

"We went to Nick's. Mom insisted, even though he told us not to come." I hear him take another deep breath, this time through his nostrils. "It wasn't pleasant for any of us, and not just because we were missing Zach. Nick is…not well." There's another long pause, another hitching breath. "Watching Zach die has broken him in a way I don't know how to fix."

Gabe sounds so sad and confused and lost, and my heart

heaves for him, just rises up in my chest and rolls over. I want to reach through the phone and wrap myself around him in a tight hug, hold on until this awful day has passed and it's tomorrow. From everything I've learned about Nick, Gabe didn't just lose one brother that day on the battlefield; he lost them both.

I tell him the only thing I can think of: "I'm so, so sorry."

"Yeah," he whispers. "Me, too."

"Is there anything I can do?"

"You can talk to me. I don't care about what. Anything. Just...talk."

So that's exactly what I do. I sink onto my couch and steer the conversation far, far away from war and death and dying. I point it instead to a long, drawn-out tale of the summer Mandy and I spent waiting tables in Tahoe, drinking and partying and kissing far too many boys and maybe once a girl, and how our little adventure solidified Mandy's position as not just my best friend, but my sister. I tell him about Rose, how I had no idea my heart could hold so much love for one little person until she came along, and how flattered I was she wants me, and only me, to take her trick-or-treating this Halloween. I tell him about the book I'm reading and the cooking lessons I'm giving my mother for Christmas and the race my rowing team won last month. I talk about everything and nothing.

After forever, my words trail off, and the waiting stillness on the other end of the line makes me think Gabe must have fallen asleep.

And then his deep and rumbly voice comes down the line. "So. To recap, you kissed a girl?"

"I just talked for forty-five minutes straight, and that's the part you picked up on?"

"Uh, yeah. Was it Mandy?"

I can still hear the heaviness pushing at the edges of his

tone, but something lighter has blown in, something that makes him sound much more like Gabe again, the one I met those first two times at the hardware store. It pushes a smile into my answer.

"No, it wasn't Mandy. I don't even remember her name. She was just some girl I met at a bar."

"Was she hot?"

"Yes. She was hot, I was drunk, we were both in college. It was an experimental summer for me."

"I'll say. Was there tongue? Any skin-on-skin action?"

I can't stop the giggle that sneaks up my throat. "Gabe. Can we please move on?"

"One more question." He pauses, and his voice drops an entire octave. "What are you wearing?"

My giggle turns into a full-blown laugh, and Gabe joins me. I know he's only joking. I know his questions and his flirting are little more than a distraction tactic—albeit a fairly effective one—to lighten up the weight of the day, but I can't help the way his interest makes my skin tingle. The way *Gabe* makes my skin tingle.

"Are you going to be okay?" I ask.

"I think so. Thanks for talking me off the ledge."

"Anytime." I check my watch, see it's closing in on midnight. Gabe and I have been on the phone for well over an hour. "Only twenty more minutes and we'll have talked into tomorrow."

My unspoken offer hangs in the air for only a second or two before Gabe snaps it up. "You forgot to tell me how the bathroom is coming along."

I flick off the table lamp behind my head, pull an afghan over my body and fill him in on the bathroom, as well as my ideas for the powder room down the hall. Twenty minutes stretch into twenty more, and those twenty into another hour. We talk about TV shows and restaurants, about vacations and books and movies. It's the kind of conversation that says nothing except neither of us wants to get off the phone. Finally, at some time past one, our words fade into whispers and then into silence.

"Abigail?" he says, his voice just another shadow in the room. It pulls me back right as I was drifting off.

"Yes?" I whisper, but I'm already smiling.

He's quiet for a moment, then, "Talk to you tomorrow."

"Talk to you tomorrow."

We hang up, and I fall asleep right there on the couch, my phone clutched close to my heart.

16

On Wednesday, I'm returning from a mid-morning run when I find Gabe on my front porch steps. I've been gone only an hour or so, but he looks as if he's been waiting for all of it. He's hunkered into a thick Patagonia fleece zipped high against the wind, his hands stuffed into his pockets, an Orioles cap pulled low on his forehead.

"Hi," I say, waving as I jog up the front walk. "I didn't know you were—" He lifts his head, and his face kicks my already double-time heart into redline territory. "What's wrong?"

"We need to talk."

It's not just his carefully controlled expression but his ominous tone that drops my stomach onto the cobblestones under my feet. "Oh, God. What happened? Is Nick okay?"

He seems a little surprised at my question. It flashes across his face before he wipes it clean.

"No. No. Nothing like that. It's just..." He trails off, and I realize something is wrong, very wrong here. I can see it in how the line of his mouth is set under a good three or four days of scruff, how his shoulders are tense and tight beneath his leather jacket. But it's more than just his obvious tension; there's something about the way his gaze won't quite stick to mine. "Can we go inside?"

"Just tell me!" I prop my right foot on the top step, unfasten the key from where I'd tied it onto my shoe and hustle us both into my foyer. "What's wrong? What happened? Did I do something?"

"You tell me." He drops his head and hands me a folded piece of paper he pulls from his coat pocket.

I take the paper from his fingers, and my entire body tenses. My shoulders, my back, my legs, every muscle bunching and bracing for whatever's written on it. I know from everything about him that it can't be good.

I peel the page open, my gaze falling on the army logo and the CONFIDENTIAL knifed in big, black, block letters across the top of the page, and the combination buckles my knees.

"Where did you get this?" It's my voice, but the tone is all wrong. Quiet and controlled and strangely detached, as if I'm asking him if they've fixed the sinkhole on Wisconsin Avenue.

"Somebody leaked it to our lawyers. Anonymously, of course. It hasn't gone public yet, but it will."

It's the last thing I hear before I read the paper further, and everything stops making sense.

As you are well aware, Corporal Zach Armstrong was killed on November 21 while on active duty in Afghanistan. Since his death, media interest in his story has been high, and high-ranking officials, including the United States President, have made increasingly public comments about his death at the hands of the enemy. However, all United States officials should avoid making any comments that paint his death as heroic. Unknowing statements such as these by our country's leaders may cause public embarrassment should the circumstances of Corporal Armstrong's death ever become public.

And there, slashed across the bottom of the page, is my father's name and signature. The world warps under the weight of them, as if the entire room is teetering, tilting every atom in my body off-kilter.

I check the date at the top. Just three weeks after Zach's death, well before the investigation began, and a little over three months before my father retired.

"Abigail."

I blink up at Gabe. "Huh?"

"I said you need to get out of those wet clothes. You're shaking like a leaf."

His words cut through the ocean roaring in my ears, but I can't seem to focus on them. My head is reeling, repeating and tripping over my father's instead, in the Oval Room bathroom hallway. The words that suggested he's still following me. The words that asked me if I trust him. The words telling me, in no uncertain terms, to back off and let it go.

Well, no fucking wonder.

My gaze sticks to his name at the top of the memo between my fingers, and the letters go dark and blurry, then explode in a burst of white. I wait for my vision to clear, for the white to fade into a tunnel of dancing black spots, and then before I know it, I'm wandering through my downstairs rooms, drifting, strangely numb, as if maybe my head has figured out my father's involvement, but the rest of my body is still struggling to catch up.

Now what?

I wander through my office, into the hallway, pausing at

the door to the kitchen. Gabe stays close on my heels the entire time.

My father knew. He knew the truth about Zach's death, almost from the very beginning, and yet he didn't tell the Armstrongs. Even worse, he did everything in his power to cover up his involvement—from them, from the public, from me, the daughter who compiled silly articles for a silly health care web magazine and whom he thought would be the very last person to take an interest in the story.

I'm standing at the kitchen table when it comes over me, slowly at first, like a storm rumbling in the distance. My breath quickens. My fingertips and toes start to tingle. Something cold and hard forms in my belly, growing and pulsing until it grips me by the guts.

My father *knew*.

"Jesus!" My voice is high and loud and furious. I whirl around, bounce right into Gabe.

He steadies me with a palm to each elbow. "Are you okay?"

I give Gabe a you've-got-to-be-joking grimace. Clearly I am about as far away from okay as you can get. "It all makes sense now, you know. Cornering me in the castle, following me to the bathroom. His tail's probably calling him as we speak, reporting back that you're inside my house."

"What are you talking about? Whose tail?"

"My father's tail. That's the only way he could have known." I wrench my arms from Gabe's grip, look around for my keys. I spot them on the counter under the microwave.

"Could have known what? Where are you going?"

I look at him as if he just asked me if I had a date with the president. "Where do you think I'm going? To talk to my father, of course."

And that's when I hear it again, Gabe's earlier words when I asked him if I did something. *You tell me*, he said. The words blow through the fog in my brain, stoking the fire already licking at my insides. "What did you mean, 'you tell me'?"

He hesitates, just a second, but I see it. Gabe knows exactly what I'm referring to. Still, he pretends not to, scrunches his brow in mock confusion. "What?"

I narrow my eyes, step right up to his big frame. "Don't play games with me. When I asked you if I did something wrong, you said, 'you tell me.' You thought I knew about my father's involvement, didn't you? Even after you clinked your glass against mine and toasted to a fresh start, even after I let you talk me into calling Graciela with some bullshit story about her brother, even after all our midnight confessions. You assumed I knew."

He shifts his weight, looking uncomfortable. "If it helps my case any, I certainly don't anymore."

"Jesus, Gabe!" The heat spreads through my body, licking at my limbs and flushing my face. "You really are an ass-hat, aren't you?"

He gives me a good-natured grin. "And you're only figuring this out now?"

"Nothing about this is funny. This is the opposite of funny."

"You're right, and I'm sorry. But if I were my therapist," Gabe says calmly, rationally, "I'd tell you now is not the right time to talk to your father. You're too angry. You need to calm down first, think things through."

"What I need is for you to get out of my way." I plant both palms on his chest and shove, but it's like trying to push through the Washington Monument. Gabe's feet don't even budge.

He shakes his head. "No good decision is ever made when you're this upset."

I snort. "Said the man who got drunk at his own brother's funeral."

God, that felt good. I get it, I think suddenly. I understand why Gabe allows his temper to get the best of him. How good it must feel for him, too, to sneer and bark at journalists, to shock them with his *no fucking comments*. It's release, pure and simple, and it feels freaking awesome.

He flinches at my comment, but he doesn't take the bait. "Exactly. I should know."

That he somehow manages to keep his own temper in check pisses me off even more, stirs the giant vat of anger brewing in my gut until it explodes in a ball of fire. I shove at his chest again. "Damn it, Gabe, let me through!"

He reaches for me, but I lurch backward, and one of my flailing arms connects with a vase of yellow roses on the kitchen table. Gabe springs forward to catch it but is too late, and as I'm flying into the hallway, I hear the unmistakable sound of the vase smashing into a million tiny pieces on the kitchen tile.

By the time he catches up, I'm already in my car.

I find the general puttering around in the backyard in a pair of ancient wellies and Mom's floral gardening gloves, planting a bed of orange mums by the garage window overhang. He looks up when I come through the garden gate. A smile climbs his cheeks when he sees me, then falls just as quickly when he gets a load of my expression, and the half-crumpled sheet of paper in my fist.

"Don't look at me like that, Abigail." He straightens, leaning his weight on the shovel, and bobs his head at the memo. "That document doesn't contain all the facts."

In the car on the way over, the closer I got to confronting my father, the more my rage melted into plain, old-fashioned fear. Not of what I would say, but more of the extent of his involvement in the matter. I'm terrified of finding his fingerprints on more than just the memo, and yet the former journalist in me has to ask.

"But you wrote it." It's the first time I've actually said the words out loud, and they feel like okra, prickly and slimy on my tongue. "Three weeks after he was killed, you wrote a memo that insinuated not only was Zach Armstrong killed by friendly fire, but that the army was doing everything possible to sweep that little tidbit under the rug."

Dad picks up a shovelful of dirt and dumps it onto a pile on the bricks. By turning back to his work, he's not dismissing me per se, but rather taking the importance of our conversation down a notch.

"I wouldn't be so quick to judge me, darlin'. At least not until you know all the facts."

"Then tell me the facts." I sink onto a stone bench at the edge of the terrace. "Please."

He shakes his head and reaches for a potted mum. "You know I can't do that."

"Okay, then. Tell me you didn't do it. Tell me you didn't write this memo."

I know it's irrational to demand such a thing when I'm holding the evidence in my hand, but I'm desperate. This is the man who taught me about loyalty and integrity and respect, about selfless service and personal courage, and now I'm like Dorothy, peeking behind a curtain at something I don't want to see. The lasso around my lungs pulls tighter. Did all those lessons mean nothing?

Or did he get so caught up in duty, honor, country that he lost sight of what's right?

Screw duty. Screw honor and country. I just want him to explain how he could have written the goddamn memo.

"I don't know what to tell you," he says. "I'm not at liberty to discuss this matter with you."

At his easy dismissal, my frustration morphs into anger, pulsing and pricking under my skin. My father keeps telling me I don't understand, asking me to give him the benefit of the doubt. Yet how can I just trust in him blindly, when it's written here in black and white?

"Okay, then," I say, "why don't I tell you what I know instead? Zach Armstrong was killed by one of his own men, but for some reason, the army made a conscious decision not to tell the family. Instead, you painted him as a hero and used his fame to bolster public opinion of a war gone bad."

"Me, huh?"

I shrug, pointing to his name on the paper, printed there in black and white. "Your name is on the memo. Can you imagine how that poor family felt when they read it?"

"I'm sorry they had to."

"How else were they supposed to find out about their son? Oh, wait. That's right. They weren't."

"Don't be sassy with me, young lady. We didn't want to give the Armstrongs half-baked information, that's all that memo is saying."

"And yet the army gave them a contrived story about how he'd been killed by enemy fire. Hell, even the president was bragging about what a hero Zach was to the press. It was utter bullshit!"

"We did what we had to do at the time."

"What about now? What about doing the right thing now?"

"There are things going on here you don't understand. Things that are none of your business. You do *not* have all the facts."

I groan. "Why don't you tell me, then?"

"You know me, and you know I can't do that. You're going to have to trust me on this one."

"I don't..." My voice almost breaks from the sob trying

to sneak up my throat, but I swallow it down before it can escape. "I don't think I can do that."

The hurt in his face is instant. His cheeks collapse and his jowls sag, and his upper body curls into itself as if I just punched him in the gut. He covers it by reaching for the shovel, but it might as well be made of lead. It takes him forever to haul it upright. "Then maybe you should pay more attention to the word *confidential* written across the top."

"And maybe you should pay attention to your own conscience. Because this?" I shake the memo in the air. "This is reprehensible."

I can see I've gone too far. He spikes the shovel into the dirt so hard it stands at attention, even when he lets go to clench his fists at his sides. "What do you want from me, Abigail? Because I'm not going to stand here and discuss this matter with you any longer. This is where the story ends."

"This is *not* where it ends. Because it's about to become everybody's business. This memo is going public. You know that, right?"

"I do." He scoops up a mum by its roots and jams it into the ground, thrusting dirt all around it.

Right now, I suppose the best I can hope to hear is that he knows the way the army handled Zach's death was wrong, that he regrets his involvement in it, that he's sorry. But my father would clearly rather murder his mums than offer up either an explanation or an apology.

Victoria's words push up from somewhere dark and depressing. *Somebody always gets hurt, but nine times out of ten it's the bad guy.*

"You have to know how it looks, Daddy. You have to know." By now I'm crying openly, the tears sliding unchecked down my cheeks. "This memo means you're the bad guy."

His hands freeze in the dirt, but he doesn't look up. "I'm

sorry you feel that way, darlin'. I'm only doing what I have to do."

My heart heaves and cracks, but he's still my father, and even though his actions might not deserve it, at the very least I owe him a warning. "Then so am I."

I call Victoria from the car. "Check your email," I say as soon as she picks up, trying not to flinch at the bitter pill pushing at the back of my throat, an acrid mixture of fury and sorrow and self-reproach. "I just sent you something."

"My Magic 8 Ball told me you would eventually." I give her a few moments to click around her computer, then she sucks in a breath. "Holy *shit*, Abigail."

"I know. I *know*. Just promise me no spin. Report the facts, nothing more."

"I will, but you know others won't. Once the rumor rags get a hold of it, there's no telling what will happen."

"That's why I'm bringing it to you first. Set the tone, and make sure it's a fair and impartial one."

And then I punch the button to end the call, slam my brakes in the middle of Key Bridge and throw up onto the pavement.

That night, I lie in bed, watching shadows dance on the ceiling. Long after the sky turns black with night, long after the city is dark and quiet and still, sleep refuses me. My body hums with energy.

At some time close to one, I roll over, reach for my phone. Gabe's voice when he answers is low and gravelly. "Hey."

"Sorry to wake you, it's just…" I trail off, suddenly searching for words. When Gabe had called earlier, I didn't pick up. I was still sorting things through in my own mind, still trying to figure out how the man who had taught me to be good could do something so bad. I wasn't ready to talk. Now I am, so why can't I get the words out?

"No. It's fine. Is... Are you okay?"

"Not really." I can hear the tears clogging my throat, feel the heartache rising yet again in my chest.

"Do you want to come over?"

"Yeah," I say, flipping off the covers, trying to pick my clothes out of the shadows on the floor. "I really, really do."

17

Gabe's house, I see over the roof of my car, is very much like mine. Same front porch, same low profile, same twin windows on either side of what I know is the living room fireplace. Only, Gabe's house is mine on steroids. Healthy and robust and bulked up a good two to three sizes, and even in the dark, I can see what looks to be a fresh coat of paint and matching flower boxes spilling over onto a thriving front yard.

I'm winding my way up the brick pathway when the porch light flares, and a barefoot Gabe opens the door. He looks as if he just rolled out of bed, jeans and T-shirt and all. His hair is mussed, his chin and cheeks dark with scruff.

"I'm sorry for what I said about you at your brother's funeral," I say, trudging up his front porch stairs. Before I say anything else, I have to get that off my chest. "It was mean and spiteful and unforgivable."

Gabe shrugs off my apology. "Please. If anyone can understand saying something you later regret, it's me."

I want to tell Gabe not to compare my situation to his, since his brother is dead and my father is not, and then I realize that even though my father may still be alive, the man who I thought he was is not. Fresh tears prick at my eyes.

Gabe sees them, and he snags my wrist with a hand, yanks me into him, wraps his arms and his heat around me. It's only then I notice how icy cold I am, all the way down to the hollowed-out part of my bones. I shiver, and he pulls me tighter. It's the middle of the night in the freezing cold, and he stands here in his bare feet, holding me as if there's nowhere else he'd rather be.

"How are you?" he says after a while. "I was worried, especially when you didn't pick up my call earlier. I thought maybe you were still mad at me."

I tip my head back, find his gaze in the dim porch light. "For what, telling me the truth about my father?"

He shakes his head. "For being suspicious. I mean, I would have been pissed if I found out you already knew, but I wouldn't have blamed you. I figured if anything, you were trying to protect your father. How could I fault you for that?"

I hear his words, hear the compliment concealed behind them—Gabe would have understood me lying to him in order to shelter my father from blame—and something unpleasant squeezes me breathless. This situation is just so unbelievably confusing. My father. The memo lighting up the internet sky, thanks to me and Victoria. Gabe, watching me with an expression that makes me want to forget everything but him. It's as if the universe is pulling me in a million directions.

Gabe must read the misery on my face, because without another word, he guides me into his living room, parks me on his designer couch and hands me a glass of amber liquid. Kentucky bourbon, according to the bottle on the coffee table. I take a huge gulp, and then another. The liquid hits my stomach and eases through my veins, warming me up by a good ten degrees, but it doesn't melt the aching lump that seems to have lodged itself permanently in my throat.

"If you want to talk about it," he says, his voice warm and soft and inviting, "I'm a good listener."

It's all I needed to hear. The day bubbles up in my throat and boils over in a rush of words I can't hold back. Gabe deposits my glass on the table and pulls me into him, and I tell him everything. About someone breaking into my house and swiping the transcript, and how after today, I suspect it might be someone sent by my father. About our conversation at Mike's and in the Oval Room hallway and the most recent one, when I confronted him in his backyard. About sending the memo to Victoria, and how I'm heartbroken my father is one of the bad guys from her ominous premonition. About Ben and Chelsea and Maria and the new videos flooding the internet, the latest from just yesterday with a darker, younger, kinkier man, and how Floyd is clicking away in his mother's basement as we speak, following in her cyber footsteps. About the guilt and the regret and the heartache.

He holds me the entire time, his chest humming occasionally in sympathy or encouragement, his palm drawing long strokes down my back. When I'm finally empty of tears and words, a wave of exhaustion crashes over me, threatens to suck me under, and I think how nice it would be to fall asleep right here, with Gabe's arms around me and his heart beating strong and steady against my cheek. Gabe was right, I think, drifting off. He really is a good listener.

"Abigail," he says, and the rumble in his chest pulls me back. "Do you want my take?"

I push off his chest and straighten, mopping up my face with both sleeves. "Yes."

"Drop it," he says, his tone gentle and firm at the same

time. "Before it harms your relationship with your father any further."

For the longest moment, I'm stunned silent. After everything that's happened to bring us here, to a place where beyond a common goal to find Ricky we seem to have found a...I don't know, what is this, a special friendship? Regardless, I wasn't expecting him to try to talk me out of helping him. "I—I thought you wanted the truth."

"I do, and I still plan to get it. I'm just suggesting you think about whether or not your involvement is worth harming your relationship with your father any further. If there's one thing I learned from Zach's death, it's that family is a precious commodity." He smiles at me then, a smile so genuine and comforting it makes my heart ache. "You have to cherish them while they're still here, no matter what they've done. It's called unconditional love."

"Of *course* I love him unconditionally. That's what makes this so hard." A new wave of tears gathers in the corners of my eyes, and I shake my head. "But even if I stopped now, it's too late. It's already harmed. I don't trust him, not after that memo, and I can't just blindly trust that the army or my father or maybe even Ricky had a good reason for the way they handled Zach's death. And because of all that, I won't let it go. I can't."

Gabe reaches over, tucking a stray chunk of hair behind my ear, brushing a tear away with a butterfly finger, watching me not with pity but with tenderness. The gesture undoes me, more than a little, and my throat tightens at the same time something in my chest whispers and stirs.

Maybe it's the bourbon that makes me bold. Maybe it's the intimacy I forced by crying into his chest. Maybe it's the hole my father's betrayal carved in my heart, the empty spot in *my* chest, the feeling of missing something so essential I have nothing left to lose. I latch on to the fabric stretched across his torso, fist it into a ball and pull his lips to mine.

The kiss starts out slow and sweet, and I can feel him holding back. He pulls me close but then doesn't take it any further, not until I wrap my arms around him and urge him on with a long, low moan. It has the intended effect. Gabe leans into me and turns up the heat, pushing me into the couch, covering me with his hard and ready body, pressing down on mine in all the right spots. He deepens the kiss and tugs at my clothes with rapidly building urgency, and I know, just as surely as the earth revolves around the sun, what happens next.

And then he puts on the brakes.

"Abigail," he whispers against my lips, and my eyes flutter open. "I don't think…"

Rejection heats my cheeks. Gabe doesn't finish, but he also doesn't have to. There are very few words that can come after a start like that, and at a moment like this one. I try to push him off, but Gabe won't budge. He latches one palm on my waist and the other behind my head, his big body caging mine on the couch cushions.

"Let me rephrase. I want this. You know how much I want this." And just in case I miss his meaning, he presses down and I feel how much he wants it. "But you've had a rough day. Are you absolutely, positively sure this is the right time?"

The weight of the day falls around me like a lead blanket. My father's name on the memo. His expression when I confronted him in the garden. The sound of my heart breaking in two.

Talk about an anticlimax.

I blink up at Gabe, thinking how much I want him, and with an ache that pounds in the middle of my chest, bitter and sweet at the same time because he's right. Maybe not now. Maybe not for all the right reasons.

I shake my head, and the disappointment I see reflected on his face matches mine. "Rain check?"

Gabe presses his forehead to mine and nods, and his voice is just the right combination of strained and eager when he says, "Please, God, yes."

18

That Friday, at precisely six o'clock, I ring my brother's doorbell, praying it's not Mike but Betsy who answers. My brother and I are not exactly on the best of terms. He's furious about the memo, about Victoria breaking the story, about it turning his neat and tidy life into front-page news. And I'm still livid about his reaction, which was basically to pound down my door and condemn me, and in loud and rather colorful language, for all of it. Long story short, Mike sides with Dad. Unconditionally. I am a traitor and a snake and a fool. I am the worst kind of daughter. Our reunion tonight is going to be beyond awkward.

But no matter how much I want to avoid seeing Mike, I want to take Rose trick-or-treating more. For kids, Halloween is the most sacred of holidays, and the fact that she wants to spend the evening with me and only me makes braving another round of my brother's vitriol well worth the cost.

The double oak doors open to reveal Rose in a green fairy costume, glittery wings flapping at her back. She's flanked by a barking Ginger, who looks more like a maniacal insect than a dog, thanks to antennae that hang lopsided over one eye.

"Trick or treat," I sing, opening my wool cape with the back of an arm and bending in a deep curtsy. Rose's eyes widen at the sight of my costume, and she giggles behind a tiny hand.

According to Party City, this particular ensemble is called "Renaissance Maiden," but so far the only thing it's been is annoying. A full-length, multi-layered skirt. Puffy sleeves with finger loops and bat wings. A corset that digs into my ribs and a headpiece with long, netted drape. But on a bright note, at least I'm not a slutty nurse.

Mike appears behind Rose, his face set in a perma-scowl. She plucks a plastic pumpkin container off the foyer floor and skips to the door, bouncing up and down and screaming, "Let's *go*! Let's *go*!"

I hold out my hand for hers, but Mike stops us. No, he stops *me*. "She can't go out like that, Abby. Jesus. What is the matter with you?" He snatches a navy peacoat off a chair by the door and punches the air with it.

"Nothing's the matter with *me*," I say pointedly, swiping the coat from his outstretched hand. Mike is the king of passive-aggressive jabs, but he and I lived under the same roof long enough for me to have picked up a trick or two. "You, however, might want to remove that giant stick from your A-S-S." I soften my tone and turn to Rose. "But your father's right. It's cold out, and you need a coat."

Rose looks down at her costume, essentially flimsy green chiffon over thin white tights. "But Tinker Bell doesn't wear a coat."

"Then Tinker Bell doesn't go trick-or-treating," Mike says, in an and-that's-final-young-lady tone.

Rose doesn't move, except to jut her bottom lip out a little farther.

But now I'm in even more of a hurry to get out of here, and Mike to have me gone. While I prod Rose into wearing the wings on the outside of her coat, he gives me a short and short-fused discussion of logistics. At the end of the driveway, Rose and I are to turn left and follow the road toward the golf course. On the way, we will stop at all the lit houses on the right side of the street, leaving the left side for the trip back. And no matter what, I must, must, must have her home by eight o'clock sharp. His instructions are classic Mike. Even when he's not in control, he tries to be.

"Okay, Tink," I say as soon as he's done. "You got your pumpkin basket?"

She holds it high so I can see.

"Your pixie dust?"

She shakes her head, giggling behind her free hand.

"Let's go get that candy!"

Outside, a quiet twilight is settling over the neighborhood, bathing the streets in a hazy, purple glow. There are few people out this early, mostly parents with young children with bedtimes as early as Rose's. I grasp her tiny hand in mine as we cross the street, kicking up leaves and pulling to a stop at the first house we come to.

"Do you want me to come with you?" I ask. "Or would you rather I wait here?"

Rose eyes the house, an imposing structure of brownish-gray stucco under a canopy of giant trees. There's a smoke machine somewhere by the door, spewing a white mist over the entire front porch. Fake tombstones litter the yard, planted askew amid skeleton hands and feet clawing their escape from the grass.

Silently, she yanks on my hand, and I follow her past a

ghost, its eyes glowing a bright, evil red, hanging from a tree by the stone walkway. Quite frankly, I can't say that I blame her for preferring an escort.

After the first house, our rhythm is established. I begin by punching the doorbell while Rose bounces on the mat in anticipation. Once the door swings wide, she squeals, "trick or treat!" loudly enough for all of Maryland to hear and then spends a few minutes eyeballing a giant bowl of candy. Once she's satisfied she's found the very best treat, I prod a "thank you" out of her and we head to the next house. We do this three more times, and then she stops in the middle of the road.

"This is the scary dark part," Rose informs me, except with her articulation, it comes out sounding more like "scawy dahk paht."

Regardless, I see her point. To our left is a wilderness of shrubs and tall weeds, and to our right, a partially built home, its doors and windows yawning black holes on a tall wooden frame. The road ahead is the length of half a football field with no streetlights, fine for now, in this in-between stretch of dusky twilight. On the way back, however, it will be blanketed in pitch-black darkness.

We cross through it and Rose grows quiet, and I can see she's nervous. I distract her with light, mindless chatter.

"Tinker Bell is my favorite Disney character, did you know that? And you, my dear, make a very fine Tinker Bell. You saw the movie, right?"

Rose stops her wide-eyed staring at the tree line and nods.

"Well, then. Do you remember what you have to do to prove you believe in fairies?"

Her lips lift in a tiny smile. "Clap."

"That's right!" I clap my hands in front of me. "Let's clap, so the real Tinker Bell knows we believe in her."

Rose drapes the plastic pumpkin strap over her wrist and

claps her pudgy hands. Together, the two of us giggle and clap until we're well past the scary dark part.

"See?" I point to the road behind us, now bathed in dark shadows. "Not scary at all."

Rose grins and reaches for my hand.

By the time we make it to the end of the street forty minutes later, the sidewalks are overflowing with both children and adults, and Rose's plastic pumpkin is brimming with designer candy. Rose and I collapse onto a low stone wall to split a Snickers bar, while a constant stream of costumed children runs past us toward the golf course.

"What's down there?" I ask Rose, pointing after them.

She shrugs, hardly pausing in her chewing to check. When she's done inhaling her candy, I wipe her mouth with my skirt and suggest we go check.

Less than ten seconds later, Rose and I gasp when we see what all the fuss was about. An entire double lot, every inch of grass and stone and concrete covered with about a thousand Halloween-themed yard inflatables. We are hypnotized by its tackiness. We join the group of children we just watched stream past us, gaping and squealing in delight at the spectacle.

We spend some time moving through the blowups and studying each one up close. Grinning jack-o'-lanterns and an animated black cat and a host of spookier types—skulls, ghouls and monsters who, cast as plastic inflatable creatures, are not scary at all. Frankenstein has an impish grin, the grim reaper looks positively cuddly, and the giant bloody eyeball is simply laughable. Rose is mesmerized by every single one.

"It's Cinderella's *castle!*" she squeals and takes off running, weaving her way through a group of animated witches toward a pink princess castle on the edge of the lot.

I'm rounding the corner to follow when I notice a man ducking behind a skeleton poised at an organ. He doesn't fit the bill of the yard filled with children in costume, their watchful parents and the slew of mingling neighbors, sipping what I suspect to be adult beverages from red plastic cups. This man, by contrast, is alone and trying very hard not to be conspicuous. An uneasy tingle clenches my insides.

Instinctively, I move to where Rose is standing, snatch up her hand and hold on tight. Out of the corner of my eye, I keep a careful watch on the man. He pauses, too, pretending to inspect a dancing Garfield on a witch's broom.

For a moment I'm uncertain. Am I imagining things? Am I paranoid? Maybe he's the father of one of the fifty kids running around the lot. But why, then, is he not chasing after a child?

And then I recognize his coat, a beige Members Only jacket with a grease stain on the right-hand cuff, and my heart rides into my throat. I've seen it, and on him, before. I look again, and now I'm positive. It is the pumpkin-inspecting man from Handyman Market.

I keep a careful distance. Close enough to not show fear, far enough to be prudent. How long has he been following me? How many times have I not noticed him? I think back to the first time I saw him, a week or so ago, and a jolt of fire explodes up my torso, straightening my spine and bathing everything around me in a red haze. I don't know who he is, what he thinks he's accomplishing by trailing me and my four-year-old niece—my niece!—around a neighborhood, but I do know one thing.

I know who sent him.

I dig my phone from my pocket and stab at the screen until I've found the right number. My father picks up with a distracted, "Wolff."

"Call him off, Dad."

"I'm gonna need a little more to go on here, darlin'. Call who off?"

"Your tail." I look over and there he is, watching from behind a juggling Snoopy. I give him a look that tells him I'm onto him, right before Rose grabs my skirt and drags me over to the next blowup. "The stocky guy with the comb-over. Tell him to back the hell off."

"Darlin', he's not—"

"Did you send him into my house, too?" Rose lurches to the next blowup, and I follow closely behind. "Did he pinch my copy of the medic's transcript, because—"

"Abigail." Dad's voice snaps an order, and it's for me to shut up and listen. "I need you to stop moving around so much. Grab on to Rose and stand still until I tell you otherwise. Can you do that for me?"

Something dense and deadly has slid into my father's voice, something that sucks the steam right out of me and sends a million tiny pinpricks of fear crawling like electrodes over my skin. Because his words aside—he knows I'm with Rose, and that we're moving around—I know my father well enough to know what that warning in his voice means.

It means it's not my father's tail.

I whip my head around, searching for the man in the crowd, but now either he's ducked behind a blowup, or he's gone. After my obvious taunt, my money's on the former. Why did I have to provoke him? Why couldn't I have just kept pretending he wasn't there?

My father's voice booms down the line. "Abigail, you still with me, darlin'? Talk to me."

I open my mouth to answer when Rose takes off running across the yard. "Rose!" I scream, but she doesn't look back. Two seconds later she's swallowed up into the crowd.

For a single, hysterical second, I'm frozen.

"Rose!" I scan the crowd for a little green fairy in a navy peacoat, but there are too many people, too many blowups blocking my view. I spin around, my heart lurching into my throat. Nothing. I zigzag through the blowups, screeching her name over and over. "Rose!"

A couple of mothers recognize my look of frantic terror for what it is, and they huddle around me, peppering me with questions. What does she look like? What's she wearing? How old?

I stop long enough to give them a hasty description, then take off through the blowups again.

"Rose!"

What if he has her? The thought slices through my mind, and tears prick at my eyes. I picture him snatching her up, one hand clamped over her mouth, and carrying her kicking and screaming to some beat-up van. Surely Mike's given her the stranger-danger talk, but *Jesus*! What if he's got her?

Oh, God. My breathing accelerates, my stomach plummets, and my vision begins to swim. I'm walking the edge of an anxiety attack. The shakes are rolling up my muscles, and I can't seem to get enough air.

"Rose!"

"What's wrong?" a little voice says from right behind me.

Relief turns my bones to slush. I spin around, fall to my knees and pull Rose into a titanic hug. "Omigod, I thought I lost you. I thought—"

She tries to wriggle out of my arms. "Leggo. You're squishing my wings."

I'm also scaring her. Her eyes are wide, and there's a distraught edge to her voice. I loosen my hold and haul a couple of deep breaths, trying to get a handle on my hysteria, but I still don't know who the man is or where he went. I haven't seen him since he disappeared behind Snoopy.

Even though I can still feel him watching me.

I feel around in my pockets for my cell phone, thinking I'll

call my father or maybe even 9-1-1, but it's not there. I must
have dropped it in my frantic search for Rose. The thought of
combing the yard while the Members Only man smirks behind a blowup makes me feel both vulnerable and foolish for
losing it in the first place, and I resign myself to forking over
the cash for a new one.

Because beyond finding my cell, what I really want more
than anything is to get the hell out of here.

In the span of a couple of shaky breaths, I run through my
options. First and foremost, I can't enlist Mike's help. Our relationship is on shaky enough ground as it is. What will he
say when I tell him I may have put his daughter in real, physical danger? I can't take her back the way we came, either, not
without leading my tail right back to my brother's house. And
I don't even want to think about what could happen when we
come to the scary dark part.

As far as I can tell, there's only one option, but it will have
to be subtle.

I snatch Rose's hand, pull her in the direction of the front
door and stab the bell with a shaking finger. After the extrava-
ganza in the front yard, I'm a little surprised at the well-dressed,
fortysomething man who answers. He doesn't look like the
type to coat every inch of his property in plastic blowup toys,
but then again, who am I to say? I haven't exactly been the
best judge of character lately.

Rose stabs her pumpkin in the air. "Trick or treat!"

As he's dropping a handful of candy into her basket, I use
my superhuman powers to get us inside. "I'm really very sorry
to ask, but do you think I could use your phone? I lost my
cell, and I need to check in with home."

"Of course." He waves us inside without hesitation, parks
us in the foyer as if we're completely trustworthy. "I'll just go
get the handheld. I think I left it somewhere upstairs."

And then he disappears up the stairs, leaving us alone in his foyer.

I can barely believe my luck. As soon as he's gone, I put my fingers to my lips, grab Rose's hand and sneak us down a rose-papered hallway. Muffled music and squeals from the front lawn push through the windows, and a TV news program floats on the air from another room, but otherwise the house is quiet. No other people as far as I can tell.

I crane my neck around the corner, peeking into the empty kitchen. Just as I hoped, at the far end is a back door.

"Found it," the man calls out from somewhere deep in the house, and heavy footsteps hit the stairs.

I hurry Rose through the kitchen and out the back door, emerging onto a wooden patio overlooking a yard, and beyond it, the golf course veiled in misty moonlight. We scurry down the stairs and onto the grass.

"Where are we going?" Rose asks, and I shush her.

"I want to see the golf course," I whisper, which is so ridiculous an excuse—it currently resembles an empty black hole of shadows and eerie mist—that even she, a four-year-old child, calls me out on it. "Just for a minute, okay?"

I don't wait for her response, just pull her reluctant figure behind me, crossing over three backyards in the general direction of Rose's house. I just pray that by the time we reemerge on the street a good block down, we will have lost our tail.

Rose and I hotfoot it home, weaving back and forth between the shadows, and I listen and watch for the man following behind us. She's tiring, her gait slowing to a weary crawl, and I feed her a handful of Gummi Bears to perk her up. She seems unaware of any danger, but I'm not taking chances. I need her to be able to run.

As far as I can tell, though, no one is following. I can't spot our tail lurking in the shadows of the trees and bushes or anywhere in the gaggles of trick-or-treaters we meet along the way. There's only an eerie silence from the darkness behind us that's almost worse.

As we approach the scary dark part, by now a tunnel of empty blackness, I glance over my shoulder, picking up movement in the shadow of an elm tree. The shape of a body poking out from behind a thick trunk.

My heart climbs into my throat.

I hoist Rose onto my hip and swing the overflowing pumpkin over an arm. As I'm getting her situated, I sneak a look at the tree line and there he is, frozen in the shadows.

It's all I needed to know.

"Hold on," I whisper, and a yawning Rose wraps her arms around my neck.

I lift my skirt with my free hand and take off at a dead run.

19

Rose and I slip into the tunnel of darkness.

She clenches her eyes and buries her head in my neck, which is uncomfortable as I tear down the road, but it doesn't slow me down. The thin soles of my ballet slippers clack against the pavement in time to my heartbeat, pounding more from fear than from exertion. As the adult in this scenario, I'm pretty sure my frenzied sprint is doing nothing to calm Rose's nerves, but I don't have time to care.

Because heavy footsteps are gaining in the darkness behind me.

I speed up, ducking my head and powering for the glow of a street lamp on the other end. My thighs are screaming and my feet are throbbing and my arms are burning by the time we emerge into the light, and I hate to tell Rose, but we lost almost half her candy in the commotion.

I tear to the first brightly lit front door we come to and punch the doorbell, sucking air and casting panicked glances

over my shoulder into the shadows. I wait, listening. At first
it's quiet.

And then…footsteps.

I start shivering. I'm freezing cold, aching all over. Terrified all the way down into my bones but trying not to let on
to Rose. I lift a fist to beat the door down when a man dressed
as a pirate opens it. Relief turns my knees to sponges, wet and
squishy, and I want to kiss him, eye patch and all.

"Arrg, who do we have here?" he says in a heavy French
accent.

I almost laugh. *Almost*. Because a French pirate with an eye
patch? Hilarious.

Rose, however, does not see an ounce of humor in the
situation. She's still got me in a stranglehold, her little body
convulsing in terrified sobs. My arms give out, and I slide
her down my legs until she's standing, wet face buried in my
scratchy skirts, on the front porch step.

"I'm sorry," I say to Mike's surprised neighbor. "We got a
little spooked by the last block."

He squats down and puts a hand on Rose's shoulder. "Rose,
chérie? Is that you?"

She wipes her eyes on the itchy fabric and peeks at him,
nodding once. He lifts his eye patch, and her face registers
recognition, and yet she clings to my leg. Poor thing. I hope
I didn't scar her for life.

"It's okay, Rose." I squat down and wrap a throbbing arm
around her waist. "Everything's okay. We're fine."

"You're safe here," the pirate adds, and her tears dry up a
little.

I, however, am still freaked way the hell out. Who was that
guy, and even more important: Where is he now? Lurking in
the shadows, watching, waiting? I cock my head and listen, but

I can't hear anything above the roar of my heartbeat, thudding thunder in my chest.

The man distracts Rose with a giant bowl of candy, and she digs through the selection, finally settling on a bag of sour Skittles. But when it comes time for us to walk the few yards up an abandoned street to her house, a panicked look pinches her face, and her tears return.

"Would you like me to walk you home?" he offers, as much to me as to Rose, and our nods are immediate. He closes the door behind him and extends a hand in my direction. "Jacques Martin. I'm Mike and Betsy's neighbor."

"Abigail Wolff. Mike's sister."

We head for home, flanking an exhausted and sniffling Tinker Bell, and it takes every bit of effort to not constantly peer over my shoulder for the man in the Members Only jacket. I only pray that the glow of the streetlights and a neighbor in a pirate costume have scared him off.

So why do I still feel so exposed?

Jacques rests a giant palm on Rose's head. "If it makes you feel any better, *chérie*, I don't like that part of the block, either." He looks over to me, explaining. "The neighborhood association has tried to get another streetlight installed there for years now. I can't tell you how many letters we've written, but the bureaucracy." He says it the French way, *bureaucratie*, and waves a hand dramatically through the air. He sighs. "Maybe by the next Halloween."

My father pulls into the driveway as we're walking up, prompting a miraculous recovery from Rose. She wrenches herself loose and runs to him. "Grandpa!"

My recovery is instant, as well. My heart slows at the sight of his ramrod figure unfolding from his car, and I feel as if I can breathe again. I know how ridiculous that seems, thirty-two and still counting on my father to save me, but he's a career soldier and a three-star general, for Christ's sake. If anyone knows how to protect us from harm, it's him.

Even if he is still so clearly furious at me.

By now, Ginger has alerted all of Bethesda to our return. Mike opens the door and takes in the scene on his front lawn, eyes darting between me and Dad and Jacques, while I glue my gaze to Ginger tearing across the yard. Where's she going? What does she smell? She stops at a row of bushes, and even though it appears to be nothing other than a good place to do her business, watching Ginger pee seems easier than facing Mike's blame and my father's barely contained fury.

"What happened?" Mike asks. "What's wrong?"

"They just got a little spooked," Jacques says, "so I walked them home."

Mike seems to accept the answer, but his scowl doesn't relent, especially once he focuses it back on me.

Rose provides a welcome distraction from his dark looks, tearing up the driveway with her pumpkin bucket. "I got lots and lotsa candy. I'm gonna go show Mommy." And then she disappears inside.

Jacques waves his goodbyes, and then it's just the three of us. I wait. Mike waits.

The general isn't as patient. "Mike, you go on inside. I'm gonna need a minute or two alone with your sister."

Mike whistles for Ginger, and then, after one more meaningful look in my direction, he closes the door.

My father turns back to me, his expression on lockdown. "Description."

The lack of venom in his tone startles me, as does his question. I'd expected blame and accusation for the memo, fury for putting his granddaughter in danger. Anger rides the top of his voice, sure, but I don't think it's directed at me. I search my father's expression, his sharp eyes and white-line mouth, but I don't find anything there but concern.

"Excuse me?"

"I need a description, darlin'. Tell me what he looked like."

I am soothed by the calm reassurance in his voice, even though I suspect it's for my benefit. I pull my cape tight around myself. Now that the adrenaline has stopped flowing, the shakes are about to set in. I can feel them rumbling like a train in the distance, barreling straight at me, growing in speed and strength.

"Heavyset. Mousy-brown comb-over. Probably in his mid to late forties. Just under six feet. I've seen him before, about a week ago. He seems to think beige Members Only jackets are still in style."

Dad shakes his head so hard his cheeks wobble. "God*dammit*."

I take all this to mean my father knows him. "Do you know who sent him?"

He clamps down on his lips and stalks to his car, which means he knows, but he's not telling.

I scurry after him, my teeth now starting to chatter. "Am I in danger?"

"Go home." I'm not exactly comforted by his nonanswer, and Dad notices. "I'll call you when I know more," he says, right before slamming his door.

And then with a screech of rubber on asphalt, he drives off before I can tell him that's impossible, that my phone is lying in the trampled grass a mile up the road or, worse, clutched in Members Only's sweaty palms.

I take the long way home, winding first to the north and then to the east, looping through busy streets and empty parking lots, shooting through stop signs and lingering at green lights until I'm certain no one's following me. Fairly certain.

Nearly one hundred percent certain. Even so, every bouncing pair of headlights in my rearview mirror sends a fresh wave of panic surging through me, and I can't help but give my pursuer a tiny bit of credit. If his goal was to scare the shit out of me, he certainly succeeded.

I tell myself my father would have never sent me home alone if he thought I was in any sort of danger. I tell myself he's taking care of it. But the events of the night keep coming at me in waves—the heavyset man, the terror when I thought I'd lost Rose, our frantic run through the darkness—and I'm not sure I believe myself.

By the time I roll up my block, it's after ten and the street is quiet. Keys clutched in a fist, I bolt to the front door, intent on getting inside as quickly as possible. My sleeves and cape have other plans, and they tangle themselves around my hand, making the task so difficult that I'm not aware of the footsteps approaching behind me until it's too late.

"Abigail."

I let out an ear-piercing scream. Poor Gabe looks stunned to be at the receiving end of it, even more so when I start beating my fists on his chest.

"What are you doing here? You scared the *shit* out of me!"

"No kidding." He snatches my wrists out of the air and holds on tight. "I was out for a walk and wanted to see—" Concern climbs up Gabe's face, pushing up from under what's now almost a full-grown beard. "What's going on? What's wrong?"

Somewhere nearby, a door slams, a dog barks. The sounds accelerate my pulse and prickle my skin and hurtle me back to the ledge of full-blown panic.

And then there are footsteps. My heart thunders and my head whips around, my eyes scanning up and down the street. The dog starts up again, and a fresh wave of panic tugs at me.

"Let go, Gabe! I mean it." When he doesn't, I fill the air with a hysterical, "Let *go*!" shrill enough to burn the back of my throat.

He releases me, and with shaking hands, I twist the key in the lock and shoot inside. I run from room to room, closing blinds and double-checking locks.

Gabe follows closely behind. "Abigail, talk to me. What the hell happened to you tonight?"

"Do you see anyone out there?" I stand on my toes to try to see out the window, but I'm not tall enough to have a clear view of the street.

Gabe looks at me as if I just asked him if he's seen a dancing circus bear on my front lawn. "Lots of people. It's Halloween."

"Look again!" I point to the window at the top of the door. "Is there anyone out there?"

He humors me for a second or two, peering out into my empty yard and the street beyond, and then shakes his head. "Calm down. There's nothing out there." Turning back, he pushes off the door and reaches for my hand, his eyes wide with worry. "Jesus, your fingers are like ice."

"Okay. Okay," I say, more to myself than to Gabe. I draw a shaking breath. "He didn't follow. He doesn't know where I live."

"What are you talking about? *Who* doesn't know?"

"The guy from the market," I tell him, as if that would clear things up. "The one with the Members Only jacket."

"What?" Gabe's face scrunches up, and he runs a hand across the back of his neck. "Wait. Back up. What guy?"

"I noticed him first at the market, when I came to tell you about Ricky. And then I saw him again tonight, when I was trick-or-treating with my niece. He chased us."

"He *chased* you." I nod, and Gabe's eyes harden. He leads

me to the couch, parking me and sinking down next to me. "Start at the beginning."

I take a deep breath and will the knots in my shoulders to loosen. "There's not much more to tell. I was with Rose at this house with a million of those ridiculous inflatables when I spotted him for the second time. I recognized him by his jacket. It has a stain on one of the cuffs." I point to my right bat sleeve, but it's all tangled around my wrist. "Anyway, as soon as he saw me watching him, he ducked behind a giant skeleton. I called Dad, but the tail wasn't his. I tried to shake him off without Rose noticing—she's only four, and I didn't want to freak her out—but he caught up to us, so I ran."

Gabe is rubbing both my hands in his, warming them with the friction. "And he chased you."

I nod. "Through the scary dark part. That's what Rose called it, and I gotta say, she has a point."

Gabe lifts a hip, reaches into his pocket for his cell phone. "I'm calling the police."

"No!" I pull him, scowling in protest, back onto the couch. "My brother is already furious at me for the memo, and if he knows I put Rose in danger, it will tip him into nuclear territory. He'll never let me anywhere near her again. Besides, my father would have told me if I was in danger. When he left, he said he'd take care of it."

Not exactly the truth, but close enough. And talking through the experience, I've discovered, has helped. Helped calm my heart, wash the fear from my bones, put tonight's events in unruffled perspective. Now that I've said the words out loud, I'm convinced Dad will take care of things. He is the general, after all.

And then I think of something else, something that chases the warmth from my body all over again. "Oh, my God. The Members Only man was standing right there when I told you

I found Ricky. He was down by the pumpkins. He had to have heard me."

Gabe looks away, and his jaw flexes. "I don't think we said anything else after that, did we?"

"Not there, but what if he followed us to Starbucks?" I squeeze my eyes shut, try to recall the scene in the coffee shop, but I can't. I was so intent on telling Gabe my story in between bites of blueberry muffin, I have no recollection of anyone but a couple of people behind laptops and women on their way to the gym. "He could have been sitting next to us, and I wouldn't have noticed."

"We need to get to Graciela first."

Tell me about it. As confident as I was in the beginning, assuring Gabe she'd return my calls with a certainty that bordered on cockiness, I'm starting to get more than a little worried. It's been a whole week now, and Graciela still hasn't responded to any of my increasingly desperate messages.

"Let's give her the weekend, and if I haven't heard back by Monday, I'll take a little road trip to Portsmouth."

"*We'll* take a road trip." He grins and gestures to the thick stubble hugging his jaw, decorating his chin, his cheeks, his upper lip. "By then my disguise will be complete. What do you think?"

I reach over, running my finger over where his dimple used to be in his cheek, feeling his almost-beard against my palm, the prickle of his hair on my fingertips.

The look that rolls up his face is heated and tender all at once. It's like watching desire come to life, and it makes me forget every awful thing that happened earlier tonight.

I miss the dimple is what I was going to say.

What comes out is, "I think it's time for that rain check."

20

Gabe and I end up in bed. Of course we do. After the last aborted attempt, after circling each other for the better part of a good month now, all that pent-up desire had to come out at some point.

It came out in kissing and grinding on my couch, in hands sliding under fabric and over skin baking underneath, in soft gasps and louder moans, and finally, in Gabe throwing my legs around his hips, pinning me to his chest and carrying me upstairs, shedding clothes along the way.

Which brings us to now. Gabe and me, panting and sweaty and tangled on my wrecked sheets.

"Wow," I whisper into the quiet dark. The word seems pitifully inadequate for what I just experienced. Sex with Gabe was like none I've ever had—and at thirty-two, and at the risk of sounding like an oversexed trollop, I've had plenty of sex. But this was different. Wild. Spectacular. Unprecedented. "Remind me to send a thank-you card to the mustard heiress."

He shoots me a wry grin. "Send it to whoever made that

dress of yours. I've always had a thing for corsets." I shove him playfully, and he captures my wrist in his hand, kissing the inside of my palm. "And you," he says, all teasing from his tone gone now. "It seems I also have a thing for you."

Warmth spreads across my chest, and I close my eyes and breathe him in. "I have a thing for you, too."

He slides me up his torso and gathers me into him, wedging my head in the crook of his neck, curling me into his big body. My gaze lands on the tattoo I discovered earlier, swirling black letters that trail up the inside of his left bicep that spell out *Zachary*. I trace them with a light fingertip.

"Not many heterosexual men are confident enough to have another man's name permanently inked onto their skin, you know."

Gabe gives an amused puff of breath, warm and ticklish on my scalp. "It does get me a few interesting looks at the gym."

"From the lamenting women or the rejoicing men?"

"Both."

I laugh, and so does Gabe. Outside my window, a murky mist has floated up from the Potomac, blurring the outlines of my neighbors' houses and bathing my bedroom in an eerie, purple glow. He buries his face in the crown of my head, kissing my scalp, and we lie there for a bit in comfortable silence.

"Mom says she knew the second Zach was killed," Gabe says out of nowhere. "Before Nick called, before the army chaplain showed up at her front door, she says she knew. She felt part of herself dying and just knew."

Tears come to my eyes so suddenly, there's just no blinking them away. I think about how that moment must have been for Jean, how in the middle of going about her day, while drying her hair or eating an apple or driving to work or the market, she was sucker punched with knowledge she didn't want to have. It's impossible if you think about it, really. She *couldn't* have known, and yet she did. I imagine how she spent the rest of the day trying to talk herself out of it—*not possible, Zach's fine, everything's fine*—and then later when the chaplain came, the sick dread that must have sucker punched her all over again at the sound of the doorbell.

"Your poor mom." I splay my fingers through the light hair bisecting his stomach and press my lips to his chest. "That must have been awful for her. For all of you."

"I know the risks of war, knew when my brothers got on that plane there was a very real chance one of them would not be coming back, but I never thought it would be Zach. Zach was Superman. He was supposed to live forever."

"Is that why you put his name on your arm? To keep that connection with him, to keep him close?"

He lifts his head, gives me a look that makes me think I maybe hit a nerve.

"It was part of it, yeah. But the other part is to remember. Not that I would ever forget him, but I don't know…memories fade with time. His name on my arm won't."

My heart squeezes for him, for his pain at losing a brother he so clearly worshipped, but also with something bigger, something completely separate from his brother. What I feel is one hundred percent Gabe. Inking his dead brother's name on his skin, abandoning his fast-track career to care for his family. Gabe here is the real deal. I know I used those words on his brother, but that's because I hadn't met Gabe yet. Gabe Armstrong is the *real* real deal. I scoot closer still, wrapping myself around him until there is not a sliver of space between us.

"It's not that I want revenge," he whispers into the darkness. "For the army to go to all this trouble to bury what happened out there, for your father to…" He gives his head a little shake, as if that's a sentiment he doesn't want to finish. "By now I'm pretty certain that whoever shot Zach did so by mistake, and I know it won't change anything, but I still have to know. I can't move forward until I know what happened to my brother."

"I get that." I push up on an elbow, rest my chin on his chest. "And if I can help give you closure, Gabe, I will."

He watches me for a long moment, his eyes crinkling as he studies me. "I wasn't expecting you. This. It's a nice surprise, feeling like this again."

"Like how?" I know I'm breaking every rule in the book by prodding, but I also don't care. Gabe left that door wide-open, and now I want to know. I *have* to know. "How do you feel?"

"Like tomorrow might not be so awful with you in it." He pushes me onto my back and rolls on top, planting a row of kisses from my ear to my breastbone. "Tell me you'll be in it."

At first I can't respond around the sudden lump in my throat, and then it's because his hand is on the move. It leaves a trail of chill bumps as it wanders up my side, brushing over my ribs, the side of a breast, my collarbone. I gasp as his mouth dips lower, then lower again. My fingers slide into his thick hair, guiding him, and the rough scrape of his beard lights a path down my skin, now hot with lust and need.

"Abigail." Just one word, my name, but it comes out sounding the way sex with him feels. Demanding. Intense. Just the right amount of rough. His teeth nip the skin just above my hip bone, by my belly button, lower still. "Tell me you'll be in it."

"Definitely," I say, right before I arch up to meet him halfway.

Gabe sleeps the way he lives, with power and presence. His big body sprawls across my mattress, eating it up with his size and weight, commanding the middle of the bed and most of the covers. At some point near dawn, I wake up cold and shivering at the edge of the mattress. Gently, trying not to wake him, I scoot nearer, pull the comforter back my way. I'm almost completely underneath when Gabe stirs. He rolls into me, gathers me up, wraps the comforter around us like a cocoon, and I settle back in.

I'm drifting off when he whispers into my hair, "I think you should do it."

I pull back to look at him. His eyes are still at half-mast, but he's clearly awake. The slack is gone from his cheeks, and his expression is alert. "Do what?"

"Call Mom and tell her yes. Tell her you'll help her write Zach's story."

I don't say anything for a good minute. This is the place where I'm supposed to say no. Where my head is supposed to shake and my tongue push out some excuse. Where, instead of letting the lines between personal and professional loop around and turn topsy-turvy, I'm supposed to draw one in the sand.

"Why?" I say instead, even though I think I already know the answer. For all the reasons his mother asked me in the first place, Chelsea and my father and how both of them will make me more careful with my words. For finding Ricky, for calling Graciela, for giving the memo to Victoria, for blowing their allegations against the army wide-open. For make-out sessions on couches and whispered midnight phone calls. I expect any or all of those answers.

But that's not what Gabe gives me.

"Because you're the only one who I want to share him with." He picks up a lock of my hair and twists it around a finger, his expression open and sincere. "You're the only one I trust to do his story justice."

I was already hovering on the ledge. Gabe's beautiful words just tipped me over.

★ ★ ★

I awake the next morning still tucked into Gabe's chest. I lift my head and look at the man asleep on the pillow beside me. Gabe's cheeks are flushed, his thick hair rumpled, one arm thrown above his head in deep REM abandon. Early-morning sunlight catches in the scruff on his cheeks, casting his face in shadows and angles, and happiness balloons inside me, warm and full.

With a kiss to his pec, I slip out of bed, plucking a T-shirt and jeans from the chair in the corner on my way out of the room. I pull them on just outside the door, brush my teeth and wash my face in the tiny guest bathroom, and head downstairs.

Content curation is like erecting a lightning rod and then sitting back and waiting for the storm. While Gabe and I were upstairs…well, not sleeping, exactly, my curation software was getting zapped from every corner of the world wide web, pulling out the relevant content, categorizing it and spitting it into my inbox.

While my computer sorts through the jumble, plucking the best stories from the hundreds of emails like ripe cherries, I dig my old iPhone out of a drawer, restore all my contacts from iTunes and reactivate it with my carrier. I know I've got it up and running when Floyd's name lights up my screen.

"I thought you forgot about me," I say, half joking, half not. I remember Floyd as being much faster with these types of assignments, which means either he's really busy, or Maria is turning out to be more complicated than I thought.

"Never, hon. But Maria's doing a damn good job of covering her tracks. Looks like she's stashed her cash somewhere safe, and whoever's been paying her hasn't made a peep. Until they file a complaint or she gets mugged on her way to the bank, that cash is pretty much invisible."

Well, hell. Just as I feared. Cash transactions are pretty

much impossible to trace unless you mark the money or see the exchange, and since I can't do the first, that means I'd have to have put a tail on Maria, which I didn't. Disappointment lands with an elevator-like thud in my belly.

I flip through my mental Rolodex, thinking about people I haven't thought of in years, considering which one will do the best job for the least amount of money now that I no longer have a budget to cover research expenses.

"Okay, well, thanks for trying, Floyd. I appreciate—"

"Hey, give a guy some credit," he interrupts. "I don't ever call a client empty-handed, and…"

He's still talking when another call beeps through, and I pull my cell away from my ear to check the caller ID. The number on the screen sends a string of firecrackers popping up my spine, and I cut Floyd off mid-sentence.

"I'll call you right back," I say, then, without waiting for his reply, press the button, heart thundering, to take the next call. "Abigail Wolff speaking."

"Hi, Abigail. This is Graciela Hernandez returning your call." Her voice is high and lyrical and tinged with a Southern accent, just like the one on her voice mail message, and the familiarity of it picks up my pulse. "Sorry it took me so long to get back to you, but I hardly ever check my home machine. Nobody ever calls that number but telemarketers."

I wipe a suddenly sweaty palm across my jeans. "No problem at all. I'm just so glad you called me back."

"Yes, well…" She pauses to clear her throat. "You said your fiancé knew my Ricky?"

"Yes. At least I think so. I was hoping you could maybe help me figure out the connection."

"You mentioned something about a letter."

"Yes," I say, drawing out the word, buying time while my brain churns out the fabricated half-truth I told Graciela. The problem with half-truths, I'm discovering, is that they are also half-lies. So now I have to come up with a letter, which means first, I have to come up with a reason to stall. "I have a letter, but, um, I'd really rather not read it to you over the phone. Could we maybe plan a time to meet? I'd be happy to come to you."

"Oh. That would be fine, I guess." I hear a shuffling like the flipping of pages in a day planner. "When were you thinking?"

"Anytime." As soon as I say it, though, I feel the warm rush of Members Only man's breath hot on my neck. If he knows we know about Ricky, then whomever he's working for does, too. Gabe and I have lost too much time already. "As soon as possible, actually. What does your schedule look like?"

Graciela tells me her job as a hospital nurse gives her a somewhat erratic day in the best of times, but starting tomorrow, she's putting in extra hours and will be working back-to-back night shifts all through next week. I check my watch and do the math, rounding up and planning in a little extra time for leeway.

"What about today?" I jump out of my chair and hurry to the stairs, but when I see my reflection in the hallway mirror, my hair wild and tangled, Gabe's beard burn on my chin, I tack on an extra hour. "I could be there by dinnertime."

Graciela agrees, and after a few more minutes discussing logistics, we hang up. I race up the stairs and into my bedroom, where Gabe is still passed out. "Gabe." I shake his foot. "Wake up."

He does, and the slow, sexy grin that spreads up his face when he sees me standing at the foot of the bed makes my entire body tingle. "Why aren't you naked?"

I shake off the unexpected rush, file it away for a later contemplation. "Because we have a date with Graciela."

He jolts to a sit on the mattress, his expression suddenly and deadly serious. "Which way's your shower?"

We shower and dress in twenty minutes flat. While I dry my hair, Gabe borrows my car for a quick trip home for a fresh change of clothes and his toothbrush. I wait for him downstairs, tossing my laptop, notebook, tape recorder and the contents of my purse into a tote bag, filling two travel mugs with coffee. Three staccato beeps of my car horn announce his return, and the two of us steer my car as fast as its little Prius engine will allow to Portsmouth.

"We have a teeny tiny problem," I tell him once I've merged onto 395.

He looks over, his eyes shaded under a John Deere baseball cap like the ones hanging from a rack by the Handyman register. "My beard's not long enough?"

"No." By now Gabe has moved beyond scruff into something bordering on Zach Galifianakis territory. "I can't remember what I told Graciela my fiancé's name was."

"Oh, Jesus." He turns in his seat to face me. "You're shitting me, right?"

I glance at him as I surge past an 18-wheeler. "You were standing right there when I said it. Don't you remember what it was?"

"It was your story, not mine. I figured it was some old boyfriend or something."

"Oh. Well, then. Let's see." I cock my head to the side and pretend to think. "Brooks? Justin? Scott? Dylan? Aiden? Shaun? Trey?"

He gives me an incredulous look. "Seriously?"

I roll my eyes at the same time I reach for his thigh. "Of course not. Loosen up."

"Sorry." He sucks in a deep breath and blows it out. "Well,

it must have been somebody you know, and pretty well, by the way you just threw it out there."

"David," I say, suddenly remembering.

"Yeah, that sounds about right."

"David runs the rowing program," I explain, even though Gabe hasn't asked. "Makes sense. I'd just spent the entire morning on the boat, and his was the first male name that popped into my head."

My cell phone chirps, and my mom's name slides onto the screen. I suspect she's calling to talk about my fight with Dad, and for some reason I don't have time to analyze, I would really rather this conversation not be broadcast over the car speakers. I attach my headphones to my cell, pop one in my ear and pick up the call.

Mom and I spend a few moments chitchatting and covering the basics—Betsy and Mike, everyone's health, neighborhood gossip—and then she gets down to the reason for her call. "Do you have time to meet me for lunch tomorrow?"

I do the math. Even if we spend only an hour with Graciela, it will be past midnight by the time we make it back to DC. And though I'm currently jacked up on adrenaline and anticipation, I suspect by then I will be ready to crash, especially after the few hours of sleep I got last night. I steal a glance at Gabe, staring out the side window at the roadside scenery whipping by, obviously trying to give me some privacy. "Um, tomorrow's not so great for me. How about later in the week?"

"Please, dear. I have something very important to talk to you about. We could do tea or coffee if that works better for you, or I could swing by your house. I can come by anytime."

I fall silent, thinking. Though I don't know what she intends to tell me, I suspect it will be somewhere in the neighborhood of a scolding for confronting Dad about the memo or for sending it over to Victoria, which I'm certain he very well knows I did. After all, it doesn't take a genius to figure out her connection to the story.

So if it's a scolding I am to get, I would much prefer to get it in public, where Mom is far less likely to release the full extent of her fury.

"Fine," I concede. "But just a quick lunch, okay? I'm way behind at work."

"Wonderful! I'll make the reservation. How about that cute little bistro on the corner of King and Fayette? Is one o'clock okay?"

I confirm the time and place, and before she can launch into a new topic, I tell her I have to go.

"Sorry," I say, glancing at Gabe. "My mother."

He doesn't turn his head. "I got that."

"I'm having lunch with her tomorrow."

"I got that, too."

I pause, casting a series of glances in his direction. "Everything okay?"

"Sorry." He blows out an endless sigh. "Just nervous."

"It's okay." I look over with a reassuring smile. "It'll be okay."

He reaches for my hand, lacing his fingers through mine, and presses a kiss on my knuckles.

As we near Richmond, Gabe and I fabricate a story for Graciela. Gabe is my brother, a falsehood which is both laughable and disgusting at the same time, and is lending me moral support in my quest to keep my fictional fiancé's memory alive. David, we decide, was good friends with Zach and fought alongside him on the day that he died. David was devastated by Zach's death and corresponded with me at length about it. In one of the many letters he wrote, he mentioned another friend by the name of Ricky Hernandez.

Once we have our story straight, I reach into the backseat, pull a pad of paper and a pen from my bag, hand both to Gabe and start dictating.

21

"My fiancé was stationed in Kabul until late last year." I smooth my sweater, cross my hands in my lap and try to look a very tiny, very pregnant Graciela in the eyes as I say the tale Gabe and I rehearsed to perfection in the car. "From what I understand from his letters, that's where he met Ricky."

On the hard-backed chair across from me, Graciela gives me a could-be shrug. "Ricky was there for Intergon. He was a contractor, but he was in close contact with the troops." She's dressed up for our get-together, in a floral dress and low heels, pale blue eye shadow and a strand of pearls, and the notion that she's made an effort for us to come over and lie to her face presses down hard on my chest.

Why did she have to be pregnant? Lying to the sister of a dead man is hard enough, but lying to his pregnant sister… excruciating.

Next to me on the plaid squishy couch, Gabe ducks his head so most of his face is hidden behind the bill of his ball cap. Still, those stubborn Armstrong genes push up through the thick scruff. So much so that Graciela's eyes widened just slightly when we walked through her door, though I can't be sure if it was from recognition or admiration—he isn't the type of man a woman easily overlooks, not even a married, pregnant one. Now she tilts her head and squints at him, and I'm suddenly positive she knows.

"Did he ever mention David?" I ask, pulling her focus back onto me. "David Shepherd, but some of his friends called him Dave."

Graciela takes a moment to remember. "I don't think so. But it's been so long, you know."

"I do know." I pull the letter from my bag and pass it across the coffee table to her. "Perhaps this will help."

I give her a few moments to read the letter, the text of which I know by heart. After the mundane bit about the heat and the sand and the greasy food, and just before the paragraph in which Dave extols how much he worships and misses me, are the following ten sentences:

Yesterday was the hardest I laughed since the time you accidentally tripped that waiter with the tray full of desserts, remember that? Ricky, that's one of the guys here, got his hands on one of those inflatable dolls. You know the type? Big boobs, bigger mouth. Yeah, that one. Anyway, he somehow figured out a way to inflate that thing by remote (the dude is brilliant like that) and hid it in Zach's hooch. A few of us, including our commanding officer, were hanging out in there last night when all of a sudden, the lights go out and stripper music starts blaring. Zach throws open the door and there she is, in her full naked glory, lying on his bed. We found Ricky rolling around on the ground just outside. I thought I was going to bust a rib.

Not knowing Ricky, Gabe and I had a long, extended discussion about whether or not a practical joke involving a blowup sex toy would be a good idea. What if Graciela, or Ricky for that matter, was a total prude? But Gabe insisted that practical jokes are a frequent and welcome distraction for overseas soldiers, and he would certainly know better than I. In fact, the blowup girl incident really did happen to Zach just as my fictional fiancé described in the letter, except the jokester was a soldier named James.

But as I sit here, watching the corners of Graciela's mouth for any sign of reaction, positive or negative, I'm beginning to doubt the wisdom of including such a racy joke. What if Ricky's lifelong dream was to be a priest? It's a possibility we hadn't considered.

And then Graciela drops the letter to her lap and smiles, her eyes shining. "That is just like Ricky. He was always playing practical jokes, on everyone."

Relief hits me like a Valium to the jugular, and my shoulders descend from where they'd been hovering, up by my ears.

"Did he ever mention Dave or Zach or any of the other soldiers?" I sit up straight and pause, swallowing. This is where things could get hairy, so I choose my words carefully. "The Zach in the letter was Zach Armstrong. You may have heard of him. The actor who was killed right around the time Ricky was."

Recognition illuminates Graciela's face. "He talked about Zach all the time. Ricky was devastated when he was killed. He said he saw it happen."

I notice Gabe's thigh muscle clench through the denim, but otherwise, he doesn't move.

"That must have been horrible," I tell her.

"It was. I remember wondering, when they started handing out all those medals, what his family would think when they learned Zach's death was from friendly fire. Ricky said they all knew it that same night. What a mess the army made of that, huh?" She shakes her head as if to flush it from her mind. "But you're not here to talk about Zach."

"That's okay. Any stories that help jog your memory are welcome," I say, reviving one of my old standbys from my journalism days. It's kind of like that word-association game, where one thought serves to spark others, even seemingly un-related ones. It was my favorite and most effective technique to get sources talking.

Graciela, though, doesn't take the bait. She shifts in her chair and gives me a kind smile. "I'm really sorry, but David, or Dave, is not ringing any bells. Maybe Ricky mentioned him on his blog."

Gabe and I share a look, and he is clearly as stunned as I am.

I clear my throat. "Ricky had a blog?"

Graciela's silence spikes my pulse, especially when I look back to find her staring at Gabe, her slightly squinted eyes studying his face. "I'm sorry, have we met?"

My heart stutters to a stop, then kicks into triage territory. Shit. Shit. *Shit.* I *told* Gabe to wait in the car, *told* him that Graciela would recognize those famous Armstrong genes. Even with the mountain-man beard, he looks so much like his big-screen brother that Graciela would have to be either blind or Amish to not make the connection.

"I don't think so," Gabe says, his tone easy and light.

She tilts her head and studies him some more. "You just look so familiar."

"I get that a lot." He lifts a casual shoulder. "But *you* look exactly like my high school girlfriend, so I definitely would have remembered meeting you."

"I'm sorry, Graciela," I say, hijacking her attention, pulling it back to me and to the reason we're here. "You said Ricky had a blog?"

She tears her gaze from Gabe and nods. "Blogspot lost it, though. They told me it was a computer glitch. One day it was there, and the next it just vanished from their system. Thank God I made a printout of all the entries for our grandmother. She doesn't have a computer."

Deep breath. Calm down. Focus.

"Could I maybe take a look at those printouts?"

"Sure. Be right back." She hoists herself from the chair and waddles off, leaving Gabe and me alone in the tiny living room.

"Mother mother motherfucker," Gabe whispers.

I don't dare to respond, don't dare to even look at him for fear of losing every last bit of my cool. We sit there in silence, the weight of what we just heard pushing down on us from all sides, until Graciela reappears, toting a three-inch binder and a short stack of well-thumbed envelopes.

"I brought a few of his letters, as well, from May of 2010 on. That's when he went to Baghdad. Maybe we can find something about Dave in there, too."

I look up at her gratefully, a sudden pang of guilt at her kindness curling at my belly. This is where the lines *really* get crossed, I think, where personal relationships skew integrity and lead to questionable behavior, like lying to a poor, pregnant woman grieving her dead brother.

"I'm so sorry to intrude on you tonight, Graciela."

She waves off my apology, and I swallow down my remorse, concentrating instead on the letters. There is, of course, nothing in any of them about Dave, but we do find a few mentions of Zach and Nick. That the three of them waited out a late-spring sandstorm by arguing politics. That Nick came down with a mean case of food poisoning. That Zach was learning Arabic.

And then finally, Gabe passes me a letter, pressing his knee against mine as he does so, that almost makes me gasp out loud. He catches my eye after I've read it, and I know what I need to do. I place the letter atop the pile on the coffee table and push to a stand.

"Graciela, could you please show me to your restroom? I could use a little break."

"Of course."

I help her heave her enormous belly out of the chair, and she leads me down a short, dark hallway, flipping on lights as we go. We pull to a stop outside a plain, wooden door halfway down. It's taken us all of three seconds to get here. Not nearly enough time.

"I really can't thank you enough for everything you're doing," I say, stalling. "I know it's painful, and that you probably have a million things you'd rather be doing than carving open old wounds, but—"

She stops me with a palm to my arm. "If you and I don't talk about Ricky and David, then who will? Talking about them is how we keep our men alive, keep their memories fresh in our minds, right?" When I don't answer, she tilts her head and gives me a sad smile. "Right?"

"Right," I whisper. Hot tears spring to my eyes, not because of all the reasons she thinks, but because I so thoroughly, completely, desperately hate everything about this conversation. The lies. The faking. The bullshit fictional fiancé that brought me here. I hate everything about it.

"Oh, sweetie…" Graciela pulls me into an awkward embrace, smoothing a petite palm across my back. "I'm sorry. I know how hard it is to lose someone you love."

She releases me, and I don't have to pretend to be traumatized as I slip into the tiny bathroom, because I am. Traumatized and sick, literally nauseous from the revolting lies I just spun to this poor woman. I grip the laminate countertop, throat burning and hands shaking, glaring at myself in the mirror. Flowers, as soon as I get home, the biggest bouquet I can afford. The gift won't smother the guilt, but at least it will serve as a miserable sort of penance.

Suddenly, getting out of here, out of Graciela's house, out of her life, is my newest and most urgent goal.

I return to the living room, pausing at the end of the couch. Gabe's face is buried in the blog binder, but he slides me a look that tells me he's got what we need.

I turn back to Graciela, pinching out the first excuse I can think of to get us out of here. "Would it help if we made copies of what's in the binder? That way we won't keep you up."

"Would you mind?" She rubs a hand over her giant belly, looking beyond grateful at the suggestion. "I am pretty tired."

It's all Gabe needs to hear; he slaps the book shut and stands, tucking it under his bicep. After a bit of discussion, we agree to leave the notebook between the front and screen doors so she can go straight to bed, and Graciela shows us, stunned and shaken and slightly giddy at our discovery, to the door.

I steer the car around the corner, slam the brakes and freak way the hell out.

"I lied to her, Gabe! About her dead brother. Right to her face. I looked her in the eyes and lied! Oh, God." I rest my forehead on the steering wheel. "I hate myself."

Gabe slides a palm up my shoulder, grips the back of my neck, gives it a gentle squeeze. "You had to."

"You don't know that. Maybe she would have told us. Maybe she would have been just as forthcoming if we'd told her the truth about why we were there. If anybody would understand, it would be her. She lost a brother, too."

My last point hits home with Gabe, I can tell. He removes his cap, rubbing a palm over his flattened hair. "Sometimes the end justifies the means."

The uncertainty in his tone brings fresh tears to my eyes. "That's bullshit! It's bullshit, and you know it. What if that had been your mother in there? What could possibly justify lying and stealing in your mind if it had been her?"

Gabe doesn't have to think about his answer. "The truth."

"*Your* truth. Not hers."

Gabe's cell rings, and both of us ignore it.

"Maybe," he says, "but I can't fix things until I know what Ricky knew. Not until I know what happened to Zach. We're so close, Abigail. I can feel it in my bones."

It's then that the realization hits with the force of a wrecking ball. Gabe and I may say we're on the same team, sprinting toward the same goal line, but are we really? Gabe wants the truth, and I want it for him, too. Of course I do.

But getting it isn't game over for either of us, is it? Who knows what Gabe and his family will do with whatever is in Ricky's blogs—seek retribution, fight for justice, demand amends. The answer for him, I suppose, will depend on the explosiveness of what we find.

For me, however, this game ends in…what, exactly? When I began, I told myself it was to seek amends, to rehab my karma. I told myself it was pure, unabashed curiosity and nothing more that drove me to find Ricky, that sent me on this quest to ferret out what he knows, to uncover what really happened to Zach. But somewhere along the way, things got personal. Emotions became entangled. My father. Jean. Gabe. It's all so convoluted now. I no longer know what's right, as evidenced by my repulsive lies to a dead man's sister.

"I can't do it, Gabe." I shake my head, trying not to focus on the calm determination that lines his brow, trying not to think about how it must look so different from mine. "I have to go back there. I have to apologize."

Gabe shakes his head, and he opens his mouth to answer when his cell rings again. "Hold on," he says, digging it out of his pocket. "I just need to make sure it's not…" He flips it around so I can see the screen, and his mother's name on the caller ID. He holds up a finger with one hand, swipes the screen with the thumb of his other.

"Hey, what's up?" He pauses to listen, and his gaze holds mine the entire time. "Yeah… I'm with her right now. You want me to ask?" Apparently, Jean's answer is yes, because he drops the phone to his lap. "Mom wants to know if you've given her offer any thought."

I nod.

"And?"

And I can't even think about Zach's story right now. All I can think about is the look on Graciela's face in the bathroom hallway, the way her eyes filled at our supposedly shared misfortune, her voice calling me sweetie.

Gabe sees my distress, wraps his free hand around my head, cupping it, and leans his forehead against mine. "I swear to you, when this is over, you and I will go back, both of us, together, and we'll apologize to Graciela. We'll tell her everything. But for now, I'm begging you to let it go. Please, Abigail. I *have* to know what's in those blogs."

It's not his tone that does it, or his hand on my neck. It's not his breath, warm and familiar on my lips, or his quiet desperation to learn the truth. It's not even the way his eyes turn liquid and soft, watching me in a way that almost makes me forget about Graciela. It's that one little word. *Us.* The promise of a future—*together*, his word—and of something magnificent blooming between us.

I give him a tiny, almost imperceptible nod.

He kisses me then, the barest brush of his lips against mine, but the tenderness and hope and desire feel like my reward, and they melt through my heart and solidify into something warm and golden. I'd promise him my soul right now if he asked.

"And Mom?" he whispers. "What should I tell her?"

"Tell her I say yes," I say, at the same time telling myself it hasn't been my answer all along.

Part Three:
The Space Between

22

After we make copies and return the original blog posts to Graciela, my iPhone directs us to the closest all-night diner, an IHOP on Frederick Boulevard. Inside it's bright and warm and, rather unfortunately for us, crowded for ten-thirty on a Saturday night.

A determined Gabe winds his way through the restaurant, leading us to a booth at a deserted corner in the back. The diners we pass on the way seem more interested in their late-night pancake platters than in paying attention to either of us, but we study them carefully anyway. No sign of the Members Only man, or anyone else suspicious-looking, for that matter.

I slide into the booth on the side facing the restaurant, and Gabe sinks onto the bench next to me, positioning us both so we can keep a watchful eye on the room. He scoots in so close that if it weren't for the fluorescent lights and sticky tabletop and overwhelming scent of bacon and syrup, I could almost pretend we were in a normal restaurant, and this was our first date.

And then he smacks the pile of papers onto the table in front of us, and I remember. We have work to do.

A woman in a blue-and-white waitress uniform comes to take our order. I'm not even remotely hungry, but since I haven't eaten anything other than a couple of the granola bars I threw into my bag this morning, I order the breakfast sampler. Gabe orders the same and adds coffee and water for us both.

As soon as she walks away, Gabe reaches for the stack with the eagerness of a kid ready to tear into his presents on Christmas morning.

"Gabe, wait." I slap a palm over the pile and pause until I have his full attention. "If the truth is in there, whatever it is, I will write it. Even if it proves my father is at fault. I won't like it, but I'll do it for you. I just wanted you to know that beforehand."

It was apparently the right thing to say. He abandons the papers and slides a palm up my neck, planting a long, slow one on me in a way that makes everything else fade away— the people and the noise and the smells. I know nothing but Gabe, kissing the breath from my lungs.

"When this is done," he says against my lips, "when we get back to DC, I'm going to take you on the most epic first date ever. Flowers, champagne, candlelit dinner, the works. I'm going to start all over at the beginning with you and make you fall for me the old-fashioned way."

What if I've already fallen? whispers through my mind, but I push it away with a grin. "Okay, but just so you know, I don't put out on the first date."

"Good thing I like a challenge, then." His face is serious, but there's a teasing edge to his words because both of us know there will be no challenge. I've already fallen, and after last night, Gabe and I have already moved well past the boundaries of a promised first date.

We untangle ourselves and dive into the blog copies, passing the sheets back and forth and making notes in the margins. We agree to create two piles—one for blog entries with any mention of Zach or his platoon as well as all the entries in the weeks before and after his death, and one for those without. Our food comes, and we mostly ignore it, pausing our work only occasionally for a lukewarm bite.

What we do not ignore, what we *cannot* ignore, is the man with a denim jacket and goatee sliding into the booth next to us. Gabe and I fall silent, taking to whispers and written notes on my yellow notepad, and casting sideways glances at the man as he studies the menu.

Before long, we've learned that Ricky became friends with Zach and Nick shortly after arriving in Kabul. He mentioned both of them plenty of times in his early blog entries.

"I know Nick is…troubled," I whisper to Gabe, "but he didn't remember Ricky at all?"

Something settles over his face. Dark, uneasy, despondent. He dips his head close, his breath hot on my ear. "Nick loses it every time I bring up Ricky's name. I can't get anything out of him other than a string of profanities and paranoia."

My heart heaves for him. I slide a palm up his thigh and press a kiss of solidarity to his shoulder.

And then we return to our reading, and I am quickly swept up in Ricky's stories. His writing was honest and true, and he had a raunchy sense of humor; it's our blind luck that the blowup doll would have been right up his triple-X alley. Our coffee grows cold, and the two piles on the table before us grow higher. Within a little over two hours, we have divided all the papers. The man beside us has long since paid and gone.

"Let me see that letter again," I say.

Gabe pulls Ricky's swiped letter out of his back pocket and

unfolds it, smoothing it down on the table. We bend our heads over it, reading it for the second time.

Dear G,

I watched a friend of mine die yesterday. It is an image I will never forget, no matter how hard I try. There's really no way to prepare yourself for something like that, and as much as you see it all around you in this godforsaken place, you never get used to it, either. Especially when it happens to a friend.

But the thing that affected me even more than watching the bullets tear through his brain, is the way his brother sobbed over his body. Zach is just lying there, his skull in chunks on the desert floor, and Nick is on top of him, clutching him and wailing. It was the saddest thing I've ever seen, and believe me, I've seen a lot.

At the base afterward, you could have heard a pin drop. All of us just stood in the motor pool, sweat pouring down our necks and foreheads into our eyes, dripping off our knuckles onto the concrete, not saying a word, just staring at the ceiling, the walls, our shoes. Anywhere but at each other. The thing is, by then we all knew it wasn't the enemy that killed Zach. It was one of us. It had to have been. I just thank God it wasn't me.

And then the commander came in and confirmed what we already knew. Not in so many words, but with some bullshit message about how we should avoid placing blame on any one person. One by one, we were questioned, briefed and sent to our respective tents. When they got to me, a civilian consultant there only to fix a stupid truck valve, they couldn't get rid of me fast enough. The commander practically signed my transfer papers himself. I don't like it, but what can I do? Zach's

death is going to be a PR nightmare back home, and I
guess the army wants to batten down the hatches.

Death is so arbitrary here, G. A total crapshoot. We all
fear our deaths, pray for our lives, miss our homes, wonder if we will ever return to our families. This time it was
Zach, but it just as easily could have been me. It could
have been Nick. It could have been anyone. Who's next?

Sorry to be so morose on you, sis. This place is starting to get to me.

I love you,

R

My vision blurs, and I draw a shaky breath. "They knew.
Everyone knew." There's a hitch in my voice I don't bother
disguising. "That very same day, they knew."

Gabe's jaw clenches. "And they tried to conceal it."

Another person chooses a table too close for comfort, this
time a slender blonde in her midforties. She throws more than
one glance in our direction as she pretends to read the menu,
and that's all I need to know. We need more privacy than the
IHOP can afford. I write *HOTEL?* in big, block letters on
my notepad, and Gabe nods his agreement. While he pays
the bill, I gather up the stacks of papers and our things, and
we meet at the door.

It doesn't take us long to find an ancient motel on a cross
street, but Gabe nixes it. "Those places are crawling with bed-
bugs," he declares, so I drive on. A little farther up the road,
we find a newer-looking chain hotel, and I pull into the lot.
A disinterested night clerk checks us in and hands us two keys,
pointing us to the elevator that will take us to room 213.

"Very romantic," I say, taking in the worn carpeting, cheap
wall unit and two double beds.

Behind me, Gabe activates the double lock and straps the chain across the door.

With my thumb and forefinger, I remove the ratty bed-spread and synthetic blanket from both beds, dumping them in a pile in the corner. When he gives me a look, I say a little defensively, "I watch *CSI*. I know what's on those things."

We spread our papers out over the stiff cotton sheets of the beds and get to work, each reclining on a headboard. We re-read every entry in the Zach pile, and when we don't find anything more than what was in Ricky's letter, we reread the other pile, as well. When we don't find anything after that, we start all over again. I read until my eyes burn. I read until the letters blur and the lines run together on the page, and then I read some more. If there is something else there, something beyond what we already know from the letter, I'm too tired to see it. And from the bleak look that has swallowed Gabe's face, he's not seeing it, either.

Finally, at somewhere around four in the morning, I collapse onto the pillows behind me. "What are we missing?"

On the next bed, Gabe drops the paper he was holding, and it skates to the floor. "Maybe the letter is all there is."

"There's got to be more." My voice is boiling with desperation. "Why else would the blog just disappear? There's got to be more."

"There's not. Goddammit all to hell." Gabe slumps onto the pillows, draping an arm over his face. The past forty-eight hours have been such a roller-coaster ride of emotions for me, I can't imagine how hard it must have been for him. I go to him, gingerly moving the papers onto the other bed and curling up at his side. I kiss his temple, his scruffy cheek, his clenched jaw. Except for his quiet breathing, Gabe doesn't move at all.

"I just hoped…" His voice breaks and then falls still.

In my time as a journalist, I covered more tragedies than

I can count. I've stood among hysterical parents and shocked survivors outside schools and malls and fast-food restaurants while a gunman wreaked havoc inside. I've interviewed weeping mothers who've lost a child to an inner-city gang or a serial killer or a lunatic with a semiautomatic rifle. I've questioned rape survivors and tsunami survivors and every other survivor you can come up with, but never, *never* have their emotions touched me as deeply as Gabe's does now.

I scoot even closer and bury my face in his neck. My voice is barely a whisper. "I know. I'm so sorry."

"I still call him," he says, and the words reach into my chest and put a choke hold on my heart. "I still pay for his cell phone service, just so I can still feel like I'm talking to him. I don't ever want to stop..." He wipes his eyes on his sleeve and turns to me, and what I see in his face breaks my heart. "Stupid, right?"

"No." My eyes fill with tears for Gabe, and for a man I never really knew. I wrap myself around him until not even a whisper of air can make its way between our bodies. "No. It's *not* stupid. It's the sweetest thing I've ever heard."

"I told him about you."

His words hit me like a lightning strike, blowing me apart with a billion volts. Gabe called his dead brother, the one he spent his entire life worshipping, the one he looked up to and sought approval from, and told him about me. It takes me a couple of tries to find my voice.

"What did you tell him?" I whisper into his chest.

"That I've found someone who softens that constant ache in my chest. Someone who makes me smile again." He rolls onto his side to face me, pushing the hair back off my temple, tucking it behind my ear. "It's true, you know. You're that person."

I lie here for an endless moment, unable to breathe, thinking back to the last time anyone said something so beautiful to me. My high school boyfriend, the first to tell me he loved me. Rose this past February, when she asked me to be her Valentine. My grandmother's whispered words before she took her last breath. None of them comes even close.

I soften the ache. I make him smile. I'm that person for him.

I do the only thing I can think of to show him what his words mean to me. I undress him. I start with his boots and socks and work my way up. I let him help only when absolutely necessary, whispering for him to lift up his hips or sit up enough for me to peel him out of his sweater. This isn't about sex or physical release. This is about me helping him forget his brothers even if only for a minute. This is about me loving away his pain.

I kiss every inch of him. His forehead, his cheeks, his earlobe, the scruffy spot at the hinge of his jaw. Gabe doesn't move other than to bunch up the sheets in two tight fists. I kiss his Adam's apple, the hollow of his neck, the center of his chest, holding there until I feel it, his heart beating steady and sure underneath. Gabe's big, beautiful body hums like a high-voltage electrical wire, and I am the lightning rod. I kiss every inch of him, licking down one side and up the other, nipping with my teeth and soothing with my tongue, lingering on places that provoke a gasp or a sigh or a groan.

And then without warning, he flips me. "My turn," he says, his voice low and rough.

His hands are licks of fire as he slides them across my body, peeling off my clothes with burning, urgent fingers, an inferno boiling my blood and consuming me with heat. Every nerve ending in my body springs to attention. I arch up to meet him and moan. He answers it with one of his own.

He makes love to me then, and it's as if he is searching for something in me, some way to fill him up and make him complete again, and maybe I'm doing the same with him. It is so different from the last time, more bittersweet maybe, and far more powerful. I watch him above me, my heart pounding in my chest as if it's trying to break free, and something inside of me is breaking open, spilling out everywhere. At the last moment, right as I'm about to cry out his name, he pushes the hair off my brow and holds my gaze until both of us fall off the edge and into each other's arms.

Afterward, he holds me as if he will never let me go, and I do the same with him. As I'm drifting off, three little words bubble up in my throat but go unsaid, the dizzying realization I'm in love with the man next to me almost floating me back to consciousness, but the pull of exhaustion is too great.

By the time I reach the far side of a sigh, I'm asleep.

Sometime after dawn, I wake in his arms.

I know what we missed. What we read over and over and over and missed. Our minds got so hung up on Ricky that we didn't see Nick, sitting in the seat right beside him. All this time, the answer was right there in front of us. We just didn't see it.

Gently, I lift Gabe's arm from my hip and slip out of bed. He stirs under the crumpled sheets, but his eyes remain closed, his breathing slow and steady.

In the dim morning sunlight poking through the curtains, I scramble around until I find my T-shirt and panties on the floor and noiselessly pull them on, and then I begin sorting through the papers on the bed. Within less than a minute, I find the blog entry I'm looking for, the one dated just two days after Zach's death. My eyes skip down to the last paragraph.

On the drive back to base, I could feel the weight of Nick's empty seat beside me. He was in whatever truck had the gruesome task of carrying back the body of his brother. I thought of all the things I should have said to him as they were loading what was left of Zach into a body bag, the things I will surely tell Nick the next time I see him. That I will miss Zach, that I was blessed to have known him, that I will never forget him. But mostly I will say that Zach was my brother, too. He was my brother.

I reach for my computer and turn it on. As I wait for it to power up, I reread that paragraph again and again, rolling the words around in my brain. No matter how hard I try, I can't figure any other way around it. According to Ricky, Nick rode out on the seat beside him, which means Nick was in the *second* convoy, not the first.

Then why do all the official army reports state Nick was in the first convoy with his brother Zach?

I pull up the reports on my screen and start scrolling. In every account, on almost every page, there is some mention of both Armstrong brothers in the first convoy. It's as if the army bent over backward to make certain this point was clear, stating and restating this detail more often than necessary.

I check the blog entry again and there it is: *Nick's empty seat beside me.* But why would the army want to bury the fact that Nick was in the second convoy, unless...

My father's voice slices through the confusion in my head. *Do* not *open that Pandora's box, Abigail.*

Something inside me splits open, letting in light, filling me with understanding I don't want to grasp, dropping the bottom out of my world.

"Oh. My. God."

On the next bed, Gabe awakens at the sound of my voice.

23

It takes Gabe's sleep-befuddled brain a few beats to register the look on my face. When it does, he shoots straight up in bed, the thin sheet pooling around his waist. "What's wrong?"

I have no fucking idea how to answer that question. The only thing I *do* know is that I can't speak the words I think to be true. If neither of us says those awful words out loud, then maybe they won't be true. I'm having a nightmare. I'm being punked. I'm waiting for the punch line.

Yet slicing through the steady hum of the room's air-conditioning unit, I hear my own voice, high and hysterical, already believing.

I shake my head, stare at the veins pulsing on the back of my hands. "Nothing."

One hand still clutches the blog entry like a crumpled bouquet, and my mind searches for a way to release it without Gabe noticing, to slip it under my thigh maybe, or let it slide from my hands onto the floor. I can feel Gabe's eyes sliding over me, looking for clues, and I sit here frozen. I can't seem to look up, to meet his gaze head-on. The room is stuffed full of silence.

He snatches his jeans off the floor and thrusts his legs in, pulling them up over his bare ass. "Please, Abigail. You're scaring me. What?"

"Nothing." I try to smile, but dread swirls inside my chest until I think I'll drown. "I'm fine. Everything's fine. Really."

Bile touches the back of my throat at the lie, and I swallow down a thick, burning ball of it.

Gabe shoves aside the mountain of papers in front of me, wraps his big palms around both my biceps and shakes. "Tell me."

The shoulder he sets behind the words rattles me to the innermost point in my belly, or maybe he was trying to shake the answer out of me, I don't know. Either way, in all the commotion, Gabe notices Ricky's blog entry in my fist.

He snatches the paper up, gaze flashing over the words.

I can't watch. I don't want to see the moment when realization hits his face. I launch myself off the bed and run to the sink by the bathroom, burying my face in a hand towel. I hear him come around the corner, picture his big body filling up the tiny hallway, the paper still in his hand, and I don't dare look. Is his face bathed in confusion, or horror?

"What am I not seeing?" He pulls the towel from my hands and tosses it onto the floor, tipping my face up to his. His eyes brim with tears, ones I can barely see through my own. "Please. Just tell me."

But I can't. My lips won't form the words, my tongue won't push them out. It's bad enough that I was the one to work it out in the first place, I cannot, no, *will not* say what I think I know out loud. This is math Gabe is going to have to figure out on his own.

He looks back to the paper. "But what… I don't…"

There's a long silence, one that expands and fills the room until it becomes almost tangible. A silence that presses down on my skin and fills my lungs with cotton. That it's taking Gabe longer to fully comprehend is something I don't fault him for, will *never* fault him for, given the circumstances.

"But that's not right." He shakes his head, hard, like a dog choking on a bone, and the paper floats to the floor. "That's not fucking right. Nick was with Zach. He was—"

I look away, but by now it's too late. I've already seen it, those beautiful, horrified eyes, that angular, trembling jaw. Gabe did the math, and he came to the same sickening conclusion I just did.

"Maybe we're wrong." I'm surprised I can even speak, as thick and rubbery as my tongue feels. The words come out slow and slurred. "We can't possibly know for sure."

"We know."

"Maybe we don't."

"We know, Abigail. We fucking know! *Jesus.* Mom kept telling me to let it go, that Zach was gone and nothing could bring him back, but I wouldn't listen. I had to have someone to blame. I had to know, and now…" The snag in his voice tells me he's barely holding it together, as does the way his hands are shaking. He shoves both of them in his hair and pulls, his face twisting into a tight wad, his bare chest heaving. "I'm such a shit! Why didn't I *listen* to her?"

"Gabe." I reach out for him, sliding a hand onto his waist, and he flinches. My hand drops back to my side. "None of this is your fault."

Gabe turns and stalks back into the room. Halfway there he freezes, blinking around at the rumpled sheets and papers and pens, the empty water bottles strewn among our clothes on the floor, the piled-up bedspreads in the corner, taking everything in as if he's seeing it for the first time. His breathing has calmed somewhat, and I might think he's okay, were it not for his clenched fists and the muscles across his back, standing up under his skin like rope.

And then his shoulders broaden, his back expands and his lungs fill with air. He's bracing for a fresh gale of grief, I think, and then it comes, folding him double and pushing an awful, keening howl up his throat that knifes me in the center of the heart, a direct hit. And then before I can take even a step in his direction, he straightens, brings an arm back and punches the wall with his fist.

"Gabe!" I run to him, reaching for his injured hand, but he yanks it away, only to beat the wall again and again and again. "Gabe, stop. Stop!"

Gabe doesn't stop. He keeps going until the wall crumples and bloody streaks coat the striped vinyl wallpaper.

On one of his backward swings, I latch on to his arm by the elbow, throwing all my weight and strength into the effort. It's like dragging an oar upstream, sluggish and heavy, and it lifts me clear off the carpet. I clench down, hold on tight. The action whirls his big body around, and his expression is so downright terrifying I have to remind myself his fury is not aimed at me.

"Gabe, it's okay," I say, even though it's not. Even though it's the opposite of okay. I press both hands to his bearded cheeks, force his gaze to mine. A drop of something splats on my foot, and I know without looking that it's blood. "I'll help you. It'll be okay."

He hauls a hitching breath, and he nods, quick and eager as if he believes me. A jagged pain ripples up my throat, aching with tears I can no longer hold back, not for Nick or for Zach but for Gabe. For the man who so desperately wants me to make it okay, and for the knowledge that I can't. I can't make any of this okay.

He collapses into me, and we fall back onto the bed, on top of the papers and trash and wrecked sheets, his body pressing down on top of mine like a deadweight. My face is mashed into his shoulder and my ribs are creaking under his mass, but I don't push him off or complain, because that's when I feel it.

It starts slowly, silently, like a hurricane rolling in off the ocean. His chest jerks once, twice, again. The movements tear up his torso and throat, building in strength and speed, churning into sharp and violent sobs. Gabe is sobbing on top of me, and with a force that threatens to break my bones. His skin is damp and salty, his entire body heaving, and I would stay here under him forever, not moving, barely breathing, if I have to.

Because though I can't do anything to take away his pain, the least I can do is bear the weight of it.

Bright November sunshine streams through the windshield in slices of gold, lighting up Gabe slumped in my passenger's seat. His eyes are dull and lifeless, but his cheeks glint with silver tracks of dried tears, disappearing into the dark scruff of his beard. He hasn't said a word for the past hour, and though I'm trying to be supportive and give him some space, his silence is eating away at me. I don't know what to do, what to say, how to help. I'm way out of my league here.

I toss my bag onto the floor behind my seat and climb behind the wheel. "What now?"

Gabe stares out the side window, onto a row of scraggly bushes at the edge of the hotel lot.

"Gabe." I touch a finger to his arm, and his skin flinches like a horse's hide swatting away flies. "What now? Do you want to go home?"

"Eagle Rock, Virginia," he says without looking over, his voice flatlined.

For a moment, I'm confused. "Is that where Nick is?"

He gives me a quick bob of his head and nothing more.

"Is that... Gabe, are you sure that's a good idea?"

"Just take me there."

Sighing, I punch the coordinates into my navigation system, which tells me Eagle Rock is nudged up against the West Virginia border, a good five-hour drive to the northwest.

I think of all the things I should do. Call my father and beg him to meet us there. Swing by the Naval Medical Center for a psychologist trained in dealing with PTSD. I don't know what Gabe hopes to accomplish by confronting Nick with our discovery, but nothing about this feels like a good idea.

"Maybe he doesn't remember. I'm not sure you should be the one to tell him if he's repressed it." I don't know much about PTSD, but if ever there was cause for a licensed professional, I'd imagine this would be it. "This is way over both of our heads."

"I have to know." Now, finally, he looks over, and what I see there breaks my heart. "I have to know for sure. So either take me there, or take me to a Hertz counter."

I put the car in gear, follow the little white line guiding me toward the highway and take him there.

As we roar up I-64 in haunting, suffocating silence, I use the time to turn every bit of information we learned over and over in my mind, but no matter how I twist or turn it, I can't come up with any other explanation than the one I already have. Gabe and Jean were right. The army was lying about what happened to Zach, but with good reason. The best possible reason. The only reason that could make a lie like theirs okay.

My father's words suddenly echo in my ears, the words lighting up across my mind in gleaming strobe letters. *Just because something's the truth, that doesn't make it right.* My father knew about Nick and Zach. He *had* to know. But in trying to steer me away from Ricky, was Dad covering his own ass, or attempting to spare Gabe and his family the devastation of ever discovering the truth? The last one clamps down on my heart, threatens to pinch it in two.

And then I remember his other words, the ones telling me not to open that box, and my vision swims and blurs. My father knew about Nick all along. When he confronted me in the bathroom hallway. When I confronted him with the memo. He told me I didn't have all the facts, that I should not be so quick to judge, that I didn't want to get involved in a matter I knew nothing about. He did everything to stop me from learning the truth, even—oh, God—asking me to trust him. To *trust* him.

Thinking about it makes me light-headed with guilt. After Eagle Rock, after whatever happens there, I am driving straight to my father to apologize.

Just past Richmond, I need a bathroom and gas break, and I pull over at an Exxon. I fill my tank, use the restroom, purchase two sodas and two packs of peanut butter crackers, and return to the car, only to find Gabe in the exact same position. The soda and crackers remain untouched in the console between us, and we drive the rest of the way in silence.

At some time past five, just as the sun is sinking behind the bald trees, I roll up the two-block stretch of homes and businesses that comprise the entire town of Eagle Rock. I pull onto the gravel on the side of the road and tap Gabe on the arm.

"We're in Eagle Rock."

Gabe looks up, and he speaks for the first time since Portsmouth. "Find the diner."

Maw and Paw's Diner is a little farther down on the right, and I pull to a stop in front of it. I'm parked in the middle of the two-lane street, but in a town like Eagle Rock, it doesn't really matter. There's not exactly a whole lot of traffic.

"Take the next right," he instructs me, "and go two miles up the hill."

I follow his directions, keeping a careful eye on my odometer as I climb higher and higher into the Jefferson National Forest. Just as I'm approaching the two-mile mark, Gabe points to a mailbox at the edge of a dirt road, and I turn into the shadowy tunnel. We're swallowed up by the woods, thick trees that rise up all around us like giant headstones. We emerge in a clearing with, at its center, a lone wooden cabin. It sits dark and deserted, blending into the forest as if it's been here forever.

I still my engine as the front door swings open, and a tall figure in jeans and a flannel shirt steps out onto the long front porch. The first thing that comes to mind is Bigfoot, even though I recognize him immediately. It's Nick but hairier, long strands of it covering his face, draping over his eyes and brushing the tips of his shoulders.

Gabe reaches for the handle, and for the first time since we left Portsmouth, his gaze finds mine. "Wait here."

24

Alone in my car, I check my cell phone for the first time in I don't remember how long and wince. Seven voice mails from my mother, two from the real David, three from a number I don't recognize, five from Floyd and a whopping thirteen from Mike. I listen to Mike's first message, but when I discover he only called to lay into me, yet again, for Victoria's article, I don't bother listening to the rest, and I don't call anyone back. I don't have the first idea what I would say to any of them.

I compose a quick text to my mother, who must be sick with worry, apologizing for missing our lunch date and promising to call her as soon as I'm back, and then I text roughly the same to David. I ignore the rest, saving them for later. After the texts are swept away into the network, I power down my phone and store it in my bag.

The cabin shows no signs of life, its windows dark and still. The silence inside could just as well be a good thing as a bad, and I try to put myself in Gabe's position. What would I say to Nick? Confront him with the facts? Beg him for an explanation? Wait for him to confess? I have no idea, and quite frankly, I'm too dizzy with exhaustion to consider it for very long. I recline my seat and close my eyes, and I fall asleep almost instantly.

"Abigail."

At the sound of my name, I jerk awake. By now it's pitch-black out, so dark I can barely see Gabe's figure hovering in my open car door, bent over and watching me. The forest over-head has blocked out whatever light the stars or moon may be making in the nighttime sky, and the only illumination at all is a lone bulb by the porch and my car's dim interior light.

"I'm staying the night," he says.

I consider my options, but it doesn't take me long. A Quarter Pounder, a bath and a bed, in that order. I reach for the start button. "Call me when you're done."

"No." He blows out a loud sigh, and I hesitate. "What I mean to say is, it's late. Let's stay here tonight."

"Are you sure?" I rest my hand on the wheel and blink up at him, but darkness blankets his face. "I think I saw a hotel near the last exit."

He holds out a hand for mine. "Come on."

I reach for my bag, putting my hand in his palm and lacing my fingers through his. I know this is neither the time nor the place, but I'm aching to suction cup myself to him and never let go. There is an empty crater in my chest, and though I'm certain it's nowhere near the size of his own, I don't want to spend the night alone. As selfish as it sounds, I'm craving the feel of Gabe's body next to mine, tonight more than ever.

Together we go toward the door, but before we reach the first wooden step, I pull him to a stop. "I know this is a ridiculously stupid question, but how are you doing?"

He rubs his free hand through his hair. "I have no fuck-ing clue."

"And Nick?"

"Who knows? I can't get anything out of him about that day. I'm not even sure he remembers it."

"Is he getting any help?"

Gabe nods, avoiding my eye. "But now that I know what I know, clearly not enough."

I have nothing to say to that.

Gabe lowers his voice to a whisper. "A couple of things before we go in. He's calm most of the time, but if he gets belligerent, don't freak out. Let me handle it. It usually blows over pretty quickly. He's not going to trust you, and he probably won't even be nice to you, so don't take it personally. Don't tell him you're a journalist, and whatever you do, do *not* tell him who your father is. That'll only set him off. Okay?"

I nod, strangely nervous about what I'm walking into. "Are you sure you don't want me to find a hotel? Because I'd be fine with that."

Gabe shakes his head. "Let's just stay the night here, and we'll figure things out in the morning."

We climb the two steps to the door, and then at the last second, Gabe pulls me aside as if he's forgotten to tell me something. "Oh, and he paints. You'll see."

He releases my hand, and together, we go in. I blink, my eyes adjusting to what is not a whole lot more light than outside the tiny cabin, and follow Gabe to the most basic of kitchens. I drop my bag on the floor by a square, wooden table. Nick is standing by the counter, peeling open a can of black olives.

"Nick," Gabe says to his older brother. "This is Abigail."

Nick doesn't look up or acknowledge me in any way. He reaches two fingers in the can and pulls out a handful of olives, popping them one by one into his mouth.

"Abigail is going to sleep here tonight," Gabe tells him.

At that he looks up, pausing in his chewing to scowl.

"She's cool," Gabe adds.

Nick narrows his eyes. "We don't know that."

"*I* know that."

Nick slams a fist on the countertop hard enough to rattle the can. "Nobody is accountable. Criminals are in charge. Blundering, egotistical, incompetent, malevolent, virtueless, vacuous criminals. We can't trust any of them."

Good grief. Nick might want to lay off the internet chat rooms for a while.

Gabe steps around the counter to him, puts a hand on his shoulder. "That's true, but Abigail's not one of them. I'm going to let her crash in my room, and we'll be out of here tomorrow morning, okay?"

Nick shrugs and returns to his olives. "Whatever."

Gabe ushers me to the other end of the cabin. On the way, I take my first quick glance around, and it's overwhelming. To say Nick paints is the understatement of the century. Every surface—the walls, cabinets, tables, even the floors and ceilings—is covered with angry swaths of dark color, mostly blacks and army greens and deep bloodreds, and scrawled text. I can't decipher most of it, but I do pick out a few words. Words like *illegal*, *apathy* and *torture*, like violent cave drawings scribbled across the walls and furniture.

We go down a hallway, stopping at a tiny room barely bigger than the single bed that fills it at the end. Gabe flips a switch that lights a lone bulb on the ceiling, avoiding my eye. "I'll take the couch."

"Gabe." I reach for his arm and pull him to me. There is so much I want to say to him—that no family deserves this to have happened to them, that I want to be here for him if he will let me, that I love every inch of him, body and soul—

where on earth do I start? I decide with the most pressing. "I'm so sorry this is happening."

He gives me a tight smile. "You and me both."

He goes to take a step backward, but I press my forehead to his chest and hold on to his sweater, clutching it into a ball with both fists. "Will you come back later? I don't want you to be alone." *I* don't want to be alone.

"I'll try. We'll see." He untangles us and slips out the door, pulling it gently closed behind him.

I collapse onto the bed.

Behind me, the window rattles with a sudden gust that blows clear through the pane, and I shiver and wrap the quilt over my shoulders. A ball of worry balloons in my belly, crawling through my limbs, growing teeth and claws, strangling the calm, reasonable voice that keeps telling me that I can fix this, that all will be well, that Gabe and I are still an us. Even though I can already feel him pulling away, creating a distance between us, digging an emotional grave for the feelings we've just begun to share. I shiver again, but this time, not from the cold.

Before long, the noises from the other room fall away into silence. My doorknob, dull and dusty from disuse, doesn't turn. I sit in the quiet, pitch-black room, waiting, hoping, pleading, until the seconds blur into minutes, until time coils into itself, until all there is left to do is pray. Pray that I can heal the gash I helped carve in my father's reputation. Pray that Gabe and his family come out of this in one piece. Pray that the chill I just felt creep up my spine was another gust through the glass, and not a terrible foreboding.

I wake up and know something's wrong, very, very wrong. Holy-motherfucking-hell wrong. Only, I can't figure out what.

I blink into the quiet dark, try to get my bearings. For several disorienting seconds, I don't know where I am, whose scratchy, musty sheets are pressed against my skin. I know only this unmistakable sense of doom.

And then I hear a *whump* followed by a male voice I only vaguely recognize, and I remember.

Nick's cabin.

I jerk upright, and the squeak of the bedsprings slices the silence.

There's more noise from deeper in the cabin. More voices, the crash of something breaking, a hard thump that rattles the walls, like someone fighting off an intruder.

I throw off the covers and feel my way along the wall to the door in my T-shirt and bare feet. Carefully, I pull on the knob and peer down the empty hallway. At the far end, on the table by the front door, a lone lamp glows, its crooked shade casting pale yellow shadows on the wooden floorboards.

"They're taking fire," Nick says, too loudly, his words anxious and thick. "Shit."

"Nick." Gabe's voice, calm but insistent. "Wake up, bro."

Relief rushes through me, at the same time something more ominous twists in my gut. Their voices are too strained, too urgent for this to be just a nightmare.

I creep into the hall, on tiptoe and breathless, worried I'm intruding on a private moment between brothers, terrified of what I'll find around the corner.

"Too much smoke... I can't see!" Nick's voice is louder now, and he's panting as if he's just run a marathon in July, as if he's hyperventilating. "Where's Zach? Where the hell is Zach?"

I chance a peek around the corner. In the dim light of the room I get a side view of Gabe, in jeans and a rumpled T-shirt, both hands high in the air as if he's being held at gunpoint. "Nick, man, it's okay. You're safe."

Nick's answer doesn't make any sense. "Roger that, four o'clock. Enemy at six."

I lean farther into the room.

A naked Nick, huge and hairy, crouches behind the counter by the kitchen, his eyes empty, his face straining with tension. The overhead light shining down on his skin makes him look slick, as if he's covered with sweat even though the air in the cabin is downright chilly. Veins bulge, as fat and raised as a bodybuilder's, on the shiny skin of his arms, but it's his hands—oh, God, his hands—that stop my heart.

They're holding a gun, a Beretta M9 exactly like the general's, and it's pointed at the center of Gabe's chest.

"Nick, it's me. Gabe." Gabe takes a step forward, and a scream lodges in my throat. That weapon holds fifteen rounds, and no telling how many are in there. But if Gabe senses the danger, he doesn't let on. He holds his hands higher and takes another step. "You're in Virginia, man. There's no enemy."

It's as if Nick is deaf. He jerks his head back and gapes at the ceiling above my head, his mouth moving in a silent scream. Swinging the gun up, he fires once, twice, three times, into the wooden beams, prompting a shower of wood and dust and dirt. The air, permeated before with tension and sweat, grows even thicker with the smell of smoke and gunpowder.

"Nick, there's nobody there. It's only you and me. Your brother Gabe."

Something registers. Not Gabe's words, necessarily, but at the very least his presence. Nick responds by waving his gun back and forth, from Gabe to the ceiling and back. When he pinches off another shot that lodges in the wall to my right, I can't hold back my scream.

Gabe freezes, but Nick's gaze swings to me.

So does his gun.

I dive behind the wall, skidding on rough planks and bare knees and elbows down the hallway floor to safety.

But what about Gabe?

"Hold your fire, soldier!" he shouts, his voice deep and unyielding and loud enough to penetrate, I pray, Nick's fog. "That's a goddamn order."

Gabe's plan works. Nick holds his fire.

I hold my breath, straining with everything I have to hear what's happening behind the wall. For the longest moment, all I hear is silence, and then deep gulping gasps of air that build up to what sounds like a sob.

"Zach?"

My heart breaks at Nick's voice—just heaves and snaps into two—calling for his dead brother. And then again for Gabe, whose voice cracks when he says, "Zach's gone."

Now Nick is definitely sobbing. "Oh, God. Oh, God. I thought... I didn't know... Fuck!"

"Nick, I need you to drop the gun..."

A new and different note of panic in Gabe's voice has me scrambling on hands and knees back to the doorway. I don't want to see where Nick's gun is pointing, and yet I have to know. Gabe's heart? Nick's temple? Because judging from the sounds coming from both brothers, it's somewhere lethal.

Nick's wailing escalates into a chant. "OhGodohGodoh-GodohGod—"

I duck my head around the wall, and my heart stutters to a stop, then takes off like a fighter jet.

His chin. Nick is aiming the gun straight up his chin.

"For Christ's sake, Nick, drop the motherfucking gun!"

I glance around, thinking through the options, what I can do to help. Ice water shoots through my veins at the answer. Nothing. There is absolutely nothing I can do to help but pray.

Meanwhile, Nick's chant climbs both in speed and volume. "—ohGodohGodohGodohGod—"

"Don't do it! Don't you pull that goddamn trigger!"

"—ohGodohGodohGodohGodohGod—"

"What about Mom?" Gabe's words are like an atomic blast, releasing ten thousand tons of energy into the cabin and lurching every living thing to a stop.

Nick stops wailing, but he doesn't drop his weapon.

Gabe bends at the knees, crouching down to his brother's level. "Think about it, man. Are you going to let her lose another son? Because you kill yourself, and you're killing her, too. She won't survive losing you, too."

Silence. Nick looks at his brother, but other than his own chest rising and falling in great, gulping pants, he doesn't move. I hold my breath, press a shaking palm over my mouth and pray.

"And, God, Nick, neither will I." A shudder travels across Gabe's shoulder blades, and he sucks in a hitching breath. "Now please, for God's sake, drop the gun."

The thunk of metal on wood when Nick obeys hits me square in the solar plexus, and my bones go mushy with relief. I collapse back onto my ass, taking my first full breath in what feels like a century.

"It should have been me," Nick says between sobs. "Why wasn't it me?"

Gabe tackles his brother in a desperate embrace, and they tumble to the floor, and I can't tell who's crying harder, them or me. And then Nick throws his head back and howls, and it's Nick, by a million trillion miles. I don't mean to watch. I don't even want to. But there are some things you just can't look away from, and this is one of them.

After forever, I haul myself off the floor, trudge back down the hall to the tiny bed and—for the second time tonight—cry myself to sleep.

25

The next morning I awake, shivering and alone in the tiny room, the threadbare quilt tangled around my legs. My head pounds and my tongue is like sandpaper and I feel hungover, even though I didn't have a drop of alcohol.

Fratricide. A brother shooting another brother. An awful, terrible, devastating accident, but still. How can such a thing be possible? How could that kind of tragedy happen? It's as if the planet suddenly decided to grind to a halt on its axis and reverse directions. Summer turns into winter, bypassing fall. The sun sets in the east. The world feels the complete opposite of how it's supposed to be.

I press two fingers to my temples and rub, but it only makes my headache worse.

In the light of day, Nick's artwork assaults me from the walls and furniture, deathly shapes resembling bodies and mangled tanks and explosions of color, as do the memories of last night. The painted walls sway and darken in my vision as I think of what almost happened. What I almost *watched* happen. Thank God Gabe had been able to stop Nick from harming himself, but what about next time? When Gabe and I pack up and leave, who will stop Nick then?

I crawl to the tiny window at the end of the bed, blinking into the bright morning sunshine. The cabin, I now see, is at the edge of a large lake, a dark, shining pool surrounded by thick forest. If there are any other homes dotting its shores, they are well hidden behind the trees. As far as I can tell, Nick is completely alone in his refuge here.

As am I.

Gabe never came.

The sharp smell of bacon and eggs awakens my empty stomach, and I sit up straighter in bed, listening. Gabe's voice says something I can't decipher through the pine door, but from far enough away that I think he can't be addressing me. I thrust my feet into my shoes, press my ear to the door and listen for more. Pans clank, and a man's footsteps rattle the floorboards, but no one speaks. When the sounds fade away into silence, I sneak down the hallway to the bathroom and slip inside.

The first thing I notice is the lack of a mirror—which kind of explains Nick's hair, if you ask me—and I don't know whether to be sorry or grateful. After all the tears I shed last night, I'm not certain I would want to catch even a passing glimpse of myself.

But there is, hallelujah and praise Jesus, toothpaste, and I swipe a good squirt of it across my teeth and tongue with a finger. I squat above the filthy toilet, wash my hands and splash my face, and then I make my way into the cabin.

Gabe is at the stove, staring into the bubbling, popping frying pans and looking even worse than last night, if that's possible. His face is pinched and wan, marked with worry lines I haven't noticed before, darkened by new shadows below his eyes and his cheekbones, dipping into his beard. The table behind him is set for three, and my bag has been transported to a spot on the floor by an ancient couch. I glance around the room for Nick but find no sign of him.

"Did you get any sleep?"

At the sound of my voice, Gabe glances over his shoulder, noticing me for the first time. "No."

"How's Nick?"

He pokes at something in one of the pans with a wooden spoon. "He didn't sleep, either."

God. Given what Nick holding that gun to his chin did to my heart, I can only imagine what it must have done to Gabe's. A desire to touch him centers right in the middle of my chest, an ache that is so much more than physical. I go to him, threading an arm under his, the one with Zach's name on it, and press my palm against his chest until I feel his heartbeat, steady and true, beating against it. He stills at my touch, but he doesn't turn around.

Nick walks in then, carrying an armful of firewood, and I unwind myself from Gabe.

"Can I do anything to help?" I ask, and Gabe points me to the fridge, to the orange juice and milk and whatever else we'll need for our breakfast.

Nick ignores both of us as he dumps his armload into a basket and sets about making a fire in the wood-burning stove. As far as I can tell, that rickety hunk of metal is the only source of heat in the cabin, and I hope for Nick's sake it can produce plenty of it, and quickly. It's barely the beginning of November, but just as frigid inside the cabin as out. I don't know how he can stand living here once winter really hits.

Gabe distributes our breakfast over the plates, and we settle in at the table, Nick and I at Gabe's elbows. I'm ravenous and desperately thirsty, and I chug the glass of orange juice

Gabe pours me in four seconds flat. And then we eat, mostly in silence.

After breakfast, Nick slips outside to God-knows-where, and Gabe and I clean the remains of the meal in silence. Gabe is meticulous in his work. Long after I'm done he's still scraping the pans, scrubbing the sink, hunching over the countertop, scratching at the dried smears of paint with his thumbnail until every last one of them pulls loose.

"Gabe." I drape a palm over his hand, and now, finally, he stops. "What now?"

He straightens, and that's when I see it. Pure, primal terror. His eyes are wide and bloodshot, rolling around like a terrified horse, and I feel a pang of sympathy angst, like a fist closing around my heart. After what almost happened last night, Gabe has so much to be afraid of. It's only a matter of time before Nick has another flashback or, God forbid, holds a gun to his own head again.

"Did you clear the house of weapons?"

"Yeah, but what's to stop him from going up the street and getting another one? This is hunting territory. There's a goddamn gun shop on every corner." He tosses his sponge back into the sink and dries his hands on his jeans.

"Nick should be in a hospital. You know that, right?"

"He'll never agree to it."

I say it as gently as I know how: "I don't think at this point the decision should be up to him."

Gabe doesn't nod, but he doesn't shake his head, either. He just stares at the floor for a long moment, looking so bereaved, so wilted and lost. And then he pushes off the counter and crosses the room to the window, searching, I assume, for Nick. Nick didn't say where he was going when he walked out the door, and I could tell it was killing Gabe not to ask, the same way it's killing me now to watch Gabe's obvious struggle.

"Why don't I call my father, get him to pull some strings? He'll know which institution is best for these types of situations, who to strong-arm to find Nick a…" Gabe turns, and my words trail off at the look on his face, the way it clamps down and closes off. "What?"

"You can't talk to your father about Nick, Abigail." His voice is low and lethal, and there's something about the way he's looking at me. "You can't talk to *anyone* about Nick. If you do, if this story gets out…"

He doesn't finish, but he also doesn't have to. Talk about words being deadly. If the truth about Zach and Nick ever broke, I don't know how any of the remaining Armstrongs would survive.

"My father is not just anyone, Gabe. He probably already knows, and he can help, at the very least by finding the right spot for Nick."

Gabe folds his arms across his chest. "What if your father was the one who gave you the transcript? Have you considered that possibility?"

"No, because that's…that's ridiculous. Dad was the one warning me away from you and your mom, remember? He was the one telling me not to open Pandora's box."

"Because he was the top of the chain of command. Maybe he's ultimately responsible for splitting up the platoon, putting two brothers in a position to fire on one another. Maybe *that's* the truth he didn't want released into the world. That this whole disaster is all his fault."

"Now you're just grasping at straws. If any of that was true, if Dad wanted to cover up his part in any of this, then why would he have given me the transcript? Your theory doesn't make any sense."

"You sure about that? Your father wrote that memo, and he retired awfully suddenly. Why do you think that is?"

I hesitate, hardly a pause at all, but Gabe notices, and he knows he's hit a sore spot. Dad's retirement *was* sudden, and it never made any sense to me. He lived and breathed US Army, and even though he's kept himself busy since retiring, he's seemed a little aimless without it.

"Positive," I say, and my voice tilts. It's more than just Gabe's obvious suspicion toward my father, and my defense of him. It's that this conversation suddenly feels like a runaway train headed for a sharp curve. I'm watching it fly down the tracks, barreling toward doom and danger, and I have no idea how to stop it. "My father did not give me that transcript."

"A couple of days ago, you weren't so sure. In fact, you were so positive he was guilty, you sent the memo to your former boss. You said he was one of the bad guys, remember?"

His words slice into me with a knife's edge. I don't need this little reminder of the enormity of my transgression where my father is concerned. I have more guilt than I can stomach already. But it's the way that Gabe says it, with unconcealed accusation in his tone, that gives the blade that last little twist.

"Because that story was going to break with or without me. Because I knew Victoria would be fair and impartial. That's why I sent it to her."

"There's no fair and impartial with this story. This story has got to die."

The train picks up speed, its wheels and joints groaning, the squeal of metal against metal. The curve looms in the not-so-far distance.

"What story?" I tilt my head, narrow my eyes and fold my arms over my chest, everything about the gesture a dare he make his accusation out loud.

"Words are as deadly as warfare, you said so yourself. These are words that will kill my mother. This story will destroy what's left of my family."

"What story, Gabe?" I lean forward as I say it, my last attempt at leaning on the brakes.

For the longest time, Gabe just stands there, his big chest puffing. Not all that long ago, I told him what happened with his brother gave his behavior a free pass, but he just nudged up awfully close to my boundary lines. What he says next will either turn this thing around or shoot us off the rails.

"I'll call Mom," he says finally. "I'll tell her you've changed your mind. I'll make up some excuse."

"Fine."

"She's going to try to talk you out of it. She's going to be relentless. When she calls, just don't pick up."

"Tell me what you want me to say, and I'll say it."

"I don't want you to say anything. I want you to let me handle it."

I hear his words, understand the weight of them, read between the letters for the real intent: Gabe doesn't want me speaking to his mother, at all, ever again, because he's afraid of what I'll say.

"I see," I say, and I do. I see the train skipping the tracks, shooting over the edge, bursting into flames on the rocky canyon floor. "You think I'm going to tell her about Nick. You think I'm going to write the story. You don't trust me to keep Nick's secret."

His eyes search the floor, and I realize *this* is what it is really about. What it's been about since that rainy evening he spent on my couch, when he came to apologize and request a fresh start. Gabe doesn't trust me. He may have needed my help to find Ricky, he may have even grown to like me along the way, but deep down, he didn't trust me. The pain of it steals my breath. After everything that's happened between us, after his couch and my bed and Portsmouth, it guts me all the way through.

"You used me, Gabe. You *used* me in order to get to Ricky. You knew I liked you and—" I try to finish my sentence, but the words die in my throat as suddenly the horrifying extent to which he used me crystalizes in my mind, as clear and sure as the barbaric paintings covering the walls. I take two steps back until I'm pressed against a rickety table by the wall. "Oh, my God. You even *fucked* me to get to Ricky."

He shakes his head in surprise, and his brows slam together. "Is that what you think?"

"Tell me I'm wrong."

"You're wrong," he says immediately, and then…nothing more.

"Okay, then. Tell me this. Why don't you want me talking to your mother?"

Gabe hauls a breath to speak, then doesn't. He doesn't say anything at all. He doesn't have to. His silence says more than words ever could.

My father always said every good warrior knows when it's time to retreat. Now is the time.

I push past him, head for the door.

"Abigail, wait." Gabe takes off behind me, his boots echoing off the scarred pine floor. "Where are you going? We can't leave Nick."

"*You* can't leave Nick." By now I'm out the door and rushing down the rickety steps. Patchy late-morning sunshine filters down through the heavy forest overhead, lighting up the still mountain air with golden sparkles. "But I can, and I am."

"Abigail, are you—"

I whirl around so fast, my shoes send up a spray of dirt and gravel. "Am I what? Planning to write a story? Running home to tell your mom? Or do you have another accusation you'd like to throw in the mix?"

"I'm just trying to manage the crisis, to prevent the bad

from getting worse. I'm just trying to get the train back on the tracks."

If Gabe's analogy wasn't so goddamn heartbreaking, it might actually be funny. "So am I. Which is why I'm going to see my father."

"You're not… You're not going to like this question, but I have to ask it anyway." He takes a cautious step toward me. "What are you going to tell him?"

"First, I'm going to beg his forgiveness. After that—" I lift my entire upper body in a shrug "—you're just going to have to trust me."

26

From Eagle Rock, I drive straight to my father.

Gabe might not trust Dad, but I've had the past four hours to think through what I know, and the only thing I know for sure is I don't share in Gabe's suspicions. Anger? Sure. I still have plenty of that. Dad still penned that awful memo, and he still tried to bully me away from the Armstrongs instead of giving me a reasonable explanation. But there's no way he's the one who snuck me the illicit transcript, not when he was so adamantly warning me away.

But also, I have guilt. Lots and lots of guilt. I tell myself I can unravel the damage I've done to his reputation. I tell myself I can make him forgive me. Because if I've learned anything from last night, it's that whatever issues I may have with my own father pale in comparison to the Armstrong tragedy.

Mom greets me at the door with a kiss and a fierce hug, and though she certainly looks annoyed, she doesn't look the least bit surprised to see me. "Your father and I have been worried to death."

"I know, and I'm sorry. Did you get my text?"

"One text. One, and all it told me was that you were alive. Not how you were doing." She pushes the hair off my shoulder, tucks it behind an ear. "You look exhausted. Are you hungry?"

I could tell her I inhaled a Double Whopper and large fries on the way into town, but I don't. If Mom likes to express her love with food and hugs, who am I to complain? I nod and tell her I'm starving.

"But first I need to talk to Dad, okay?"

"Better scoot." She turns me around by the shoulders and nudges me in the direction of the hallway leading to the far end of the house. "He's been waiting, and not very patiently."

The general looks up when I come into his office, and I brace myself for fury and blame I don't find. Dad's long arms stay folded and relaxed on the polished cherry surface, his eyes soft and kind behind the tortoiseshell reading glasses perched on the bridge of his nose.

"Hi, Dad," I begin, then come up short.

The thing is, I know how to apologize for Jean and Ricky. I even know how to apologize for Victoria. But what I can't seem to come up with, what I can't seem to think of one single, miserable word for, is how to express my shame at believing Dad could be one of the bad guys. *I'm sorry* just isn't going to cut it. I open my mouth to say...what, I don't know, when he holds up a palm.

"Hold that thought, Abigail. I need to say something to you first." He motions to one of the cracked leather club chairs behind me, and I sink into it. "Do you remember that girl you used to ride the bus to school with?"

It takes me a beat or two to switch gears, and then another few to come up with her name; the last time I rode the school bus on a regular basis was middle school. "Katie Richardson," I tell him after a moment.

"That's her. I ran into her a few weeks ago at the grocery store. You wouldn't recognize her. She's grown into a beautiful woman. Tall, long legs, great smile. Quite the looker."

A smile sneaks up my face at his old-man description, as well as the knowledge that the laws of karma really do apply in Katie's case. Back when I knew her, she was, to put it politely, extremely unfortunate-looking. Pudgy and short, thick glasses, the world's worst fashion sense. But she was sweet, despite the torture the girls at school inflicted on her, and she had a wicked sense of humor. I liked her. She moved away the summer before seventh grade, and despite our tearful goodbye and the best of intentions, the two of us lost touch. I always wondered what became of her.

"She told me to tell you hi. She also told me to tell you she still owes you one, said you would know why." He pauses to regard me. "Do you?"

Uh, yeah. Dad's talking about the time in sixth grade Katie and I got caught playing hooky. We were both grounded for a month, even though our reason was, to us at least, perfectly valid.

A couple of girls at school who were just as evil as they were popular concocted a plan to fill her locker with a thousand pink, scented tampons. I got wind of it the afternoon before, when I overheard them giggling about how purple her face would turn when the avalanche of feminine products she did not yet need came tumbling to the ground. Too bad they forgot to check the stalls for anyone who might put a dent in their scheming.

I warned Katie the very next morning. When the bus dropped us off at school, the herd of kids turned right and Katie and I veered left, hoofing it a mile and a half to the mall.

We spent the day having perfume fights, trying on the biggest bras we could find and eating ice cream for lunch. We timed it just right, too, arriving at our homes at exactly the time the bus would have returned us there. And we would have gotten away with it, were it not for a nosy school nurse who called our mothers to see how we were feeling.

So, yes. Of course I remember.

"I couldn't understand at the time why you got so worked up about it. You were in sixth grade, for Pete's sake. How bad could it possibly be?"

"Pretty bad." I make a face. "Especially for Katie."

"Yes, well, my point is, knowledge is a powerful thing. You used your knowledge that day to do good, and for someone who needed a hand. Do you remember what you said when your mother and I sat you down that night?"

I try to shake loose the memory, but the only thing I can come up with is the injustice I felt at being punished for helping a friend. "Please, don't ground me?"

He smiles, just a whisper of a curve to his mouth, but not enough to detract from the point he's trying to drive home. "No, and we grounded you, all right. But I'll never forget the words you said to me that night. You said we could punish you all we wanted, but in your heart you knew what you did for that girl was the right thing."

If this were the movies, now would be the moment when the music swells, when the cameras pan out, when the heroine turns to one of them and busts through the third wall. That's what my father's words just did, busted through my internal third wall. I am still for a long moment, slowing my thoughts and listening to my own inner heroine tell the audience she gets it. She understands. Her father was punished for doing the right thing, too.

"You leaked the memo, didn't you?"

Dad's brows rise up his forehead, but he doesn't deny it.

"Of course you did. You had to. Gabe and I were getting too close. You were trying to distract us from Ricky."

Dad sighs and takes off his glasses, pinching at the two pink footprints they leave on the bridge of his nose. "It was more than that, sugar. Maybe one day I'll be able to talk more freely about it, but for now my reasons are still classified."

And that's when the full extent of my father's fall hits home. Dad knew exactly what he was doing all along. When he leaked that memo, he knew it would go public. In fact, he probably even predicted Victoria and I would be the ones to do it. Whether out of guilt or morality or for penance, my father sacrificed his reputation for Zach Armstrong's family.

I look across the desk at my father, at the familiarity of the lines fanning out from his hazel eyes, the dark stubble that hugs his jaw, the salt-and-pepper hair that never seems to need a cut. The sight of it breaks my heart just a little, but it also opens it up a little, too.

"Oh, Daddy…" I whisper. My tears mount without warning, as they've been doing ever since Portsmouth. "I'm so sorry. For everything. If I could go back and do it all over again, I'd do pretty much everything different."

"I appreciate that, darlin'." He smiles, and I can read the absolution all over his face. "I'm sorry, too. I should have been…I don't know, a little more specific in my warnings. I shouldn't have treated you like one of my subordinates. The only thing I won't apologize for is having you tailed. I hope you know it was for your own protection."

I grow an inch or two on the club chair. "Wait a minute. So Members Only guy *was* yours?"

"That son of a bitch who came after you and Rose?" Anger flickers over his expression, followed closely by something else, something I can't quite read. "Hell, no. You won't be seeing him anytime soon, I can guarantee you that much. Mine was a she, and she took out your tail long before you took off running."

"So who chased me, then?"

"Her name's Helen, and she says you could beat a Kenyan in a marathon. Even with Rose hanging around your neck, Helen could barely keep up. And by the way, should you ever feel the need to confess anything about that night to your brother, I will deny every word."

"What night?"

Dad smiles. "That's my girl." He leans back in his chair and regards me over the rim of his glasses. "Now, do you want to tell me what happened with Gabe?"

"It's a really long story."

"Then you better get comfortable."

I kick off my shoes, swing my feet under me on the chair and start at the very beginning, with running into Gabe that sunny Tuesday afternoon at Handyman, now coming up on two months ago. I tell him about the mysterious package a few days later on my doorstep, about my cocktails with Victoria, about my discovery of Ricky on the contractor casualty website and the awful story Gabe and I spun for his sister, Graciela. I tell him about the IHOP and the hotel, the hole Gabe punched in the wall, the long, silent drive to Eagle Rock, about Nick's cabin, the paintings, the hallucinations and flashbacks.

When I get to the part where Nick pointed a gun first at Gabe's chest, then up his own chin, Dad picks up the phone. He uses his general's voice, and the poor sucker on the other end is clearly someone trained to take orders, because he doesn't talk much and Dad's instructions don't take longer than a minute or two. Even from the half I hear, the gist is clear. There's a spot for Nick at Salem VA Medical Center, one of the best facilities around for veterans with PTSD.

And then Dad looks back at me, and his eyes go kind. "Now I need you to get Gabe on the line for me, darlin'."

I wriggle my phone from my pocket and dial the number. Gabe's voice, when he picks up two rings later, is flat and emotionless, and it brushes against my bruised, battered heart.

"Hey," he says and nothing else. Just *hey*.

I keep my words just as short and to the point.

"My father wants to talk to you," I say, then pass him the phone.

Mom's pulling a pan of pumpkin bread from the oven when I walk back into the kitchen. She holds it up with a grin, tilting it so I can see its perfectly browned top. "Pull up a chair, dear."

The bread's scent curls around me like a warm blanket, assaulting me with a heady mixture of nostalgia and regret. The visual of Gabe reaching across Starbucks cups and wrappers and taking my hand in his flashes behind my eyeballs, and the spicy-sweet smell of Mom's bread turns sour in my stomach. Suddenly, all I want is a long, hard cry in the privacy of my own bed.

"Actually, can we do this another time? I haven't showered or slept in what feels like a week, and I'm—"

"Sit down, Abigail," she says in that don't-argue-with-me voice I remember from my high school days.

I pull out a bar stool and sit down.

Once she's satisfied I'm settled in to stay, she takes her time removing the bread from the pan, humming as she lays it on a rectangular platter and dusts it with powdered sugar. Finally, when everything is just so, she plates two generous slices and passes one to me. And then she rounds the island and climbs onto the bar stool next to me.

"Now that you've mended fences with your father, I thought you and I could have a little chat of our own."

"Okay." The word comes out like silly putty, long and stretched thin. The best thing to do when Mom's on one of her missions is hold on and hope for the best. I break a corner off my bread, pop it in my mouth and grab on to the counter with both hands. "What about?"

"Well, why don't we start with why you look so pitiful and lovesick, and then I'll fill you in on all the things your father couldn't say."

Her words zap me like a taser, sticking my breath in my lungs and melting my backside to the stool. Not so much that she knows about me and Gabe; Mom always could read my emotions as she did one of her cookbooks—easily and with practiced skill. I'm more surprised she knows what Dad and I had to discuss. What happened to top secret and need-to-know? To duty, honor, country? Why would he tell his wife and not his daughter, when I was the one peeling back the lid of the box, spilling out the secrets, releasing all the evils?

"Were you listening at the door or something?"

Mom laughs as if I told a joke, even though I'm beginning to suspect the joke's on me. "Thirty-seven years I've been married to that man, and I've been finishing his sentences for longer than that. I don't have to listen at the door to know what he's in there telling you, and what he's holding back. Now tell me about Gabe, dear."

"It's a pretty depressing story, actually." I inch my plate toward the center of the counter, try to staunch my tears by looking up at the ceiling. When it doesn't work, Mom passes me a paper napkin. "A classic tragedy."

She rests a hand on my arm and regards me. "Gabe has a lot going on. A lot of pressures."

I nod, catching her meaning immediately. Gabe is the

strongest man I know, yet he carries the heaviest imaginable burden to bear. And I'm the one who led him to it.

I think of all the things I should have done in that hotel room. Slip the blog entry under the covers, bury it under the pillows, flush it down the toilet and sweep it into oblivion. Anything but allow him to take it from my hands. Now, thanks to me, Gabe is guarding a secret no brother should *ever* have to keep. I did that to him.

"Oh, sweetie…" she says, wrapping her palm around mine, looking at me as if she understands, and if so, she's the only one. I'm still trying to wrap my head around how Gabe can say such beautiful words to me one moment, then make such horrible accusations the next.

"Maybe it's better this way," I say, the tears flowing freely now. "I mean, I know what I want of Gabe, but I'm not sure it's anywhere near the neighborhood of what he's able to give me." I lift a shoulder, trying not to look completely pitiful. "Too much has happened for him this past year."

"Give him some time, Abigail. He's got a lot to work through. Big, life-changing issues. He's going to have to work through them before he can move forward with you or anyone else." She pauses to give me a kind smile. "He'll come around."

I want to tell her she is being overly optimistic. That his face, the way he ducked his head and avoided my eyes this morning in Eagle Rock, made things more than clear. That I, myself, betrayer of trust and bearer of bad news, am one of the issues Gabe must work through. That no amount of space or time could heal the hole learning the truth must have ripped through his heart. I want to tell her all of this, but I don't, mostly because I so profoundly, desperately, painfully want to believe her.

Mom pats my arm as if she understands. "My turn?"

I nod and give her a shaky laugh. "Please, distract me."

"Okay. Your uncle Chris is a sneaky son of a bitch and a pompous ass. How's that for distraction?"

Considering the fact that Mom never cusses, pretty damn effective. My tears dry up with the shock of it. "Are you referring to the tail Chris put on me? The one who came after me and Rose?"

It's not a long stretch to make. When my father refused to claim Members Only man as his tail, that left just one other general he could belong to.

Mom nods. "Yes, and that phone call from you and Rose almost sent your father over the edge. But I'm also talking about the transcript. Both things had nothing to do with you, and everything to do with Chris and your father. Do you understand what I'm saying to you?"

I think about her words for a beat or two, but it doesn't take much longer for the meaning to drop. "So by getting me involved, Chris was sending Dad a message?"

"Bingo. Your father still has a lot of important people's ears, and Chris wanted him to back off, to let him handle the Armstrongs. From the start, Chris has been the motor behind this whole mess. I swear, that man would still be running all over town, hawking Zach's story as his own personal PR campaign if your father hadn't stopped him. That memo of his was effective in stopping Chris, but it came with a whole host of unintended consequences."

"Like early retirement?" I think of how it came up out of nowhere, how he explained it away with a wish to go on trips he never took, how ever since he whiles his days away by moving bushes around the backyard.

"Like early retirement," Mom confirms. "He didn't have much of a choice after that memo."

An overwhelming sadness surges in my chest. My father didn't just sacrifice his reputation for Zach Armstrong, he sacrificed the career he loved, and walked away from the organization he'd spent his entire life serving.

Talk about duty, honor, country.

"The truth was supposed to be the end," I say, reaching for my napkin to staunch a fresh wave of tears. "It was supposed to give everybody closure."

Mom sighs, loud and long. "Sweetheart, that's what makes a tragedy a tragedy. There's no rhyme or reason to it, only heartbreak. The only thing you can do once the ground stops shaking and the waters recede is try to save whoever's left."

27

The next few days are a blur. I barely eat, I sleep in fits and starts, I lose all sense of time. I cry until I think I have no more tears to shed, and then I cry some more. I stare at my phone, which lights up often but with all the wrong numbers. The digits on my voice mail and text icons climb well into the forties. I ignore all of them.

But I do finish the bathroom.

I work like a woman possessed, grouting the tile, installing the vanity, cutting and fitting the moldings. I seal, I sand, I paint. I hang towel holders and toilet roll holders and mirrors, put down candles and soaps, mop and scrub and polish until fatigue burns like cinders in every inch of my body. And then I peel off my filthy clothes and stand under the showerhead for what feels like a week, until my skin is wrinkled and red, until the water turns lukewarm, then cool, then frigid, until my teeth are chattering hard enough to chip a filling.

A door slams, and Mandy's voice floats up the stairs. "Abigail?"

I shut off the water, wrap my shivering body in a towel. "Up here."

Her heels make dull thwacks on the hallway hardwoods, pausing every now and then to check a room, then finally, stepping through the bathroom door. She's still in her coat, still clutching the stack of mail she must have pulled from my mailbox, a good week's worth of flyers and catalogs and envelopes, to her chest.

She takes me in, shivering and wet and dripping onto my brand-new bath mat. "You do know I called you, like, a thousand times, right?"

I nod.

"And that I left increasingly frantic voice mails, the last of which saying I was on the way to the police station to file a missing-persons report?"

I duck my chin into the terry-cloth towel.

"You didn't listen to them. Of course you didn't." She sighs, tossing the mail onto the sink. "Do you want to talk about it?"

She knows, of course, about Gabe and me, about my growing feelings for him, about how we found Ricky and were in touch with Graciela. I told her everything, all the way up to the morning that Gabe and I motored down to Portsmouth. The rest—what happened with Ricky, with Nick and Zach— is not my secret to tell.

I shake my head.

She shrugs as if she couldn't care either way, but I can tell it's a front. Mandy believes in doing things, fixing things, changing things. Whatever things I don't *tell* her, she can't help me mend. She doesn't like it, but she lets it go.

She focuses her attention on my bathroom instead, doing a slow loop around the room, admiring the sparkling tile and inhaling the new-paint smell, running her fingers over the white porcelain of my sink, the walls, the brushed nickel hardware. And then she's standing back in front of me, looking impressed.

"You did all this yourself?"

"All except the plumbing and the shower." I gesture to the shower pan Gabe told me how to build, tucked behind a thick plate of glass jutting up from the ledge. He was right; it *is* perfect. The height of the lip, the slight pitch of the floor, the way the water rolls right into the drain. "That was his idea."

Mandy gives me an I'm-not-touching-that-one look, gestures to the first thing her gaze lands on. "I like the pebble backsplash. Nice touch."

"Thanks." I try to sound as if I mean it, but my voice is dull and detached, kind of like Gabe's *hey*. It slices through my mind, reminding me that he still hasn't called, still hasn't texted, still hasn't *anything*, and I wince.

Mandy shakes her head, and she looks at me so tenderly it makes my eyes sting. "Throw on some clothes and meet me downstairs."

"Where are we going?"

She turns and disappears out the door, calling out from halfway down the hallway. "To get you good and drunk."

Alone again in the bathroom, I notice the envelope.

Actually, scratch that. It's not the envelope that I notice sticking out of the pile of mail, but the neat block handwriting that spells out my name and address across the front. The fat, round letters, the way they tip to the left. I've seen those letters before. I know whose hand wrote them.

Maria Duncan.

I check the date on the stamp. October 28, a little over a week ago. I rip open the envelope's gummy seal and reach my hand inside, closing my fingers around cool metal. A key, silver and so nondescript that it could be for just about anything, and a hot-pink USB stick. I peer inside the package and find nothing more.

If I were still a journalist, I would call this my lucky break, that pivotal moment when a story cracks wide-open. I would race to my computer, pound out a story, file it with Victoria and watch my byline light up the internet sky. Instead, I pull on a bathrobe, carry everything downstairs, slip the stick into my laptop and wait for whatever Maria wanted to tell me.

A table of contents pops onto my screen, and I scroll through what must be twenty different files.

"What's this?" Mandy says, and a glass of clear liquid on the rocks appears over my left shoulder. I take the drink and click on the first file.

"Amateur porn." It was a guess, but it's the right one. The video opens with a close-up of her naked torso, then jerks back for a wider shot. For about ten seconds, the image stops just under her neck, and then…full frontal of her face, glossy lips and plastic-doll eyes.

"Is that—"

"Maria Duncan," I finish. "Otherwise known as Maisie Daniels."

Mandy leans in closer to the screen. "Holy shit. Her boobs are—"

"Ginormous," I interrupt again, Ben's word rolling off my tongue. There's really no other word that does them any sort of justice. "I know."

"Your job is so much more interesting than mine." Mandy pulls up a chair and settles in next to me. "I feel like we should have popcorn or something."

I snort and take a long pull of my drink, and God bless her, it's a stiff one. The vodka hits my empty stomach and bursts into a welcome cloud of warmth.

Maria's costar says something from offscreen, and it takes

me a second or two to realize I understood him. This is the
unedited, uncut version of the clip. No Darth Vader voices,
no blurred-out faces. So Maria wants to show me who's been
financing her lifestyle. I lean back in my chair, sip my vodka
and soda, and watch.

The first two are men I recognize from the social pages
of newspapers. Mandy comes up with their names, and they
sound vaguely familiar in my ears. Playboys, and from what
she knows of them, not very wealthy ones. Maria quickly
moves on to bigger fish. Politicians, businessmen, athletes.
It's like watching Maria climb a social ladder of progressively
influential and wealthy men. Naked men, and it strikes me
that most do not live up to their illustrious reputations. I snort
and polish off my drink.

After about the fifth or sixth clip, Mandy ducks into the
kitchen to refresh our drinks. I keep my eyes on my computer screen, but I'm only half watching. I'm more focused
on the key, and what's behind the door that it opens. Money,
most likely, but where? And why does she want me to have
access to it?

"Why are we still watching these?" Mandy says when she
returns. "If we're going to watch porn, let's at least pay for
the good stuff."

I pluck my drink from her fingers. "I'm still waiting for
Maria's message."

"Which is?"

"I have no idea."

And I really don't. Why would Maria send these to me?
What is she trying to tell me? I pick up the envelope and check
inside again. Nothing. No note, no card telling me what the
key's for. I go back to the table of contents, scroll through the
files again. All video files. I click on the next one, working
my way down the list, watching and waiting for her message,

but by now the vodka is clogging my brain, and I'm having trouble stringing thoughts together. What is Maria trying to say? What does she want? What's her message?

Message! The image of my voice mail icon, its little number ticking up, up, up, flashes across my mind, and I sit back with a gasp.

"What?" Mandy says.

I dig my phone from my bag on the floor and scroll through the voice mails until I find the ones I'm looking for. The ones with a string of numbers my cell phone doesn't pair up with a contact name.

"Oh, *now* you're going to listen to your voice mails?" Mandy rolls her eyes. "Figures."

I start with the oldest and work my way forward. "Hi, Abigail, this is Nathalie calling from Bloomingdale's. Friends and Family starts this—"

I delete it without listening to the rest, scroll to the next string of numbers.

"Oh, my," Mandy says, pointing to the screen. "Do you think she does yoga? She's very bendy."

"Shh," I tell her, putting the phone back to my ear.

As soon as I hear her voice, high and breathy, every atom in my body goes completely still.

"Abigail, hi. It's Maria... Duncan, in case you were wondering. Surprise!" A high-pitched giggle. "Anyway, by now you should have received the package I sent you. At least, I hope you've gotten it. The memory stick is pretty self-explanatory, but the other item...well, I'd really rather not talk about that in a voice mail, so, please, call me. 443-555-4303. I need to talk to you in person."

"Holy mother of God," Mandy says, her voice breathy and low.

With shaking fingers, I move on to the next.

"Me again. Maria. I haven't heard back from you, and I'm starting to get a little worried. Scratch that, I'm a lot worried. Are you still mad at me? Is that what this is about? Because now is not the time to be holding grudges. Now is the time to be calling me back." A long pause, then, "I think I might be in trouble."

"Seriously, Abby," Mandy says. "You need to see this."

I swivel my chair to give Mandy my back, then click on the next one, working my way through the rest—seven in all. In each message, her tone becomes increasingly frantic, and she sounds more and more...loony. Certifiably insane. A slightly hysterical tinge to her voice, the words wild and at breakneck speed. How did I never hear it before?

Finally, I reach the last of them, this one from five days ago.

"I will not stand for this. I will not be ignored. Are you not appreciative of everything I did for you? I put your name on the front page of every news website there was. I made you viral. And this is how you thank me? Not everything is about you. This is about married men using *me*, using *my* body in every possible way, for their sick, disgusting, perverted pleasures, so stop judging me and *call me motherfucking back*!" She puffs a trio of sharp breaths that seem to calm her voice by a thousand degrees. "No. You know what? Never mind. I'm over it, and I'm over you. I want my key back."

I'm going back to listen to them all over again when Mandy latches on to my arm and physically turns me around on my chair. "Abby, look at the screen."

That's when I hear another voice, a male voice drifting up from my laptop speakers, and I don't have to look at my screen to know. I hear his moans and grunts and dirty talk, and I want to cover my ears so I don't.

I recognize his voice. I recognize his face. I recognize everything about him.

The man on my screen is Uncle Chris.

28

The vodka is slowing me down. It's making my limbs heavy and useless, sticking my ass to the leather seat of my swivel chair with superglue. Even my jaw is malfunctioning, hanging from my head like a broken branch. *Close your mouth*, my mother would say. *You'll catch flies.*

I stare at the flickering images on my computer screen and try to make sense of what I'm seeing, but my normally sharp brain cells laze around in my skull. And every time I manage to corral them into a coherent thought, it's this one: Maria and Chris. Maria and *Chris*! My married, father-of-two godfather-slash-honorary-uncle, the one who changed my diapers and bounced me on his knee, who taught me card tricks and introduced me to bluegrass music, who took me skydiving when I turned eighteen and bought me my first beer when I turned twenty-one, is a lying, cheating pervert.

And now I've seen him naked.

"What is going on here?" Mandy says. "Why did Maria send you all these videos? Does she know Chris is your uncle?"

"I don't know."

After everything I've learned these past few days, I suppose I shouldn't be so confused, shouldn't feel so shocked. I shouldn't have to sit here in the glow of my computer screen, hearing their voices, seeing *both* their faces, watching their bodies twist and contort in order to believe. I shouldn't, and probably it's the vodka, but it takes watching the video three entire times, from beginning all the way to the end, before I do.

I freeze the video screen, switch over to Skype, click on the number for Floyd. He and I have never Skyped before, but his number comes up on my screen, and I don't want to use my cell. I want to keep it free in case I need to play Maria's voice mails for him.

The line connects, and a handsome-ish face fills my screen. "Floyd?"

"No offense, hon," he says, and it's Floyd, all right, "but I had higher hopes for you. You look like you just got home from a three-day bender."

"And you look so much better than I expected."

I was right about Floyd's computer-geek look, wrong about pretty much everything else. His blond hair is neat and stylish, his jawline long and lean as a marathon runner's. And judging from his clothes, a designer polo and horn-rimmed glasses just this side of ironic, he doesn't live in anybody's basement.

"Why does everyone assume that just because a guy's a computer genius, he's a fat slob, living in a filthy frat house with a bunch of other fat slobs, drinking beer and playing video games all day long?"

"Mostly because every time I talk to you, you're drinking beer and playing video games. And I thought it was your mother's basement."

He presses a hand to his chest and winces dramatically. "Ouch."

"I'm not alone. This is my friend Mandy." I pull Mandy's head closer to mine, and she waves into the camera. "She knows about Maria, too."

Floyd gets a load of Mandy, and his brows slide up his forehead. "Well, hello there, Mandy."

"She's married," I say, moving us right along to the point of this call. "In the interest of time, I should tell you I haven't listened to any of your voice mails. Start at the beginning."

His lips spread into an I'm-the-man grin. "Hon, all you need to know is Wesley Wainright IV."

"The former senator?"

"The former senator's *son*, and the sick-ass who was porking Maria. And when I say porking, I mean porking. The dude's a total pig."

It makes sense. The Wainrights hold the kind of prestige that wouldn't do well with a scandalous sex tape floating around the internet, and they have enough money—the kind of wealth that goes back to the Gilded Age and includes textile and railroad empires if I'm not mistaken—that nobody would miss a briefcase or two full of cash. And lately, rumors have been swirling that the former senator is preparing for a bid for the White House. I imagine he'd pay just about anything to keep his son's pornographic trysts off YouTube.

I turn to Mandy. "Did we see Wesley on the videos?"

"No, but there are at least three or four more to go."

And that's when Floyd's message hits me. "Wait. How do you know it's Wesley? I thought you said the transactions were all cash."

"They were. Maria's a smart cookie and she hid the cash well, which means unless one of her donors comes forward..." He lets the words trail off, but I don't need to hear it. He's telling me the cash is untraceable. "But I don't like dead ends, so I followed her. I saw them."

"Porking?" Mandy and I say in unison.

Floyd laughs at either our use of his word or the way we lean into the camera with identical, wide-eyed expressions. "No, not porking. Making the exchange. But I knew it was him because of the finger."

"What are you talking about?" I shake my head, still not understanding. Mandy looks just as clueless as I am. "What finger?"

Floyd rolls his eyes. "Jesus, girl, it's been all over the news. Where the hell have you been?"

"Virginia," I say, knowing it's not the answer he was looking for, not wanting to detract from the bigger question at hand. "What finger?"

He is silent for a moment or two, and I hear rapid-fire clicking of his keyboard and mouse, and suddenly I'm looking at a split screen—half Floyd, half his internet browser. He types a website address into his browser.

While the video is loading, Floyd tells us that sometime in the past week, while I was busy doing whatever I was doing in Virginia, a handful of new clips made their way onto the internet, all of them starring Maria and Wesley Wainright IV.

"How do you know it's him?" I say. The man's face is blurred beyond recognition.

"I already told you, hon. Because of the finger."

I search out the man's hands, but both of them are tucked behind Maria's naked thigh.

But unfortunately for me and Mandy and everyone else with working eyeballs, everything else about him is in clear, sharp focus. Wesley's sexual tastes are perverted and violent and dip way into repulsive territory, and though I'm not the squeamish type, there are more than a few parts Mandy and I cover our eyes for. Floyd is right; the dude's a total pig.

And then Floyd holds up a long finger. "Wait for it. Wait for it…"

At just the right moment, he taps his mouse and the picture goes still. He instructs us to look at the lower left corner of the screen, where the man's hand clamps onto Maria's breast in a way that can't be even remotely pleasurable. Less like a fondle, more like a five-fingered vise. Only, one of them, his right ring finger, is shorter than all the others, cut off at the second knuckle.

Floyd leans back in his chair. "Boating accident, the summer after his freshman year in college. He's lucky he didn't bleed out. His blood alcohol level was .21, and that's not even taking into account the pot and cocaine."

"Okay, so he's a pervert with a drug and alcohol problem. So?"

"So one of his fraternity brothers drowned that day, but somehow, despite the alcohol and drugs, despite them all being underage, the police never pressed charges. Why do you think that is?"

"Because he's a Wainright."

"Ding, ding, ding." He reaches for his mouse and hits Play, and the clip starts up again. "But not even a Wainright can get Wesley out of this one."

At first I assume he means the awful images blowing up the internet and my computer screen and how Maria is using them to finance her ostentatious new lifestyle, but something about his expression grows spider legs that creep up my spine.

"Get Wesley out of what?"

"They arrested him this morning for murder."

"Of?" I say, even though I already know. Even though I'm already reaching for the desk, bracing myself for his answer.

"Maria Duncan. Who else?"

★ ★ ★

Autumn returns that weekend for its final hurrah of the year. Crisp air, blue skies and sunshine light up the trees with leaves of red and orange. I stay inside every second of it, glued to my computer screen, watching for news of Maria.

Wesley confesses on a bright Saturday morning to a flurry of cameras and Google hits, all of which catalog a long line of evidence pulled from his basement. His *basement*. Poor Maria. Her tragedy began and ended in a dark, damp basement.

His lawyers schedule a press conference that nobody pays any attention to because eight hundred miles away, an explosion at a fireworks facility blows a crater into a residential neighborhood north of Milwaukee. An entire city block and all the people in it gone, blown to bits. A death toll in the hundreds and climbing amid allegations of bribery and misconduct and idiocy in the form of a lunatic with a cigarette.

And Chris's name is never mentioned. Not any of the other names from the videos Maria sent me, either, which means Maria was too busy getting the life squeezed out of her by Wesley Wainright IV to alert the media to any of the other men financing her lifestyle.

But surely I'm not the only one who knows about the videos.

I imagine by now the police have combed every inch of Maria's apartment for evidence. They would have fired up her computer, found the video files and cataloged them as exhibit A. They would have sniffed out the money trails, followed them to expensive brownstones and penthouse condominiums all over the District. Maybe they're keeping quiet on purpose, trying to build their case without media interference. Or maybe now that the attention has moved on to bigger, more explosive topics, the media has simply stopped caring.

Whatever the reason, I can't stop thinking about her. I've

played and replayed her messages a million times. I've taken notes, transcribed every word to paper, searched behind every letter for clues. Every time, every single time, I end up coming back to that one sentence: *I think I might be in trouble.* Did she call me looking for help? To keep her safe from harm? Why send me the videos, as collateral? For safekeeping? Did she want me to expose her partners, show the world whose faces were behind the blurred-out pixels, or did she want me to protect her from them? Now that she's dead, I'll probably never know the answers.

Or for that matter, where she stashed the money.

I took the key to one of my old detective contacts, who in an ironic twist traced it back to Handyman Market. How strange to think that Gabe could have been the one who sold it to her, could have been the one to tell her this particular lock, a commercial-grade shroud padlock, is practically indestructible, which is why every self-storage facility in town recommends it for theirs. I picture the pile of cash Maria must have amassed by now, gathering dust behind a roll door somewhere, and the look on the face of that particular *Storage Wars* winner. If only Maria had told me which storage facility, then maybe I could get to that money first and use it to help her brother, Matthew. He's the real tragedy here. With Maria no longer paying his bills, he's being transferred to a state facility for the indigent in early January.

But all my efforts have led to exactly nowhere, and in the end, I'm left holding the key—literally—to a mystery.

A few days later, on Veteran's Day, I'm curled up on the couch, channel surfing, when Gabe's clean-shaven face flashes across my television screen. Seeing him feels like a punch to the gut, especially when I see the rest. His banker's suit and tie, his mother and Nick hovering at either elbow, their solemn expressions. I lurch to a sit and stab at the volume button until Gabe's voice throbs in my ears.

"My brother Zach was the best man I ever knew," he says to a million flashing bulbs and mugging microphones. "He was honest and loyal. He was compassionate and sincere. He was brilliant and brave and a hero long before he stepped onto the battlefield. He was the glue that held our family together, and without him, we are left with an ache in our hearts and a void in our souls that nothing will ever be able to fill."

Nick drops his head and sobs into his chest, and Jean reaches around Gabe's back for his hand.

"If Zach were here now," Gabe says, and though his eyes are shiny, his voice never wavers, "he would hate everything about this investigation. He would tell us to get back to mourning our loss instead of pointing fingers and assigning responsibility for his death. He would tell us to look forward instead of back, to let go and forgive, to heal as a family and as a country. The best way for us to honor his memory is by honoring his wishes, which is why we're dropping the charges against the US Army, effective immediately."

And just like that, the Zach Armstrong case is closed.

I lie awake that night in my bed, alone and achy and confused. My ears strain in the dim light of my bedroom, listening for familiar old-house moans, but all I can hear are Mom's words to me in the kitchen playing on a constant loop through my head.

There's no rhyme or reason to a tragedy, only heartbreak.

Maybe Mom is right. Maybe there is no rhyme or reason to the string of disastrous events that ended in Zach's death, but to Chelsea and Maria? I wrote a story that resulted in not one but two people's deaths. I am that person. It will take some getting used to.

But what about all the others? The people in my wake, the survivors, those left standing in the wreckage and half buried under the rubble. Ben and his father. Gabe and Jean and Nick. Maybe now it should be about stitching and dressing their wounds, about finding some way to give them comfort while their bones and skin and hearts knit back together. I keep talking about rehabbing my karma, about repaying my debt to the universe. Maybe this is the way.

So for now, lying here in the light of a new day, I will stop asking the wrong questions—how did this happen, who seduced whom, who pulled the trigger? For now, the most important questions are these:

What now?

What's next?

Where do we go from here?

29

The bell rings at Baltimore Montessori Public Charter School, and I push off the wall to the left of the double doors, watching for Ben. A familiar mop-headed, stick-figure kid emerges moments later, blinking into the bright November sunshine, searching me out of the bodies milling around on the stoop. I straighten, lifting an arm in a wave, and he pushes through the crowd.

"Sorry," I say, glancing over to where a couple of his classmates are clustered, their heads pressed together, watching us with open curiosity. "I should have suggested a better place to meet."

"It's all good." Ben shoves at his bangs with a palm, but they fall right back over his eyes. "I think you're upping my coolness quotient."

I smile and steer us away from the crowd and along the street. Neither of us talks as we make the trek down a few blocks. He breathes hard and quick through his mouth, eyes fixed straight ahead, and his obvious discomfort makes me even more nervous about what I came here to say. I hope I don't screw this up, screw this kid up forever.

We slow on a quieter, residential block of plain brick town houses with wide sidewalks and yawning sets of stairs. I point to the first ones we come to, suggest we take a seat.

"Is this about Maria getting killed?" Ben asks as we're getting settled. "Because I watch the news. Some rich guy strangled her, and then he dumped her in the river."

"This isn't about Maria. Well, actually it is a little, but it's more about your mom." I wipe my palms down the thighs of my jeans, swallow a spiky lump in my throat. "I came here to apologize."

Ben's gaze hitches on my face. "How come?"

"Because a good journalist knows when there's something wrong. Even if they can't quite put their finger on it, they know. When Maria came to me with the story of her and your mom, I knew there was something she wasn't telling me. I had a feeling her reasons for going public with the story had more to them than just charging your mother with sexual harassment, but I pushed my doubts aside. I was so focused on the byline, I didn't pay attention to that squirming in my gut. I didn't do my job, and your mom died because of it."

Ben falls quiet for a long moment, chewing a raw spot on his bottom lip, his mouth twisting into a scrunch. He's fidgety and nervous, and he seems as if he's working through something momentous. I give him all the time he needs. A car whizzes past, sending a tornado of trash and leaves circling up into the air, then falling back to the ground.

"My shrink says it wasn't anybody's fault." His voice is high and squeaky as if he's about to cry, which makes me feel as if I'm about to cry, too. "He says Mom's mind wasn't healthy, and it clouded her thinking. He says what happened had nothing to do with anybody but her, because she couldn't see any other way out of her situation than by killing herself."

"That's all true. But I'm the one who put her in a situation she couldn't find her way out of."

"I thought Maria did that."

"Okay, then. I'm the one who told the world about it."

He stares down at his denim Chucks, and I see tears snagging in his lashes. I wonder briefly if that's his reason for wearing his hair so long, so that people don't see him cry, and the possibility makes me incredibly sad.

He wipes his eyes on a sleeve. "I don't know... I'm still mostly pissed at Mom for leaving the way she did. For not loving me enough to stay."

"You just told me her death had nothing to do with you."

He looks at me through a slit in his bangs. "I told you my *shrink* said that, not that I believed him."

I give him a sad smile he doesn't return.

"I hate Maria for what she did. *Hate* her. I'm *glad* she's dead. I know it's wrong to say that about another human being, especially one who was murdered, but my shrink says I'm allowed to feel rage."

"I imagine most people would in your position."

"So, why do you think she did it? Maria, I mean. Why do you think she went after my mom?"

"I don't know. Maybe she liked her, or maybe she was looking for attention. Now that Maria's dead, we might never know her reasons. But honestly, does it really matter why she did it? I mean, I get that you're pissed and it probably feels good to have someone to blame, but I guess all I'm saying is, is your anger helping you or holding you back?"

The look he gives me is exasperated, and maybe a little annoyed. "It's not like I have a choice or anything. I don't want to feel so angry. I'm *sick* of feeling so angry. I just want to go

THE ONES WE TRUST   271

to the movies and laugh and feel normal again. I want that more than anything."

His words hit me at a cellular level. Switch out *angry* for *guilty*, and Ben's words could have been mine. I don't want to feel so guilty. I'm *sick* of feeling so guilty. It occurs to me that we're not so different, Ben and I. We both have to find a way to live with what happened, a way to swim for shore.

"A very smart woman once told me that anger can feel like a life buoy, like it's the only thing keeping you afloat. But that in order to heal, you have to let go."

He looks up with a start, and I can tell Jean's message has struck a chord with him, too. "Let go. That's it? Just...let go?"

I nod. "Let go and swim for shore."

He thinks about it for a long time, his brow scrunching in concentration. Then, finally, he says, "Okay." That's it. Just *okay*. I don't ask whether his okay is an *I'll try* okay, or a *Shut up and leave me alone* okay, or a *Whatever you say, lady* okay. This is a journey he's going to have to make on his own. I can only pray that, sooner or later, he'll get there.

Instead, I say, "I'm sorry I couldn't give you the answers you were looking for."

He shrugs. "It was a long shot anyway. Even if Maria could still talk, she didn't seem like the type to ever admit to anything."

"You know your mom better than just about anyone. Why do *you* think she got involved with Maria?"

I'm probably overstepping every boundary imaginable by asking something so personal, and of a kid I really scarcely know, but who could have ever imagined such a situation? It's not like either of us is working from a rule book here. Ben is not your average twelve-year-old kid, and I've never been an objective bystander. After everything that's happened to bring me and Ben to this particular stoop, after all the sorry ways I was mixed up in his tragedy, I want him to be okay. I *need* him to be.

"Is this like one of those *the answer lies inside you* Jedi mind tricks? Because, believe me, it doesn't. I've asked myself that question a million trillion times, and the only answer I can come up with is I don't know. *I don't fucking know.*"

He's clearly miffed, so I let it go. We sit there for a moment in painful silence, and then I wipe my palms on my jeans, push to a stand. "I should go."

Ben nods, but he doesn't otherwise move. He looks up at me through his bangs. "She used to tell me she loved me to the moon and back, like, all the time. I'd like to think she wouldn't leave me for anything less than that kind of love." He shrugs, the gesture an apology. "Maybe if I say it enough, I'll start believing it."

I don't say anything for a long moment, afraid it will come out all wrong or too pie-in-the-sky to be anywhere near right. Later, I know, I'll come up with a million things I should have said, but for now the best I can think of is, "You seem awfully self-aware for a twelve-year-old."

"Nah, I'm pretty fucked up."

I laugh. "Join the club, kid."

Ben ducks his head, but I catch a grin twitching at the corners of his lips. "I can get you the number for a pretty decent shrink if you want."

Another cold afternoon, another crowded stoop. This time it's the steps of the Lincoln Memorial.

I don't immediately pick Chris out of the throngs of tourists milling about in puffy winter gear, but I know he's here somewhere, and I know this is part of his schtick. Making me wait gives him the appearance of the upper hand, and for now I let him have it. I select a spot on the freezing-cold steps, burrow down into my down-lined peacoat and wait.

Seven and a half minutes later, he sinks down onto the step beside me and gives me a one-armed hug. "Hey, cupcake."

Uncle Chris is in his civilians, something that surprises me at the same time as it doesn't. When he suggested we meet here, at such a public spot, I figured he suspected it was because of something having to do with the Armstrongs, and he wanted the anonymity of a crowd. A general's uniform isn't exactly designed to blend in. But Uncle Chris should have stuck to his service uniform. It does a better job at disguising his widening middle than his turtleneck and pleated slacks are doing.

"Thanks for meeting me." By now I'm shivering, more from nerves than the icy wind blowing up from the Potomac. "I know you're busy."

"Never too busy for my goddaughter." His smile is broad and white, and I don't believe it for a second. "So, what's this urgent matter you wanted to discuss?"

So far we're both keeping our tones warm and pleasant, but I suspect neither of us are harboring any notions this meeting will be either. After slipping me a top secret document, after having me tailed and chased through a suburban neighborhood, Chris has to know whatever I brought him here to say can't be good.

"My father seems to think the tail and the transcript were a message."

Surprise flashes across his expression before he wipes it clean. "Oh? And you don't?"

I shake my head. "I think they were a mission. I think you wanted me to find Ricky."

"I don't know what you're talking about," he says, but in an overly patient voice. Uncle Chris knows *exactly* what I'm talking about, and he knows I'm onto him. He looks out over the sea of tourists and the reflecting pond beyond. On the opposite end, the Washington Monument reaches tall and majestic up from the ground, like a giant finger poking at low-hanging clouds.

"It must be so hard," I say, following his gaze, "being surrounded by all those heroes, watching them come home to parades and ceremonies. Meanwhile, nobody's waving a flag for you. Nobody's giving you a medal. They're just screaming at you to get them out. To bring our soldiers home."

He turns to me with a tight-lipped smile. "You're playing with fire here, cupcake. Say what you mean to say."

"Okay. What I mean to say is, when word of who shot Zach Armstrong gets out, when somebody leaks that little news flash to the world, if you play your cards right, you could look like the hero for keeping the shooter's identity a secret all this time. You could be all like, *we sure made a mess of things, but those poor Armstrongs, we did it for their own good.* Just think how noble you'd look. How heroic."

And this is what has kept me awake for much of the past week, my stomach twisted in knots. Because if Uncle Chris gave me a copy of that transcript, what's to stop him from slipping it to someone else now that I haven't taken the bait? Maybe he already has. After all, now that my father's retired, who's there to stop him?

"You think I made a mess of things on purpose?"

"No. I think you made a mess of things because you were using Zach Armstrong's death as the army's personal PR campaign. If you hadn't, Jean never would have raised such a fuss, and my father wouldn't have been forced to retire from a job he loved, because he hated everything about how you were handling a family's tragedy more."

His brows slam together, and his mouth twists. "You don't

know what you're talking about, little girl. The US military is one of the strongest, most respected brands in the world. Our soldiers appear in ads for everything from the NFL and NBA to beers and cars and nonprofits. They don't get paid for their participation. They don't get a lick of credit, other than maybe fifteen minutes of fame. Corporal Armstrong is no different. He knew what he was getting into when he enlisted."

My father's words roll right off my tongue. "Just because something's the truth, Uncle Chris, that doesn't make it right."

He heaves a disgusted sigh and starts to push to his feet. "We're done here. You're wasting my time."

"Wait." I latch on to his sleeve, pulling him back down to the cold steps, and hand him my phone. "You haven't seen the best part."

He frowns down at my phone, looking at it as if he's suddenly discovered a turd resting on his palm. "What the hell's this?"

I lean in, unlock the screen and push Play. "This is tomorrow's front-page news."

Within seconds, Chris's loud "Suck it, baby" slices through the tourists' chatter. Shocked faces swing our way, and I can't deny a stab of glee at the look of utter panic that swallows his expression, the way he startles so hard the phone almost pops out of his fumbling fingers. "Jesus! Turn this goddamn thing down, would you?"

I reach over and calmly lower the volume until it's not quite so booming but still loud enough for everyone within a five-foot radius to hear. His moans, the smacks of his palm against Maria's bare skin, his many enthusiastic compliments, over and over and over, of how "nasty" she likes it. At the twenty-third second, their bodies shift, and the camera focuses on an image so crisp you can count the stubble hairs on Uncle Chris's face.

He flings the phone at me. "Turn it off. You've made your point."

"I have so many questions, not the least of which is Maria Duncan. *Really?* Surely you have better intel than that, or were you so hot to get her out of her clothes that you skipped the background check? Did you not recognize her? How much did you have to pay—"

His words come out in a spray of furious spittle. "Turn it off!"

I fiddle with the screen until it goes dark and quiet, and then I slip the phone back in my coat pocket. Granted, I've had more time than Chris to get used to the video, the fact that for whatever reason, Maria sent me an unedited copy, the idea I can use it as leverage. Poor Chris is still trying to get a handle on the situation, still trying to figure out how to shut it down before his career implodes on an even more spectacular note than my father's.

"So," I begin, "now that we're on the same page, I have something to say."

His eyes are nuclear, and his chest heaves with fury. "Stop wasting my time with these games of yours, and just spit it out."

I push to a stand and stuff my hands in my front coat pockets. "Take responsibility for the mess you made of Zach, *all* of it, and guard that family's secret with your life. If word about Nick gets out from anyone other than the Armstrongs, if my father has to shoulder one more day of blame for something he had no hand in, then your little video will be my comeback story."

And this is the point where my plan could backfire. If the police have a copy of these tapes, if they've already questioned Chris about his naked appearance on one of them, then he'll already feel the breath of discovery hot on his neck, and the possibility scares me more than a little. A man backed into a corner has nothing to lose.

But it's been a week, and I'm counting on the fact that they haven't. Maria's memory stick was filled with wealthy and influential men with everything to lose. Maybe one of them, maybe even Uncle Chris, cleared her house of evidence before the police could get there. I have no real proof of this, of course, other than the silence from the police department and my gut telling me that it's true.

After forever, Chris's chin dips in a nod, and considering the context, I try not to gloat too much.

Still. I can't help one last little jab. "Tell Aunt Susan I said hi, and I'll see her Thursday at lunch."

And with that, I turn and walk away.

30

And then, suddenly, it's November 21. The anniversary of Zach's death. Three hundred and sixty-five days. The day blooms with an epic thunderstorm, low-hanging clouds that dump rain from the skies in thick sheets, battering the roof and swallowing up all light and sound. It's like a greater power is marking the day with the gravity it deserves. Dark. Wet. Depressing.

I wake up early, far too early to start the day, and lie there for an eternity, listening to the steady downpour batter the roof's shingles above my bedroom ceiling. Today marks both an end and a beginning for Gabe and his family, and I wonder which is harder for them: closing the book on Zach's first year gone, or facing a new blank page without him on it.

I linger in bed until my bladder can't wait another second, and then I trudge down the hallway, freshen up in my brand-new bathroom. I'm brushing my teeth when I hear it, my doorbell, followed by a heavy pounding on the door that spikes my heart. I fling my toothbrush in the sink and hurry down the stairs.

It's Gabe, clean-shaven and bleary-eyed in his favorite jeans and a black puffy coat. He takes in my bare feet and rumpled pajamas, my bed-head hair, the sheet marks slashing up a cheek. "Sorry. I didn't mean to wake you."

"I was brushing my teeth," I say rather inanely, though I'm happy to hear my voice sounds halfway normal. The sight of Gabe's familiar figure after all this time has wound a rope around my chest and pulled it tight, and I'm surprised I can talk at all.

Gabe nods as if he knows, and I'm confused for a moment until he reaches up, brushing something off the corner of my mouth. Toothpaste. He wipes it on his jeans. "I don't know if you heard, but we dropped the charges."

"I saw the press conference."

"It was the right thing to do. Mom needed closure. *I* needed closure. It's better this way."

"Good. I'm happy for you." I mean it, too. If dropping the charges gave him the closure he needed, then I *am* happy for him.

Vaguely, I'm aware of a car idling on the street, of the rain beating down in sheets, of the tips of my bare toes tingling in the freezing November air. It's a strange feeling, standing so close to him again, and I think back to the first time he stood on my doormat, the night he came over to apologize. I didn't let him in then, either, though for totally different reasons. I'm dying to reach out and touch him, to wrap myself around him and not let go, and I can't be one hundred percent sure I won't try the minute he steps across my threshold.

"It's cold as balls out here," he says with a little smile, resurrecting the same words he used that night, and I know he's remembering it, too.

Still. I don't step back.

He gives a resigned nod, doesn't push it any further. "Mom still has no idea about Nick. Though…I don't know how we can keep it a secret forever. My therapist tells me Nick will have to tell her in order to fully heal." He draws a deep breath, blows it out. "I don't see how that can go well."

"She's already lost one son. I can't imagine she would push another one away because of a tragic accident. I'm not saying it's going to be easy, but he'll need her forgiveness in order to forgive himself."

"You sound just like my therapist." His smile, sincere and warm, makes my chest ache.

I drop my head, and we fall silent for an awkward moment. As interested as I am in his family, I can't help but wonder what brought him to my doorstep this morning, today of all days, but I don't know how to ask without coming across as unsympathetic or, even worse, hopeful. So I ask the question that's been piling up on my tongue since I opened my door a few minutes ago.

"How are *you*, Gabe?"

"A mess, obviously." He swipes a palm across the back of his neck. "I'm sure you know what today is."

I nod, the words sticking in my throat. Of *course* I know.

"I meant what I said at the press conference. Zach would have hated the investigation. No, that's not right. He would have been *furious* at me for taking on the country he died serving. He would have said it made his death pointless and took my scope off the people who needed me most. Mom. Nick. You." He pauses to shake his head ruefully. "Not that you ever needed me, but, Jesus, Abigail, I need you. I can't breathe I need you so bad."

And I can't breathe with him standing here. Because no matter how either of us feels, the fact remains that he didn't believe in me. He doesn't. Is this it? Is this how we end? With Gabe's admission that he needs me but not enough to believe I won't hurt him in the worst possible way? The idea of it breaks my heart, and I feel myself start to crumble.

"I'm sorry," he says. "I hate myself for letting you drive away from me like that at Nick's. I wish I'd stopped you and said—" he takes a deep breath, blows it out "—well, pretty much anything other than the words I did say. I wish I'd told you I knew you weren't writing a story, that I knew you wouldn't."

"But then you would have been lying."

He starts to shake his head, and then he freezes, gives me the tiniest of shrugs. "Yeah, maybe. Maybe I would have been lying. But just so you know, I *wanted* to believe in you, but every single thing that's happened this past year has taught me not to. It's taught me to think the worst of everyone. That's not an excuse, only an explanation for why I've become such an ass-hat. I didn't used to be."

His face is so open, his expression so boyishly repentant, that I forgive him pretty much immediately. After everything that happened between me and Dad, how could I not? I thought the worst of my own father, and what's my excuse? Gabe was only trying to protect his family, while I was willing to betray mine.

"It's fine. I get it. I didn't exactly give you reason to trust me."

"It's *not* fine. It wasn't fair to you, especially after everything you did for me and my family." He looks at me, struggling for words. "I think… I think… I don't know, I think I was so traumatized I *couldn't* think. I couldn't concentrate on anything but my terror that Nick would hurt himself, that Mom would find out, that I would lose another person I loved. Please, tell me I didn't lose you, too."

"I can't be with someone who doesn't believe in me, Gabe."

It's not an accusation, simply a statement. I know I could fall into his arms and feel better for an hour or two, but the relief would only be temporary. He would still resent me, and I would hate myself later for it. I choose long-term self-respect over short-lived pleasure.

"If Zach were here, he'd tell me action over words. Show over tell. He'd say go for the grand gesture, Hollywood style." He spreads his arms wide, more a resigned gesture than a come-and-get-me one. "But I'm not Zach. I don't do Hollywood style, and I have nothing to offer but me. Just…me." His mouth twitches in a teasing grin, and his hands fall to his sides. "Honestly, if I were you, I wouldn't take it. It's a pretty shitty deal. I'm damaged goods."

"You're not." I bite down on a smile. "You're a work in progress."

"I am. And part of what I'm working on is putting myself out there again. Learning to let go and to trust. Which brings me to why I'm here. To ask you—no, to beg you to please come with me." He steps forward, takes both of my hands in his freezing ones. "Mom and I are spending the day with Nick. She's waiting for us in the car."

I close my eyes, savoring the moment, feeling it puff and inflate in my chest. Gabe wants me to spend this day—this most momentous, private, heartbreaking day—with him and his family. He didn't fall to his knees or fill my house with flowers or write his request across the sky, he just asked, without bargains or contracts or terms.

"Abigail, please," he whispers, and I open my eyes to watch his face contort into an openly repentant expression that's completely unnecessary. I've already forgiven him, and I've already made up my mind. "Please, come."

I think about my father, who left the career he loved out of principle, on account of a family he had never really met.

About Zach, who walked away from millions of dollars to do the right thing for his country, only to make the ultimate sacrifice. And about Gabe, whose proffered sacrifice is no less significant: his family's vulnerability for our future together.

I gesture to my pajamas, to my bare feet poking out of the bottom, but I'm smiling. "I'm not dressed."

"I'll wait."

"What about your mom?"

"She'll wait, too."

"No, I mean...what do you want me to say to her?"

The corners of his mouth lift in my favorite Gabe smile. "You'll think of something."

31

"Let's sit over there, shall we?"

Jean points us to a bench under a giant cherry tree, its limbs heavy with clouds of pink blooms, and the two of us pick our way across the lawn. Behind us, the brick buildings of the Salem VA Medical Center campus glitter under a brand-new April sky that seems to stretch for forever. I push up my sleeves and welcome the sun's warmth on my skin after the coldest, wettest, longest, most miserable winter on record.

And I'm not just talking about the weather.

Nick's official diagnosis of PTSD didn't come as a surprise to anyone, and all those horrifying statistics linking the disorder with suicide are true in his case. Including the attempt I witnessed at the cabin, Nick has tried to take his life three times now—and those are just the times we know about. The phone call from my father came at exactly the right time. Gabe drove him straight here, to one of the best inpatient programs in the state. Lord knows Nick needs the very best help available.

Gabe, too. After learning the truth about Zach and caring for Nick, he has his own post-traumatic stress issues to deal with.

The three of us make the four-hour trek every Thursday—Gabe and Jean for therapy and to visit with Nick, me to lend emotional support wherever I can. I haven't seen Nick in months, not since the anniversary of Zach's death, but Gabe thinks his brother will be ready to see me again one day soon. I assure Gabe I'm in no hurry. I'm not going anywhere.

"I wanted to thank you," Jean says as we're settling onto the sunny end of the bench. "For everything you've done for my boys. Both of them."

I smile, indicating she's more than welcome. "I'd do anything for Gabe. You know that."

"I do." She winds an arm through mine, resting a palm on my forearm. Jean Armstrong is a toucher, a trait that, considering her three burly sons, amused me to no end until I saw how Gabe responded. With quiet reverence, as if each touch from her is a precious, priceless gift. Sometime in the past few months I've found myself doing the same.

We look at each other for a long moment as a breeze whips up around us, sending leaves and petals skittering across the grass. There's still a knife-edge of springtime cold in the wind, but even that will be warming up soon.

"A mother's not supposed to have favorites, you know," she says, her voice quiet but clear, her tone unapologetic. "And I love all three of my boys with every ounce of everything inside of me, but Nick has always been the fragile one. He's always needed me the most. And the kind of love a mother has for her most fragile child is special. More intense." She sighs. "Filled with worry."

I give her a sad smile. An amount of worry I can't even imagine.

"So when it comes time for him to tell me who shot Zach, I'll find a way to forgive him."

Every muscle in my body stiffens, and I suddenly can't breathe. Did I hear her correctly? Did Jean just say she'd forgive Nick for Zach?

And then I look into her eyes, ruined and haunted and positively destroyed, and I'm certain. Jean knows. She knows *everything.*

And now, suddenly, her easy willingness to let go of her desire to write Zach's story makes sense. It puts everything into clear, sharp focus. The way she smiled at me through tears when I told her I couldn't do it, the way she pulled me into a tight hug and thanked me for giving her back her son. I didn't know what she meant at the time—I thought she was referring to Zach, or maybe even Nick—but now I understand. She was thanking me for giving her back Gabe, for making him smile again.

But that's not to say I'm not writing something. I meant what I told Mandy that afternoon over lattes. My words weren't gone, they only needed the right inspiration. They were waiting for the right story. Turns out that all along, the right story was fiction. Children's fiction. My agent is currently shopping around *Ginger the Wonder Dog,* a fanciful tale about a princess named Rose, a village of evil blowups and a dog that saves the day.

"I'm not going to lie to you," Jean says to me now. "I'm not sure I'll ever be able to accept what happened, but I will not, will *not* lose another son. I stand by my initial statement. I'm surviving for Nick and Gabe. They need me. And more than anything, Nick needs my forgiveness."

No wonder the media painted this woman as ferocious. The love she has for her sons—*all* of them—is fierce and savage and wild and magnificent, and far more ferocious than the media ever understood.

I cover her hand with mine, wishing I had Jean's healing gift of touch, wishing I had words that could ease her pain. I tell her the only ones I can think of: "You are the most amazing woman I've ever met."

Just then Gabe pushes through the double doors of the hospital, squinting in the bright sunshine, and something squeezes, warm and sweet, in my chest. We watch him walk across the lawn to us, his build and gait and everything about him so much like his famous brother that I wonder how Jean can stand to look at him without bursting into tears.

Instead, she gives him a spectacular smile. "Hey, baby. How'd it go?"

"Okay." He blows out a breath, and his eyes find mine. "Better now."

I scoot over to make room, and he sinks onto the bench between us. The three of us sit there for a long while, enjoying the sun and dreaming, I imagine, of two brothers on a battlefield.

From the west another breeze kicks up, shaking the branches above our heads and showering us with a million tiny pink blooms. I let my head drop back onto Gabe's chest and watch them drift down from the sky. The petals tickle my cheeks and forehead like butterflies across my skin, promising a better season.

Somewhere out there, the seed of Nick's secret is buried. How deep is anybody's guess. I don't know how long before the truth about who killed Zach pushes through the murk, only that at some point it will. Maybe it will be Nick who breathes life into it, maybe someone else. Not my father or Chris, definitely not me or Gabe, but too many others know for the secret to stay buried forever. And if there's one thing I know for sure, it's that the truth always comes out eventually.

I have no idea how this story ends, and that frightens me, more than a little. The future is magnificently, terrifyingly uncertain, but as I sit here pressed up against Gabe's big body, it occurs to me that for all my fixation on the answers, the finales, the *endings*, maybe it's not where we land that counts. Maybe what's more important is how we get there, and with whom.

"You are going to get through this," I whisper to Gabe, but just as much to his mighty mother. "All of you."

"And so will you," Jean says.

Gabe drops a kiss on my temple. "And so will we."

Words can be deadly, yes, but they can also heal.

★ ★ ★ ★ ★

Acknowledgments

As always, enormous gratitude goes to my agent, Nikki Terpilowski, for taking a chance on me all those years ago, and for still believing in me now. To my editor, Rachel Burkot, for your keen eye and patience. Thank you for asking all the right questions and pushing me to be a better storyteller. To the entire publishing team at MIRA, from editing to design to sales and marketing, thank you for making this little writer's dreams come true; I am beyond thrilled to call MIRA my home.

To my fabulous friends, all of you, but especially: Corey Prince and Nicole Wise Williams. Thank you for being so generous with your time and advice early on, and for cheering me on from the very first word. To Hannah Richardson, for sharing your knowledge of rowing, and pointing out ever so sweetly where I'd flubbed; maybe one day we'll actually get to meet? To Lara Chapman, Koreen Myers (oh, those flowers!) and Alex Ratcliff. You girls are the very best sistahs I could ever ask for, and our writing retreats are the highlight of my year. To Elizabeth Baxendale, Christy Brown and Lisa

Campagna, for the reads and laughs and always-support. I can't imagine my life without you three in it. To the ladies of Altitude—Nancy Davis, Marquette Dreesch, Angelique Kilkelly, Jen Robinson, Amanda Sapra and Tracy Willoughby. Your friendship and support means the world. Huge, squishy love to all of you.

To the readers who make all of this possible. Thank you for all the emails, Tweets and Facebook messages, for your passion for books and your love of the written word. Because of you I want to write a better story every single time.

To the bookstores, bloggers, reviewers and book clubs that have supported my work. I am humbled and incredibly grateful.

To my parents, Diane and Bob Maleski, who never, not once, laughed when I said I might like to write a book, and my in-laws, Saskia and Frans Swaak, who have always treated me like one of their own.

And finally, to Ewoud, Evan and Isabella—this, all of it, is for you.

THE ONES
WE
TRUST

KIMBERLY BELLE

Reader's Guide

MIRA®

1. Abigail feels responsible for Chelsea's suicide, so much so that she abandoned a successful career because of it. Can you relate to how Abigail allows guilt to drive her decisions? What other big decisions in the story does her guilt have a part in shaping?

2. What does the title, *The Ones We Trust*, mean to you? Discuss all the ways the characters had to learn to trust, not only others but also themselves.

3. As a journalist, Abigail believes that public enlightenment is the cornerstone of democracy, and that it is not just her job but her duty to seek and report the truth. Her father's life and career, on the other hand, were built on a need-to-know basis. Whose viewpoint do you relate more to? Why? In the end, how did Abigail and Tom reconcile their beliefs with what happened?

4. Jean's request sparks Abigail's desire to write again, "something positive and good and important," but her fear of making the same mistakes holds her back. Can

you relate to wanting something that scares you? How do your own fears play a role in the choices you make in your life?

5. Abigail claims that "words, even when they're carefully crafted, can be just as deadly as a bullet." Do you agree?

6. What scenes or developments in the novel affected you most? Which character's motivations and choices could you most relate to?

7. How does public perception of Gabe differ from how Abigail views him? What was your impression of Gabe? Did your perception of him change during the story?

8. Gabe is determined to discover the truth about who shot his brother, even lying and stealing in order to get it. Do you think his methods were justified? Can you relate to his steadfast belief that the truth would bring closure to his tragedy?

9. According to Jean, "Anger can be like a buoy. Sometimes it feels like the only thing holding your head above water, but you have to let go of it at some point. Otherwise, you'll never make it back to shore." Do you understand what she meant by this? And is letting go of anger ever that easy?

10. How do Abigail and Gabe change over the course of the novel? Which character changes the most, and which the least?

The Ones We Trust **is a story about whether the truth is enough to overcome betrayal, and how deep loyalty and trust run even in the closest of families. What was your inspiration for this story, and what did you learn from your own telling of it? What do you hope readers learn?**

The inspiration for this story began with Abigail and her relationship with her father. I'm fascinated by people like Tom, people who do bad things for (in their mind, at least) good reasons, and I wanted to explore how far you can stretch the bonds of trust and loyalty with someone you love. When things are not as they seem, it's incredibly easy to misjudge someone's behavior, to assume the worst of them, to react inappropriately because you don't understand. And even in the closest of relationships, trust is not a given, and we don't give it infinitely. There's a point where doubts start to surface, and we draw a line in the sand, where we can no longer justify what we are experiencing with the belief that the other person is behaving with good intentions.

But I also believe that trust is a two-way street. That's one of the notions I wanted to express with this story, that sometimes in order to receive trust, we must be willing to make our own leap of faith and give it, too. Tom's behavior was restricted by his loyalty to the army and the secrets he was protecting, but to me, that moment when he expressed regret for not giving Abigail the same thing he was demanding of her was so powerful. Gabe took a similar leap of faith when he invited Abigail to commemorate Zach's death with him and his family. After everything he'd been through in the past year, after all the ways he'd been betrayed and traumatized, I never underestimated how difficult that was for him.

What were the challenges you faced writing a novel about a military family's tragedy and an army cover-up? What did you want to say?

The military angle was for me the hardest part about writing this story. War doesn't just take place on a battlefield, and our soldiers aren't the only heroes. What about the parents who send off their sons and daughters, the spouses and siblings and children left waiting at home? They are just as heroic and courageous, their sacrifices different, maybe, but just as great as the men and women fighting on the front lines. Above all, I wanted to be respectful to all of them, not just the soldiers, but also the people who love them.

An inherent part of any war is tragedy. People die, and families lose loved ones, and those left behind have to find a way to pick up the pieces. Gabe is so desperate to know who shot his brother, and I think searching for answers, trying to piece together what took place in those last moments, is a very human response to losing someone. He sees it as the way to give closure to his family, and if the truth hadn't been so horrible, he might not have been wrong.

But my overarching message was that things aren't always what they seem. Gabe didn't understand Abigail's motivations at first, and Abigail didn't understand her father's. Tom looked like the bad guy for so much of the story, and it was only once she discovered the truth that she realized she'd misjudged him, that his reasons for setting the cover-up in motion were noble, especially in light of how Chris was trying to exploit Zach's death.

How did your vision for the subplot, Maria Duncan's sad but messy reality, come to light? Why did you decide to weave it in with Abigail's story, and how did it play up the larger, overarching themes of the novel as a whole?

Maria began purely as part of Abigail's backstory, but the deeper I dug into Abigail's character, the more I realized how Abigail's guilt really drove a lot of the choices and decisions she makes in the present story. I began to think about how I could make things harder for Abigail, since my job as author is to put my characters through the proverbial wringer. Weaving Maria's story into Abigail's meant she would be constantly reminded of all the mistakes she made the first time around. Guilt is such a powerful emotion, and much like Gabe and Ben with their anger, Abigail would have to find a way to let it go before she could move forward.

Which characters came to life more easily than others? How was your experience of writing Maria, a complicated and flawed individual?

For me, the biggest challenge of writing any story is taking the armature of the suspense plot—in this case, Abigail and Gabe's search for the truth intertwined with Maria's tragedy—and developing characters that are mine, that feel as if they're real and not simply reacting to the plot points I create for them. I know I'm on the right path once they start talking in my head and telling me what happens next. Abigail and Gabe were the first to start, and the rest filled in from there.

I wrote many different versions of Maria, and I wrote a lot of her story from her point of view that didn't make it into the book. Talk about a character talking in my head! Maria wouldn't shut up. She kept trying to hijack my plot, and I had to keep beating her back, because *The Ones We Trust* is ultimately Abigail's story. As tragic as Maria's story was, the most interesting thing about it was how it intersected with Abigail's.

How do you relate to Abigail? What does she do that you would never do?

The obvious answer is that we both love to tell stories, but my connection with Abigail goes much deeper than that. When Abigail goes after the truth, she clamps on like a pit bull and refuses to let go until she gets it. Like her, I am very disciplined and tend to be hyper-focused when I'm writing, and I have a hard time letting the story go to, oh, I don't know...shower and put on real pants, for example.

But Abigail has a lot more pluck than I do in real life. She's never timid in her interactions with Gabe and Jean, with Maria and Graciela, and she always speaks her mind. I'm not that open with people I don't know, and it takes me longer to warm up to them. But it's a quality I definitely admire and wish I had more of.

Why did you decide to set the book in our nation's capital? What does the DC setting add to a story about a military family looking for truth and justice? Did you consider working in more political angles?

When I came up with the suspense plot, I needed a setting with a strong military presence, and DC was a good fit. It was also the perfect backdrop for what I wanted to say about truth, justice and doing the right thing under incredibly difficult circumstances. The city comes with its own set of assumptions about back-room politics and lust for power, and I liked the dichotomy it provided—between good and bad, between loyalty and betrayal, between idealism and dysfunction—for this story.

And no, I never considered any political angles. In fact, I stayed away from them intentionally. Politics is such a charged subject, and it has the tendency to take over any conversation, including fictional ones, and I didn't want the Armstrongs' story to be swallowed alive by a debate about military affairs or foreign policy. So, though there are a few references to politicians—it is Washington, DC, after all—I don't attach political opinions or leanings to any of them on purpose.

Your previous novel is also a complicated family saga. Have you always been interested in family dramas? What about this genre is so appealing, do you think?

The stories of families, especially families in the midst of a major upheaval, have always pulled at me. I'm constantly interested in how family members respond to dark times, how they find forgiveness after a major betrayal, how they rebuild loyalty and trust. We talk a lot about unconditional love in families, and that is such a powerful emotion, yet are there really no constraints? I think for a lot of people, for a lot of families, there are limits to what is acceptable. Not every family comes out on the other side of a trauma intact, but strong families find a way to stick together, to forgive and move forward as a stronger unit. To me, the whys and hows of both scenarios are fascinating.

Do you let anyone read your early drafts, or do you prefer for no one to see a manuscript until it's finished? That being said, can you tell us a little about your next book?

Writers are typically an insecure lot, and I'm no different. I don't like anyone seeing anything less than my best work, so I keep my really early drafts between me and my computer hard drive. No one, not even my husband or mother, reads a scene until it's, well, not perfect but at least polished enough that I'm pleased with where it's going. The only exception to this is my critique partners, because their job is to highlight all my sucky words and tell me how to fix them.

And, yes! The story I'm working on currently is about Carly Rose Wilson and her mother, a country music legend who died at the height of her career. When new rumors about her mother surface, two people stand between Carly Rose and the truth—her father, a man who will lose everything if the press discovers his secret, and her Alzheimer's-ridden grandmother. An encounter with her first love, Rex, introduces her to his young son, the one person who can still coax lucid moments from her grandmother. With their help, Carly Rose discovers unsettling truths not just about her mother, but about the people she has always trusted most—while Rex's nearness resurrects memories and feelings she thought were long buried.